TANYA E WILLIAMS

GROWING INTO GREATNESS

A *Vintage Vineyard* NOVEL

FIRST EDITION

Cover Photograph of vineyard vines by David C Williams

Cover Design by Ana Grigoriu-Voicu

eBook ISBN 978-1-989144-26-8

Paperback ISBN 978-1-989144-25-1

Hardback ISBN 978-1-989144-24-4

Audiobook ISBN 978-1-989144-27-5

For Dave,
The best wines are the ones we enjoy together.
Xo, Tanya

One

SUNDAY, MAY 1960

MY FATHER IS A COMPLICATED MAN.

I raise a long-stemmed wineglass in my right hand, giving it another swirl. The glass's contents match the downward spiral of my thoughts, as they beg me to ignore the task delivered to me by my mother three days ago, the one that demands I let go of the lifelong dream I've held for my future. I shift my gaze and instead focus on the moment. Just the wine and me.

Sunlight filters through the gossamer curtains billowing in the afternoon breeze. I rest my elbow on the desk, mesmerized by the space where the light meets the curve of the glass. The deep burgundy liquid comes to life, lingering against the bowl for a moment before descending back toward the stem.

The color is rich. I bring the rim to my lips and the scent of my latest experiment wafts up to greet me. A small sip sets my taste-buds on high alert and I can't help but smile with satisfaction. The constant fussing and worrying have paid off. Not to mention the midnight harvest that Tino's father, an accomplished winemaker and my landlord, suggested was one step too far.

I take another sip, savoring the Pinot Noir as it pirouettes across my tongue. Even Mr. Parisi had to agree when I offered him a sample this morning.

"Sofia," he told me once I caught up with him in the vineyard. "You were right. This is the best one yet. Perhaps there is something to your moonlight escapade."

He wriggled his eyebrows in jest and I knew I had made him proud. This man, who gave me a home and a bucket full of hope when none existed. To this day, I cannot look at him without missing Tino, the boy who loved the vines as much as I do.

I push the blank sheet of paper aside. The task my mother insisted I do, writing a speech for the upcoming grand opening— the weight of it drops like a stone to sit heavy on my heart.

Complicated, doesn't even tell the half of it.

A sigh summoned from the deepest part of my soul rushes up from my lungs in a race to beat the demoralizing thoughts that are sure to accompany it.

I tug the flyer from beneath a stack of books resting on the corner of my desk. Doing my best to maintain my composure, I shrug off the awareness that the flyer's buried location might be an unconscious attempt to ignore the truth that is soon to become my reality. My eyes slide over the Russo Family Vineyard logo and, without fail, the word *family* hits me like a punch to my stomach.

I've been kidding myself for years. Forty of them to be exact, though I imagine I can subtract the first five years of my life when I lived blissfully unaware of all that I was to be cut out of. My brother's name, Alonso Russo, is printed in a bold script that seems to point a finger, mocking my hope that I could have ever believed I would become the future of the vineyard.

I stand abruptly, wooden chair screeching against the old floorboards of my cottage and begin to pace. Women are supposed to be supportive only, certainly not leaders in an industry dominated by male mindsets. My fury is fueled by the practice of old

European lineage that promotes the continuation of male heirs, at least where my father is concerned.

As a child, being first born, albeit by minutes rather than years, I foolishly waved the flag of oldest sibling over my twin brother's head whenever the opportunity presented itself. Sadly, in the end, it is his gender and not his age, that has bested me, stealing my dreams and any hope of reconciliation with my father.

I walk circles around the quaint-sized living room, the swish of polyester from my orange pedal pushers accompanies every stride. My oversized desk and Nonno's battered but sturdy steamer trunk have been the only pieces of furniture filling the space since I moved in fifteen years ago. With little need to entertain the infrequent visitors I receive, I positioned the desk in front of the window so the Parisi Vineyard is never far from sight. The old trunk, though less hospitable than a sofa, serves as an extra seat with its robust structure and flat lid. Countless hours have been spent in this room, reading, planning, sipping, and dreaming. All of it for naught now, it seems.

A bubble of frustration bursts out of me. I plunk the wineglass on the desk, my heavy hand eliciting a thud as glass connects with wood. Examining the flyer, I continue to pace as I scan the details, my gaze getting stuck on the section that upends my future with only a handful of words.

Alonso Russo invites you to the Grand Opening of the new Russo Family Vineyard tasting room!

Now in its third generation, Russo Wines is proud to be one of Napa Valley's premiere wineries.

Join us as we celebrate wine, family, and tradition.

Fury burns behind my eyes, sprouting renewed contempt for a father who has nurtured this outcome. I crumple the flyer into a tight ball and toss it in the bin beside the desk, giving it what for with a look spiked with daggers.

Even if I wanted to, I can't blame Al. If there was ever a person who wanted to hand over a vineyard in its entirety, it is my brother. He never asked for the ready-made, back-breaking, forever on the verge of collapse, vineyard. In all of his actions, he has quietly declined the role of winemaker for as long as I can remember. His passion lies elsewhere.

"Oh Al." The words emerge as a sigh. "If only we could switch places, then our worlds would be set straight."

Can Papa even see how both of his children are living lives they do not desire? I find it easy to think of him as *Papa* when my childhood memories rise to the top of my mind, our past over-shadowing the strain of the relationship existing between us now.

I can't imagine a future where my brother's lack of interest in running the family business will result in its success. My decision is a difficult one but simple, nonetheless. In order to cause no more harm, no more arguments, no more discord, and save what remains of my relationship with *my father*, I must concede the vineyard, and in-turn, Al must step up.

Defeat smells rotten as I slump into the desk's chair. My nose crinkles with displeasure at the task before me. I never intend to cause friction in my family and yet the vibration of discord seems to line the very fabric of connection we hold with one another.

Nonno's stoic and frequently spoken reminder bounces through my mind. Whenever a disagreement reared its head, whether it was over whose turn it was to wash dishes or dry or something far more impactful, like who will be the next in line as Russo vintner, his words were always the same. *La famiglia è tutto.* Family is everything.

I bend at the waist, heeding his wisdom, and pull the flyer from the bin. Unfurling its edges, I press it flat against the desk's hard surface and stare at it. A small picture of the vineyard, tucked into the flyer's upper right corner, catches my eye. In an instant, the photograph takes me back to one hot summer day when I was young enough to still play with dolls.

The memory is vivid, and I swear I can feel the hard porch beneath my bottom. Playing on the front porch steps, as was usual, I would straddle the divide between sun and shade and with it the vastly different worlds of Mama's household chores and Papa's glorious field of grapes.

My eyes squinted against the sun when I saw him striding toward the house, his broad frame convincing me he was capable of anything and to his little girl that meant everything. A smile stretched across his lips when he spotted me. I was eager to ask him something, but Mama's voice, calling from the direction of the road where she had been retrieving the mail, changed the course of that moment, that day, perhaps, even the rest of our lives.

Waving her arm overhead, letter fluttering above her brunette curls, she broke into a run to meet him before he reached me at the porch steps.

"It's here!" Mama shouted, an eruption of excitement lifting her voice.

Wrapping her up, Papa lifted her off her feet and spun in circles. Mama's left shoe sailed off her foot, landing with a soft thud on the dusty ground as they celebrated something, at the time, I couldn't understand.

"Open it." Mama encouraged him as he put her down and retrieved the shoe for her.

Papa's thick finger sliced through the envelope's flap like a hot knife through butter. With Mama wedged tight beside him, he unfolded the piece of paper and began to read out loud. I can't recall how far he read, or even what the letter said. The only thing I remember is feeling as though a dark, thunderous cloud had suddenly blocked out the summer sun. Even then, at the age of six, I had a feeling the sun wasn't coming back anytime soon.

Mama's hand flew to her mouth while Papa's strong shoulders folded in on him. That was the day Papa learned his wine would not be saved by a sacramental wine permit. I learned years later the permit had already been approved by the Bureau of Prohibition, a feat in itself in 1926, given the many vineyards clamoring for the financial salvation the permit provided. Yet, the problem was with the church and its leader who Papa had arranged to manage the duties of production and distribution, as they had become embroiled in an investigation by Prohibition authorities. Nearly three million gallons of wine labeled for sacramental use had already been seized.

Papa had been assured of his good standing by both the federal government and the church, but his already bottled and cellared Zinfandel was, with the arrival of that fated letter, worth far less than the glass bottles the wine rested in. Years of his hard work, dedication, and persistence became contraband in the blink of an eye.

Yes, defeat is a nasty business.

All those years ago, the joy of being a winemaker became a noose around Papa's neck.

My focus is tugged back to the blank sheet in front of me. "Surely, I can come up with something about perseverance and hard work." I mutter to myself as I pull my chair closer to the desk, serious about getting on with the dreaded task. I have never argued against Papa's work ethic. In that way, we are alike and that has to be worth something, if only to write a speech that makes him proud.

An hour later, I toss the pen across the desk and whirl out of my chair, almost toppling it in the process. Save for the scribble of ink to ensure my pen's usability, the page that is to hold what my mother suggested be "poetic" and "inspiring" words to highlight my father's lifetime as a vintner, remains blank.

"Proud. Who am I kidding?" The scoff leaves my lips as the pen finally comes to a standstill after a final spin on the far corner of the desk. Though I would love nothing more than to feel Papa's pride in me once more, I can't hide from the fact that I haven't felt the genuine shine of his adoration of me in decades. Running my fingers through my hair, I tug at the roots, needing something, anything, to shock me from this merry-go-round of disappointment. I catch a glimpse of the afternoon sun as it dips lower, casting a fresh slice of shade over the vines while reminding me the clock is ticking.

Tomorrow begins another week and like every week of the year, my vines require my attention before heading into the office at nine. Each morning I walk my small plot of land, grateful for the gift of three-quarters of an acre for my use, from Tino's father. The deal I struck with Mr. Parisi began out of necessity—mine, not his—but, has transformed into a friendship I hadn't known I was missing until it bloomed.

I give him my time on weekends and holidays, working his land and with his grapes, wherever he needs a helping hand. In exchange, I reside in what was originally the winemaker's cottage at a reduced rent with access to the land beyond the cottage's window to plant my own vines. Along with equipment, supplies, and the occasional pep talk over dinner with Tino's parents, I've gained more than I could ever offer in return.

A quick glance at the stack of wine reference books resting on top of my desk reminds me the weekend is coming to a close and I have yet to crack open a single one. The books, research for the Wine Library project scheduled to open in the St. Helena Public Library next year, slotted in under my job description when I showed a keen interest in the project. Having little time to read between my secretarial and meeting minute-taking duties while at the Napa Valley Vintner offices, I have been lugging books home every weekend for months, determined not to be the reason for a delay with the project. Knowing my input is valued by a few in the organization keeps me returning week after week despite some of the less than stimulating tasks associated with the job.

I can even tolerate the dismissive looks, being called "little lady," and the occasional inquiry as to why I have yet to snag myself a husband, when surrounded by those who dominate the business of winemaking. To them, I'm a lowly secretary. The wheels of equality for women may turn slowly in the big world of wine, but at least I can say I am in the room, paying attention, embracing innovative ideas, and helping to shape the industry from the inside out.

I hold my glass up and examine the Pinot Noir in the new hue of late afternoon. "It's lovely," I whisper to nobody.

The crunch of his shoes on the gravel announces his arrival ahead of the knock on the door. I am within reach of the door's handle, but since he is the only one to seek me out here, I take a sip of wine and call out, "It's open."

Two

"HEY, SIS." Al steps inside, ducking slightly to gain clearance from the low slung door frame.

"Hey." A quick glance at his hand, small sheets of paper held tight within his grasp, elicits a knowing smile on my lips. "Always the pictures, Al. Never the wine."

A blush creeps up my brother's neck as he steps forward, taking the glass out of my hand. "Always the wine, Sof. Never the pictures."

I laugh and feel the shift of my sour mood turning into something far less bitter. He does that—makes me feel at home in my own skin. Perhaps it's a twin thing, or maybe Al is simply the only person who truly understands me.

He plays the role of the winemaker he is about to become in a week's time and lifts the glass to examine its contents before cocking his wrist with an exuberant swish of liquid against glass. Inserting his broad nose into the bowl, he lifts an eyebrow and I imagine his mind whirring. His facial expression asks questions of the wine that can only be answered with a taste.

Eyes closed, he tips the glass to his lips. Watching him soak in the aroma, the flavors, the subtle notes of cherry mixed with vanilla is akin to watching an artist at work. Though he has never shown talent, or for that matter, interest, in making wine, his appreciation for the complexity of the process and the end product make him an excellent judge.

"This is incredible." Al looks at the glass again. "This is yours? From your vines?"

"Of course, it is mine." I roll my eyes at him. "Just bottled it last week."

"But this is only your second harvest."

I can't decide if his look of astonishment is a compliment or an accusation. "Yes..." I draw out my response, attempting to assess his concern.

"Sof, hardly anyone hits it out of the park so early in a venture." He takes another sip, savoring before swallowing. "The vines were planted in fifty-four, right?"

I nod in response, my words choked out by a rush of emotion. "You think I hit it out of the park?" A shiver of excitement runs through me at my brother's appreciation of my wine. Years of trial and error have convinced me more times than I'd like to admit that making a wine worthy of praise is out of my reach. Until now.

My thoughts collide as I consider, for the umpteenth time, why I have been unsuccessful in giving my father reason to be proud of me. He is not a cruel man, rarely raises his voice, and never has he raised a hand. Yet the lack of his belief in my abilities cuts as deeply as I imagine his grape-picking knife would.

"Has Papa tried this?" Al lifts the glass to eye level.

"No." My wall of defense rises up and locks in place at the mention of our father. "You're only the second person I've given it to." I avoid his eyes and step closer to the desk, lifting the blank sheet of paper waiting for words I have yet to muster.

"Let me guess. Mr. Parisi?" A light sigh escapes his lips. "Well, you won't be able to keep it a secret then. You know the two of them are thick as thieves. They share everything, especially when it comes to wine."

My head snaps up. "Not everything. We have an agreement. He promised to keep my progress between us." I jut my chin, defiance snaking its way up my spine. "Papa doesn't have to know everything I do."

My love of the vineyard is deeper than I can trace. Nonno used to tease me that I had wine and not blood running through my veins. As far back as I can remember, I was out the screen door, the slap of its frame eliciting an admonishment from my mother as I ran to catch up. Hanging a half-step behind my grandfather's and father's heels, I was eager to tag along and desperate to be included in their world.

In my early years, it didn't occur to me that being a girl would close doors in my face and by the time I was aware of that reality, I already had another role model ready to take Papa's place when I learned he was set on Al becoming the next Russo winemaker. A friendly librarian taught me about Josephine Tychson. I held tight to a vision of being just like her.

I glance at Al who is still admiring my latest creation.

Well, not exactly like her, since her road to success consisted of her husband's suicide and ended in disaster after the Phylloxera outbreak of 1893. But, she was a great woman of wine, certainly, and proof that a woman is just as capable as a man to tend, nurture, and create renowned wine.

Even now, with the rumblings of a women's movement gaining momentum, I haven't been swayed from my path of becoming a winemaker. Though I believe in the advocacy for equal rights that is quietly filtering out to certain circles, I fear any gains made will come slowly and aren't likely to have a profound impact in my lifetime. Instead, I've chosen to hold tight to the belief that if I can show the world and more importantly, my father, what I am capable of when it comes to wine, my female status will be far less important. I just need to be brave enough to do so.

Though I would love to hear him shout my praises from the rooftops, I have given my father little to cheer for in recent years, having kept my attempts at winemaking a secret from him.

Al's dark eyes narrow, crinkling at the edges as he peers into the glass before inhaling its fragrance again. As a satisfying grin emerges on my brother's clean-shaven face, I consider the risk. What would it cost me to share my wine with Papa? I am not likely to hear him bellow his adoration of my accomplishments, but I would happily settle for a quiet, "I'm proud of you, Sofia," from the man I've idolized all my life.

"I don't know why you'd want to keep this a secret. Honestly, Sof, if you were going to persuade Papa that your time has come to step into the role of family vintner, this would certainly be the way to do it."

My fanciful musings are instantly weighed down by reality. "I'm afraid you're mistaken, Al. I fear that ship sailed long ago and to be honest, I'm not even sure I ever had a boat in the water." I accompany a defeated smile with a shrug of my shoulders. "It's all yours now. Besides, the vines, though planted and tended by me, are on Parisi land. When it comes down to it, I have no claim to them and neither does Papa."

Al shakes his head, disappointment emanating from his being. I want nothing more than to save my brother from a life he dreads, while at the same time living the one I've always desired, but doing so doesn't make sense anymore.

I am no longer a defiant teenager. I'm a grown woman with a job and an aging father who, after decades of toil and sacrifice, is ready to lay down his shovel. This is what my mother wanted me to embrace when she asked me to write the speech honoring Papa's life's work.

Al passes me the wineglass and I quell my deep-seated frustration with a gulp rather than a contemplative sip.

The truth weighs heavily on my heart. Despite Papa's inability to see the real me, I know he loves me. He is my father and at the very least I owe him the courtesy of letting him pass the family torch to the son he always dreamed would pick it up.

Three

"WHAT ABOUT WOMEN'S rights beginning at home?" Al's taunting pulls me from my thoughts. His cheeky smile puts his confidence, real or feigned, on full display.

A trait I did not inherit, but one I've coveted on several occasions. Al is at ease pretending to know more than he actually does. I am convinced it is a coping mechanism. But, given the challenges he faces, I choose to let it lie. Reprimanding him has never been my role in our relationship, even when he is goading me, as he's doing now.

"Very funny." I punch his arm playfully and he recoils, pretending to be wounded.

Recovering, Al pushes back the stack of wine books as he rests a hip on top of my cluttered desk. "Seriously, though." His expression sobers as his eyes meet mine. "You know I would be more than happy to step aside. I don't have to be in charge of the vineyard."

I incline my head and narrow my eyes at him.

"Fine. Okay, I don't *want* to be in charge of the vineyard. I mean, I'd be fine with the office stuff, but I'm not a winemaker." He runs his fingers through his thick, dark hair. "Happy?"

"No. You know I'm not happy about this. But what are we supposed to do? Papa has made it clear for years that you are the next in line. He is just putting all that talk into action now. It isn't like we didn't see this coming." I lift my eyebrows in challenge. "You could always accept the honor, then name me head winemaker."

"Yeah, like that could ever happen." Al shakes his head at what he deems a ridiculous suggestion. "You know as well as I do that this handover of the vineyard doesn't mean his hands won't be all over it." Al shrugs his shoulders in defeat. "Besides, if I had what it took to decline Papa, don't you think I would have done so by now?"

A slow exhale gives me a moment to pause, allowing me to locate a sliver of grace instead of the hurt and anger that are barely tucked away under my calm demeanor. "Honestly, I have to take the win that there is even a vineyard left to pass down."

Al's eyebrows converge in question. "What are you talking about?"

"Maybe you never saw it." I shrug, understanding our childhoods, though shared, were vastly different experiences. "I was always in the field. I watched as he plowed under vines for the sake of progress, or survival, or who knows what else fueled his drive to destroy the very thing he loved so deeply."

A gust of wind blows the curtains into the room like a hot-air balloon, bringing with it the scent that is pure Napa. A sweetness to the air that is beyond explanation. Never simply the aroma of a single bloom or field but a combination of all of them, dancing with one another as they form nature's most delicious perfume.

"He means well." Al's voice cracks and I stiffen at both his words and the sentiment building between us in the small room.

"You should know, Sofie. He *does* mean well." Al dips his chin in an effort to draw my gaze to his. "This has nothing to do with you being female. I don't know his true reason, but I'm certain it is not because you're his daughter and not his son."

I give him an *I don't believe you* look.

A laugh erupts from Al's throat. "I realize it might come across that way sometimes, but I've given it a lot of thought and I just can't see how gender has anything to do with it."

I try to resist the urge. But, in the end, give in and cross my arms over my chest and lean back against the wall that separates the living room from my even tinier kitchen. Defenses up? Check, I tell myself silently in an animated army commander's bark.

Shifting his position on the desk, Al continues. "Remember when Mama took a job at the post office?"

I nod, fearing the mention of the war will put me in a whole other type of tailspin.

"Right around the time the war ended. I'm not even sure how long she worked there, but it couldn't have been more than a few months. Anyway, when the men started returning from overseas and returning to the life they had before."

"Yes, I know. Women were told to go home and cook dinner. Leave the real jobs for the men." I roll my eyes at the propaganda that infuriates me to this day, never having understood why a different solution wasn't even considered. One where women and men could work together for the greater good of communities and families alike.

"Right. Well, when Mama came home that day, telling him she no longer had a job, he was angrier than I've ever seen him. It wasn't like we needed the money; we were well on our way to getting the vineyard back on its feet again. But the principle of the matter was something he couldn't stand for."

"I don't remember any of this." I move to the trunk a few steps away and sit on its flat lid, resting my elbows on my knees.

"You were probably in the vineyard with Nonno. Head in the vines, so-to-speak. Anyway, apparently, he stormed right into town and into the manager's office demanding an explanation and Mama's job back." Al smiles and shakes his head. "Mama was so embarrassed she didn't go to town for weeks. But she was proud too. Of the man she loved, standing up for her like that. Therefore, you see Sof, I'm not convinced that his decision not to pass the vineyard down to you, who so clearly wants it, has anything to do with you being a girl."

"But why then? What reason is there for him to keep me at arm's length from the vineyard? Why doesn't he trust me the way he trusts you?" The frustration I've managed to restrain is threatening to spill. "I could understand it if you wanted the job. I wouldn't think of stepping in if you showed even the slightest talent—I mean interest in the position." I hide my raw emotions with a joke at Al's expense.

"Look who's being funny now." His disapproving look morphs into laughter in seconds. "In my defense, I have never professed any talent when it comes to making wine."

"Or growing grapes. Or harvesting them." A snicker slips from my lips as I remember how Al found himself knee deep in grapes, unable to pull himself and his boots out after he lost his pitchfork in the mix.

"Laugh all you want." Al grabs my glass and drains it, waiting for my fit of giggles to subside. "But you should take a bottle of this wine and convince him he is wrong. You were made to be a vintner and, yes"—Al raises the empty glass— "That is the wine talking."

I shift uncomfortably. Between the un-cushioned surface of the trunk and my brother's direct stare, I feel as though my every move is being scrutinized. I raise a hand and point at the squares of paper he has placed on the desk beside him. "Are you going to show me those, or not?"

Al beams and pats the desk beside him. "Of course. It's why I stopped by."

"Are you sure about that?" I stand and move toward him. "I thought Mama might have hinted to check in on me, or rather the progress of the speech for the grand opening."

"Are you calling me a traitor?"

"A traitor? I would never." I shift the blank page where words are clearly supposed to have been written by now and hoist myself up onto the desk. "A co-conspirator maybe, but never a traitor."

"Fair enough." Al laughs. "When I told her where I was heading, she did ask me to check on how you were doing with the speech." A sheepish glance from his downcast eyes tells me he is required to report back.

"You can tell her that I'm still in research mode." I nod once, an idea growing inside me as I say the words. "I will have something for her in time."

Al cocks his head, not convinced.

"I promise. I will." I reach out and take the paper squares from him. "Now, tell me about these drawings of yours."

His eyes light up as he begins explaining the picture on top. I refrain from calling them doodles, all too familiar with the way the word cuts him like a knife.

"This is what spurred the idea." Al points to the squiggles in the middle of the drawing. "It's the flourishes from the Russo family crest."

The red and silver swirls are familiar and as he continues, I can see what is missing from what he has drawn.

"You see the leaves, they look like vine leaves, just a little." His assuredness wavers as he glances at me in a sideways look. "I think. Enough to pass though, right?"

"I think so. Even if they aren't, it's the family crest, so they have a reason to be there, anyway." I squint my eyes and bring the paper closer. "But, what about the lion? Or the armored helmet?"

"That is the beauty of it." Al flips to the next square of paper. "The lion is too imposing, not suitable to represent wine, and the helmet is too..."

"Old school." I finish for him as my eyes are pulled into the second drawing. Using only red and silver, Al has created an intricate design that has literal family roots and his vision of leaves fluttering upward that has transformed into wings. "This is beautiful."

"You like it?"

"I do. Are those?" I point to the top portion of the drawing.

"Wings?" Al blushes and I can almost feel the heat coming from his skin as we sit side by side, our heads bent together as we examine his art. "I thought it could represent us. Covertly, of course. I'll sell the idea to Papa with a focus on the family crest but between us—"

"Between us, what?" I raise my head to meet his eyes.

"I thought I could be the leaves. The roots, so to speak. The one who is destined to remain at the vineyard. And, you could be the wings. The one who is determined to fly."

Emotion runs through me like a bolt of lightning. Moisture pricks my eyes as my heart makes its way to my throat. "I love it, Al. Thank you."

He nudges my shoulders with his own. "You don't have to get all mushy about it."

He is teasing, but I can't let this moment go without recognizing his thoughtfulness. "This is one of the nicest things anyone has ever done for me. I am grateful. It means a lot to me to know that when you look at a wine bottle, you will think of both of us, together, in Russo wine. Who knows, this may be as close as I get to being on the label. What wine were you thinking of using it for?"

"Think bigger Sof. I want this to be the new Russo Vineyard logo."

"You what?" A hand rushes to my mouth. "Will Papa even consider a new logo?"

"I think he will." Al's confident swagger reappears. "Especially if you buck up and let him taste your vintage. That wine is more than qualified to be deemed a Russo wine and you know it."

Sensing my discomfort at his nudging, Al stands to leave. "I'll let you think about it, but I can't promise I won't bring it up again." He reaches for the door's handle, then turns back to face me with a lopsided grin. "Don't suppose you have a bottle I can take with me?"

"Are you going to keep it to yourself?" I eye him suspiciously.

"Definitely. You know how good I am at keeping a secret."

I retrieve a bottle from the kitchen. "You've never been good at keeping a secret." I pull my hand back as he reaches for the bottle. "But, since there is no label to give me away, I suppose my secret is safe with you. For now."

"I owe you one," Al says as he ducks out the door. "Will you think about what I said?"

I offer him a noncommittal shrug of my shoulders. "Give my love to Mama when you deliver your report and don't worry, I'll have that speech to her before the grand opening."

I wait a beat, letting the sound of Al's retreating footsteps disappear before contemplating my next steps. Pulling the window closed, I move toward Nonno's trunk, apprehension matching my every step. Save for tossing a few things in here and there over the years, I have avoided sifting through the trunk's contents for the past fifteen years.

I grab the thick leather strap and tug. The heavy trunk fights against the wood plank floors as I inch it closer to my desk. I position my chair in front of the trunk and open its lid. Dust motes waft up to greet me. Seeing the framed photo of Tino and me resting on top makes me question my decision to follow through on this research, as I informed Al I was doing. I swallow the urge to slam the trunk's lid down and bury the past, along with my emotions.

Reaching for the photo, I run my thumb over his face, frozen in grainy black-and-white photo paper. "What would you do?"

I know his reply before I even ask the question. What wouldn't he do if it was for the love of his vines?

Taking a deep breath, I face the task at hand. Even Papa wouldn't approve of someone slinking away to avoid a confrontation. He is a quiet man, most of the time. So quiet, in fact, that on too many occasions I've felt the deep sorrow that comes from his silence. On the other hand, if he has words that need speaking, he seldom hesitates. I've been on the receiving end of those as well. I can't imagine what form his disappointment with me will take this time. My nerves battle with what I believe I must do as I suck my bottom lip between my teeth.

Surely, Papa will have respect for my decision to come to him one last time with a plea for my place among the vines. Leaving Al to live a life he has no interest in nudges me another step forward. Little by little, I am talking myself into this, more than aware that once I begin, I won't be able to let it go. I'm driven to be the best winemaker I can be, but when it comes down to it, all I ever wanted was to be a Russo winemaker, like my father.

This is my last chance to show Papa that I am a capable winemaker and that if given the chance, I would make him proud. I'm certain I can be the future of Russo wine. The only thing I have to do is convince Papa.

The thought of facing Papa on the topic evokes a shaky inhale. "Damn you, Al." I say out loud. My only wish is that my brother's urgings didn't come with the risk of upsetting the family applecart once again. Looking at Tino's photo, it's clear as day. I can't turn back now. For better or worse, my decision is made.

Four

IF I DIDN'T KNOW BETTER, the photographs would tell the story of a typical childhood. Days filled with sunshine, outdoor picnics, and a family gathered close together around Mama's peach pie. I flip the pages of the album, scanning the images for the version of my upbringing that I've harbored since adolescence. The one that remains like a sliver imbedded in my thumb.

Staring back at me, though, is a much younger version of myself, complete with wind-swept hair and a wide grin. A few photos of the five of us litter the pages, bringing a smile to my lips. One of my father gazing at something beyond the porch rail, calls to me, making me pause and question the discrepancy between these family photos, my childhood memories, and my adult view of the relationship I share with Papa. What I don't find within the album's pages is evidence of the rift between us.

For the past several years, I've told myself that I keep the trunk full of memories close by to keep my family with me, to keep Nonno near me. But now I wonder if all I've done is kept a fractured memory of my childhood, one colored by my own disappointments, at arm's length. Close enough to feel its rub while it simmers beneath the surface, acting like fuel for my unsettled emotions. Perhaps I've misjudged both the accuracy of my memories and the importance of revisiting them from time to time.

I release a steadying breath, reminding myself of the purpose before me. I am looking for something. Anything, if I'm being honest, to help me write a speech worthy of my father's life's work. My trek down memory lane isn't completely altruistic though, and I don't ignore the possibility that I'll find something of substance to help me convince Papa that I'm worthy of the role of Russo vintner.

After years and countless arguments on the topic, I'm at a loss as to how to broach the subject with him now. With his vision for the vineyard already set in motion and a date to commemorate it all rapidly approaching, I cringe knowing that even if he hears me, some part of his plan will be trampled on by what he may view as my impertinent insistence to rehash the discussion.

I sit back in the chair, taking the photo album with me, hoping to find something poignant to use for the speech. Though I have no interest in delivering it, the words I choose to say at the grand opening may double as a final apology to my father, if I am unable to convince him that I'm the right Russo for the job he is handing over. I have little expectation of an open conversation, given that the man has been consistent in his opposition of me being at the helm of the vineyard for decades, but even so, I'm desperate to ensure my words damage our relationship no further.

I flip the page and stop short at an image of my grandfather and me. Nonno, as he preferred Al and me to call him, clung to his Italian heritage with a steadfast nature I've witnessed little comparison to. There we are, together. His wrinkled and weathered hand holding my little one. Our backs are to the camera as we walk away. But it is what we are walking toward that pulls me in. What lies before us are the first rows of vines, the ones that sit closest to the farmhouse. The same ones that Nonno and a grandmother I never knew, planted. I lean closer to the album, searching for a glimpse of the white marble bench among the vines, the one that stands guard over the fields almost eighty years after being placed there.

The next page in the album shows me with a toothless grin, raising a glass of what I assume is grape juice. The pig tails sprouting from either side of my head tell me I was around seven when the photo was taken. From the stone and dark beams in the background, I place us in the cellar where the wine is made, bottled, and stored.

I can almost hear him as the memory rises up to greet me. I was smiling at Nonno, who took the photo. I remember his boisterous laugh as he instructed me in his thick Italian accent, "Sofia, wine is to be savored not slurped."

"But this is grape juice," I replied.

"One day, Sofia, you will be a famous winemaker. You must treat every glass with respect and the understanding of what goes into it."

Moisture rims my lower lids as my finger graces the photograph. "Oh, Nonno. You believed in me. You always believed in me."

Emotions getting the better of me, I flip the next few pages in quick succession, determined to keep myself on track with the task at hand. I skim past several photos of the vineyard, the images filling me with contentment and pride.

After several more pages, a photograph I don't recall catches my eye. Sliding it free from the tiny black corners that hold it in place, I turn the photo over. Scrawled on the back in Mama's handwriting is, *Giovanni and Sofia, 1925.*

I turn the photo image side up again and laugh out loud. A family story I've been teased about for what feels like my entire life, appears in black and white before me. Mama always said there was photographic evidence of my tenacious nature though I am certain I've never seen this photograph before.

There I am, five-years-old, standing with my arms crossed over my chest in front of what looks to be a rather tall and unruly weed. Papa stands opposite me, shovel in hand and head thrown back in laughter. As the story goes, I was protecting the weed I must have thought was a small vine as Papa tried to remove the intruder from the row so as to not crowd out the real vines.

I have no memory of the outcome of the situation, only that my parents and Nonno teased me about it for years. I examine the determined expression on my younger self's face.

Where is that courageous, uninhibited girl now? My eyes are drawn to my father's joyful, exuberant face. Better yet, where is that man now? A man who clearly appreciated me for who I was, stubbornness and all. What happened to us? Where are you, Papa?

Tossing the photograph onto my desk, a determination to get to the bottom of what I don't understand, spurs me forward. I grab the framed photo of Tino and me out of the trunk and tuck the loose photo of Papa and me into the corner of the frame. Pushing aside a mason jar filled with pens, I set the frame at an angle where I can keep an eye on it, willing both men in my life to guide me through whatever is to come.

I return the album to the open steamer trunk and dig a little farther. The journals I placed inside it years ago are dusty but waiting for me nonetheless. Wiping one of the leather-bound covers with the palm of my hand, I hesitate, trying to recall which journal started them all. Nonno taught me the art of journaling. He used to say that a well-documented vintner is an insightful one. To this day, I keep a journal on everything from weather to soil conditions to the age of the French Oak barrels.

Though I am quite certain I wrote gibberish within the pages for more years than I care to admit, I open the journal and read anyway.

July 1932

We walked the rows in the back field today. I learned how to rub the soil between my fingers and assess it. I am not sure I noticed a difference, but Nonno says the grapes are ahead of schedule and suspects the improved soil conditions have given them a much-needed boost. I knew he was referring to the soil we hauled over and spread from the rows Papa tore out last spring to plant grapes more suited to long-distance travel than they are for making wine, which he is convinced will save us from this dreary time that has descended upon our country.

Nonno though, remains stoic in his attention to and care for the vineyard. Grape juice isn't Russo wine, but given the alternative, at least we still have a vineyard full of grapes.

Flipping through the pages, I skim the words written by twelve-year-old me. Most of the entries are short but the memory of them takes me back, all the same.

August 1932

Today, more rumblings about the end of Prohibition surfaced in the newspaper. Papa scoffed at the headline before pushing through the back door like the house was on fire and he needed to get far away from it. Mama and Nonno exchanged a knowing look over the breakfast dishes, but since Al was sitting beside me with his nose in a comic book, I kept quiet and finished my oatmeal.

The memory dances across my mind, lifting my eyes from the page. The secret. I had forgotten all about it. So many years have passed, I can't imagine there being any worry about such things now. The sun has dipped in the sky, playing peek-a-boo among the canopy of my Pinot Noir vines. I switch on the simple floor lamp closest to the desk, tilting its beige plastic shade to provide additional light and lean back in the chair. Thumbing through the journal, I continue reading as the months and years recorded in my own hand tick by.

March 1933

After school, Al and I were walking up the road toward the farmhouse when we heard Papa's raised voice. We rounded the mailbox and there he was, standing with his hands stuffed in his pockets as a man in a brown suit and a matching wool fedora, far too heavy for a spring sun, stabbed a piece of paper with a thick finger.

Without barely a glance in our direction, Papa said. "Go inside." Taking our cue, Al and I hurried our way toward the porch, disappearing behind the closing of the front door. Once inside, Mama shooed us to our bedroom to do our homework, but not before I noticed her wringing a dish towel between her hands.

The afternoon dragged on as Papa retreated to the cellar after the man left, only returning to the house once the lights were off and his leftover dinner kept warm in the oven had grown cold. Al and I whispered our worries and fears into the darkness until sleep finally found us.

I place the journal on top of the desk, thinking back. I remember that day. Al sequestered on his side of the partitioned bedroom curtain, his nose stuck in a comic book. Me on my side, trying to busy myself with schoolwork until I couldn't stand it a moment longer and pulled the curtain back to discuss the stranger with my brother. In the end, we assumed he was an official of some sort, but Papa was quiet for a few days and then it was forgotten and life resumed as usual.

A quick peek through the curtains tells me the sun has set low, leaving an indigo sky, illuminated solely by a three-quarter moon. I stand to move toward the kitchen where a leftover pasta salad awaits me in the refrigerator when a corner of paper catches my eye.

The paper is wedged into the corner of the trunk's lid, held in place by the interior strappings of the old-fashioned traveling case. I step around the trunk, approaching the lid from a better vantage point, and try to pry the paper free.

After several attempts, I have red fingers and a sliver imbedded in my thumb. Ignoring the sliver, I retrieve a knife from the kitchen and wiggle the sharp blade under the strapping. The knife bends, but so does the strapping, giving way enough space for me to tug the paper free.

I examine the knife's mangled blade, confirming it is no longer useful as a utensil before turning my attention to the folded piece of paper. I hold the paper closer to the lamp to read the faded words typed on yellowed paper. My hand flies to my mouth as understanding dawns on me.

Five

JANUARY 1930

THREE PAIRS of eyes are on me. Gathered around the farmhouse kitchen table in the late afternoon, Al and I squeeze together, side by side, on the short end of the table as our tenth birthday celebration is about to begin. I've been waiting for this day to arrive for what feels like forever. Now that it is here, my excitement mixes with nerves as the responsibility of what we are about to embark on settles over the room in a hush of anticipation.

The cake Mama made for the occasion is smothered in chocolate icing and sits ready for cutting on the counter. Al's elbow bumps me, pulling me from my thoughts. A quick glance at the table in front of him tells me his attention is not on the moment at hand but on his latest drawing of a superhero from one of his comic books.

Nonno does the honors and uncorks the traditional Russo Zinfandel with a pop. My heart flutters at the sound and I take a deep breath to steady my nerves. The gurgle of wine being poured into glasses that usually hold milk is muted by Papa's bark in Al's

29

direction. "Stop doodling and put that away. Your Mama didn't go to all this trouble for you to sit—"

Mama lays a hand on top of his forearm, cutting his words short. An almost imperceptible shake of her head speaks volumes as Papa holds his tongue and pulls out a chair, sliding it a little farther away from the table than necessary.

With glasses before us, Nonno inclines his head. "Go on, then."

I take a sip, mindful of the importance of appreciating the tradition and the wine. This is the moment our family brings us into the inner fold, as true Russo winemakers. I have spent my childhood begging for a sip of the beautiful deep red liquid that swooshes into bottles before being stoppered and set aside from my prying eyes. The wine is the link to the vines that fascinate me. Whatever the season, the vineyard has a touch of magic that, without fail, pulls me whenever I draw near.

Mama likes to say there was never a worry I would wander out onto the road as a toddler. The only direction I ever ventured was toward the vines.

The room temperature liquid rolls around in my mouth, making my cheeks pucker as it swishes and swirls. I've breathed in its scent my entire life, yet its taste is nothing like I've ever experienced.

Nonno leans in just as my eyes grow wide with delight as the earthy weight of the wine transforms on the back of my tongue as though someone has snuck a smear of Mama's blackberry jam into my mouth when I wasn't looking.

He slaps a hand on his knee. "*Stupendo!*" Nonno looks over his shoulder in Mama's direction. "I told you, Angeline, Sofia has the wine running through her veins."

Mama's laugh sounds like a song and my heart overflows with joy. I have made them proud. I have tasted their wine and given them reason to celebrate with my appreciation of the fruits of my family's labor.

A sideways glance in Al's direction tells me he isn't enjoying the wine, or the moment, nearly as much as I am. I shoot him an encouraging look, hoping he will attempt to hide his disappointment.

I take another sip, catching Papa's expression as my chin tilts up. A scowl rests where a smile should be radiating. I almost choke on the sip of wine as the breath rushes out of me and my stomach sinks with speed toward my shoes.

My gaze drops to the timeworn farmhouse table. I am boggled by his reaction. What have I done wrong? Where did I misstep? My eyes dart, first to Nonno and then to Mama, both of them still happily content, or so it appears. I place the glass back on the table and sit back in my chair.

I no longer feel like celebrating. I thought I had shown the proper respect and appreciation, but clearly Papa does not agree. Even I was a little taken aback with how many layers of flavors one sip of wine could hold. Though I would have pretended to like the wine if necessary, my reaction was an honest one. The disappointment threatens to pool in my eyes. I stare at the table, unable to face the one person I want to make proud. I don't understand.

The scrape of a chair on the wood floors yanks my head up. Papa is up and shrugging into his winter coat. All eyes are on him as he takes two long strides toward the door. "Come with me."

I stand, beaming. Ready to do my part, whatever it may be. Excitement bubbles up inside of me like the sparkling wine Nonno opens on New Year's Eve.

All my life I've wanted to be just like him. Papa is the strongest, kindest, smartest man I know, and I want to be a winemaker and make him proud to have a daughter to pass the family vineyard down to one day.

Nonno tells me stories about how proud he was to work side by side with Papa as he was growing up. Even when they lost my grandmother too soon, father and son worked through their pain and the vineyard together. They leaned on one another and together they carried her memory into the fields with them every day. At least, that is how Nonno tells the story.

I chide myself for thinking that he was disappointed in me somehow. I'm his little shadow, after all. The one he is sure to find a short pace or two behind him, no matter how far he has ventured away from the farmhouse.

I think back to how our days and interactions changed when Al and I started school. I missed him and the vines desperately, often being reprimanded by the teacher for daydreaming. I learned to cope though, and soon found that my favorite time of day was when Papa would come in as the sun was setting. He would wrap me in a hug and I would breathe in the smell of earth and sweet red grapes, and once again I would feel our connection to one another and our land in that embrace.

I am stepping around the back of my chair, squeezing past Al who is looking despondently into his barely sipped glass of wine when Papa lets out a frustrated sigh.

"Sofia, help your mother with dinner. Alonso, come with me."

The thud of the closing door echoes in my heart. I am stuck, unable to move from the spot where Papa left me. Tears prick my eyes and I bite my bottom lip to stop it from quivering.

I feel their gaze on me once more. Swiping at the dampness on my face, I am embarrassed that my most shameful moment of being cast out by my father has an audience. Nonno and Mama exchange a look. All I feel is their pity at having witnessed my fall from grace.

I think back over the past several months. Has this been building up between Papa and me? What did I do to receive such a rebuke? I've always been his little shadow. My thoughts gain momentum. What will I be if I am not to be that?

Nonno stands and steps toward me. "It's not you, child." He tries to convince my eyes to meet his, but my humiliation has cemented them downcast. "We've had some trying years and they're catching up and wearing on your Papa now." He squeezes my shoulders with both of his hands, the warmth of his affection for me burrowing past my thick sweater to the skin beneath.

The door opens, bringing with it a gust of winter air. "I'll speak with him," Nonno says to Mama before closing the door behind him.

Mama steps forward with her own embrace and the tears flow anew once more in the safety of her arms. "Your father didn't mean to hurt your feelings, Sofia." Mama's sigh is laced with fatigue. "He loves you. You must believe that."

"But—" The words come out in fits and starts. "He—doesn't —want—me."

"Oh, Sofia." Mama pulls back, forcing my eyes up with a finger placed firmly on my chin. "He does want you." Her eyes bore into mine.

"I think..." Mama pauses, choosing her words with care. "I think Papa is struggling with how to keep the vineyard going. Times are tough and it's been a challenge selling grapes instead of wine. And now, with the financial burden sitting heavy across the country, I am not sure the vineyard will survive both Prohibition and a financial downturn."

She says it as though I have been living under a rock. Nobody in 1930 California can ignore the situation we are in. Between newspaper headlines and a steady trickle of newcomers searching for work, all us children have been cautioned about the dangers of talking to strangers since our small farming town has erupted with them.

"How about we get started on that birthday dinner?" Mama

guides me toward the sink and keeps me busy by peeling potatoes and carrots.

"Have I ever told you about the importance of keeping the farmhouse going on a vineyard?" Mama's voice lifts with what I imagine is an infusion of hope as she tries to boost my sunken spirits.

"A vineyard can't exist without someone in the farmhouse keeping the home fires burning." Mama eyes me from the opposite side of the counter. "I realize it might not seem as interesting as spending the day in a dusty old vineyard, but without home and clean clothes, and food on the table, a winemaker wouldn't stand a chance at a growing season, much less a harvest."

My disinterest doesn't go unnoticed. "Besides, we are in charge of the garden, and that is a mighty task if ever there was one. We decide what to plant and where to plant it. Just think of those hot summer days, sitting under the shade of the back porch, shucking peas and husking corn, and letting the day slip away. We've had some fine summer days, working the farmhouse together, haven't we, Sofia?" Mama pulls my gaze to hers as she asks a question I cannot ignore.

Guilt. I think. She has resorted to guilt. That's when I know I'm done in for. Can't win for trying, so the saying goes. It doesn't skip my notice that I am the only one who wants something different for myself in this family. All this time, I believed I was one of them. How wrong I truly was.

"Yes, Mama," is the only safe reply.

With dinner and cake eaten, I opt for an early bedtime. Too distraught to sleep, I toss and turn until the rest of the house is deep in slumber. The sheet that separates Al's half of the room from mine does little to shield a light, so I scramble under my covers and write in the beam of the flashlight. The one Nonno gave me with a wink and a finger to his lips. Another one of our secrets. Gripping my pencil with a firm hand, I print in my journal

RUSSO ZINFANDEL 1926 Vintage: Cheek puckering with a hint of jam.

I stare at the words for a long time, willing them to help shape me into the only person I ever thought to become. A Russo winemaker.

Six

FEBRUARY 1930

MAMA'S VOICE is barely a whisper. "The rooster crowed before sunrise, so I've made extra loaves of bread this morning."

Even with her back to me, she senses my presence, hovering between the living room and kitchen as though I've lost my way. I wipe the sleep from my eyes and pad toward the kitchen.

She says goodbye to whoever is on the other end of the call and hangs the ear piece back on the candlestick phone's hook. Before turning to greet me, she hesitates, running a finger over the carved indent on the wall behind the phone's box. The groove became necessary when the phone was installed and the handle required the clearance to turn.

"Well, good morning, sleepyhead." Mama's voice lifts in what I interpret as false gaiety and she steps toward me, hand outstretched to smooth what is surely a tangle of messy locks. "I was just coming to wake you." Her chin dips in a slight admonishment for my delayed start to the day.

I slide into a chair at the table as Mama cuts a fresh slice of bread and slathers it in strawberry jam before setting it before me.

"You know the rules, Sofia. Every Russo must wake and be tending chores by eight o'clock on Saturdays." She sends me a knowing, sideways glance. "I covered for you. Told your Papa you were helping me bake bread this morning."

"Thanks." I mumble the words, mouth full of freshly baked bread.

"You can thank me by actually helping with the bread." Mama wipes her hands on the apron tied around her waist and turns to face me. "I've got three more loaves to bake, then you're free to do whatever you like." Mama's lips twist before she adds. "But I do hope you will find something to do. Other than spending another Saturday moping about."

I gulp the milk she's placed in front of me and remain silent, knowing this conversation can only end in disappointment for me.

"Sofia, it's been weeks." Mama pulls out the chair across from me and sits. Hands folded in front of her on the table, her gaze coaxes mine up. "Sulking is no way to spend a life."

"I'm not sulking." These are fighting words. Unfortunately, their strength is diminished by the sour mood I've been carting around since my birthday last month. "I mean. I'm not trying to sulk, on purpose." The hurt that has coated everything I thought I was lies just beneath the surface of my skin.

"We've talked about this. You know how important everyone's contribution is to the vineyard. Baking bread and tending the garden and the house are our responsibility and there is no shame in that."

I hold back the eye roll that is lying in wait and drop my gaze to the table.

Mama tries another tact. "Well, if you have your heart set on being a winemaker, then I say go ahead and be one. Your father may be the head of our household for now, but one day you will be old enough to make your own decisions. If you still want to make wine like your father, then that is up to you. But, for now, you will help me with these loaves of bread and you will adjust your attitude and be a helpful member of this family. Do you understand?"

"Yes." I follow Mama to the kitchen sink and wash my breakfast dishes. She ties an apron around my waist and we work in silence, save for the ticking of the old mahogany clock that hangs on the wall in the hallway. The constant tick tock is loud enough to coax my thoughts into submission.

Hours pass and the flour mixes with water and becomes dough under our kneading hands. The troublesome rumination that has plagued me these past few weeks nudges its way forward. I push my shoulders back in defiance and find the strength I need to share my thoughts. "I don't want to be a winemaker like Papa. Not anymore."

Mama lets out a slow sigh. "I think you might be angry with your Papa. Heaven knows, I can't blame you for that. His troubles though are mightier than either of us can understand. I know it's not easy to do, but sometimes we need to give ourselves grace in order to find it in our hearts to forgive those we love if they've disappointed us."

I nod solemnly, Mama's words doing little to heal the wound Papa inflicted on me. My stubborn disposition isn't ready to forgive him. Not yet, anyway.

The afternoon is almost half gone when the last bread comes out of the oven: focaccia. It's a family favorite and Saturday evening treat. I spot Mr. Parisi's truck as he pulls into the drive. The men's voices are boisterous and laced with the occasional Italian sentiment, loud enough to penetrate the walls of the farmhouse.

"Angeline. Sofia." Papa calls out to us. "Mateo and Valentino have come for a visit."

I watch from the window as Mama peeks her head out the back door, the February chill slipping past her into the warm kitchen. "Are you coming in? I've just taken the focaccia out."

Mr. Parisi shakes his head no; a sheepish smile grows wide as his chubby cheeks color in anticipation of Mama's bread. "We are expected at home within the hour, but I wouldn't turn down a slice of your focaccia if you're offering."

Mama laughs and inclines her head before turning back inside to slice bread for our guests.

Armed with my winter coat and a plate of bread in one hand and a shallow bowl of olive oil and balsamic vinegar in the other, I tread carefully down the porch steps.

"Ah, Sofia. There you are." Papa's joy to see me appears sincere, but I hold a reservation over my heart, knowing how easily he could break it in two. He nods his head toward the plate of bread, offering a slice to Mr. Parisi and his son.

"Did you make this, Sofia?" Mr. Parisi asks me while dipping his bread into the bowl of oil and vinegar.

"I helped." I offer a shy smile at the kind man, the one who always includes me in conversation, regardless of whether I am the only child present or not.

"Someday, Sofia here will be as good a baker as her mama." Papa beams at me, unaware of the knife he's just thrust into my chest.

"No, Giovanni." Mr. Parisi winks at me before arguing back with a lighthearted chuckle. "Sofia here will outshine us all as a master vintner."

Papa joins in the laughter, but I don't miss the expression of concern that flits across his face before he hides it behind another round of laughter.

I offer Valentino, and then Al, a slice of bread, not meeting my brother's eyes for fear of giving away my emotions.

"So, Valentino." Papa shifts the subject off of me. "Your father tells me you're becoming his right-hand man. Like my Alonso here."

Al and I exchange a strained glance between us. Tino, as we've called him since we were all in short pants, lifts his chin with pride at the comment. Being a few years older than us, I surmise he has embraced the future that is following in his father's footsteps.

"I hope to do my father and my family proud." A single nod demonstrates Tino's commitment to his path in life.

"As fathers, we are blessed to have sons to carry on the family name." Papa wraps an arm over Al's shoulders. "Even if it means we are farming plums instead of grapes."

I clamp my lips closed, but a quiet gasp slips past anyway. Though I can't be certain if it is due to Papa's mention of fathers and sons or plums instead of grapes.

Mr. Parisi meets my gaze, inclining his head in Papa's direction. "Ah, Giovanni, don't give up on the vines just yet. Things are sure to turn around and you'll be back in business. You'll see."

"That is easy for you to say, my friend. A sacramental wine permit has kept you producing, but for those of us hamstrung with grapes, the future is less certain."

As if seeing a vision before him, Papa turns his full attention on me. "Sofia." His eyes glisten with excitement as emotion rushes up within him and I wonder if he has suddenly fallen ill. "Valentino is an excellent young man; one you would be well-suited to. What a marriage it will be."

My face burns with embarrassment in an instant. I catch Tino's own discomfort at Papa's announcement, as he stuffs his hands into his pockets before kicking the dirt with the toe of his shoe. Unable to meet anyone's gaze, I drop my eyes to examine the ground at my feet.

Papa, clearly unable to contain his enthusiasm, continues. "A perfect solution. Two Italian families joined by love and wine."

Mr. Parisi steps closer to Papa with a nervous laugh as he slings a protective arm around Papa's shoulders. "Giovanni, we are getting ahead of ourselves."

I'm grateful for Mr. Parisi's attempt to save Papa from his overzealous pronouncement, and possibly me from death by humiliation.

"Just think of it, Mateo. We are best friends. Our children have grown up with one another. We have the same work ethic, the same values. Our families can one day be joined together. We already know Valentino will make an excellent winemaker, as he has learned from the best." Papa nudges Mr. Parisi with a friendly elbow. "This is the perfect solution."

"One that does not need solving today, my friend." Mr. Parisi has a soft tone. "The children are—"

Mr. Parisi doesn't have the chance to finish his sentence because the plates I am holding clash together as the anger within me boils over. I take a single step away from my father, anguish and disbelief mixing with one another. "I am not interested in being a winemaker like you." The words spew from my lips. "And I am certainly not interested in marrying one."

My head shakes from side to side as I back away, taking one step then another, distancing myself from my father and the future he deems suited for me. When I can no longer stand the sight of him, I turn and run up the porch steps and into the house, slamming the door with as much force as I can muster before falling to my knees on the kitchen floor as the sobs I've held in stream freely down my face.

"Sofia." Mama is by my side, kneeling beside me in an instant. "What has happened?"

With stilted words, I relay the events as they occurred. Mama offers soothing sounds but few comments as I alternate between anger and injury.

She shifts her body to lean against the back door, guarding our sanctuary from intruders while taking me in her arms as she moves. She strokes my hair, transforming my sobs into whimpers. Mama wraps her arm a little tighter around me and leans her mouth close to my ear. "Sofia, it's time I let you in on a little secret."

Seven

I BOLT UPRIGHT. Angling my body, I scan her face for understanding. Mama's expression is serious. I am aware of my heart as it thumps heavily in my chest. A warning, perhaps. Telling me not to ask.

"What kind of secret?" I sniff then look away, the aroma of the freshly baked focaccia nudging my stomach into a hungry growl.

"Well, this is something you will have to keep between us." Mama tilts my chin up and narrows her eyes on me. "Do you understand? I cannot tell you if you don't think you are grown up enough to hold your tongue."

"I can keep a secret." Not wanting to disappoint her, I hesitate. "But I am not sure."

"Not sure about what?" Mama asks, her voice gentle.

"Does Al know?"

Mama shakes her head no. "Your brother does not know, but if it makes you feel better, Nonno knows the secret."

"Well, if Nonno thinks it's okay to have a secret with you, then I suppose it is okay for me too."

Mama's laugh filters through the darkening kitchen. "I see

where I rank in the family. First, Nonno, and then me. Is that how it is?"

"I... Well, I just think he..."

"I am only teasing Sofia." Mama gives my hand a squeeze. "It's admirable that you seek guidance yet still ask questions of others, even if they happen to be your mother." Her eyebrows rise in jest. "An honorable trait I am pleased you lean into."

Whether it is Mama's praise or her teasing, I am uncertain, but my cheeks blush with a rush of heat.

"You know I bake several loaves of bread each week."

Instantly disappointed that her secret involves the baking of bread, I question how much of a secret Mama really has. "Yes, for those who do not have the means to do so themselves." I quote her, almost verbatim, doing my best to keep the boredom from my voice. She nods in agreement.

"Well, some of those who purchase bread also purchase a bottle of wine to go with their bread." Mama pauses, waiting for my reaction. "Two loaves of bread are equal to two bottles of wine. You may have heard me mention something about a rooster crowing before sunrise over the telephone. That is a signal. A sign to let the person on the other end of the call know that I have stashed the bread and wine in their secret pick up location."

Mama pauses as she waits for me to comprehend her words.

"But Papa says we aren't allowed to sell wine." My eyebrows crinkle in disagreement. I think back to what I've learned about the current Prohibition laws from Papa's words on the much discussed topic and from my teacher in school. "Every household is permitted two hundred gallons of wine a year for personal use or with a prescription provided by the doctor."

"That's right. But our vineyard has produced over two hundred gallons of wine a year for many, many years, even before the Volstead Act came into place."

I shake my head in disagreement. "No, Papa poured it out. I saw him."

"He did. You are correct. Papa did discard a lot of wine." Mama's sigh is laced with disappointment. "He didn't know where all the wine was, though."

"What do you mean? He was the one who made it."

"Nonno and I moved several crates of wine before Papa had a chance to discard it all." Mama looks at her hands and I sense a hint of regret in her words.

"Where did you hide it?" I've been all over our vineyard and doubt there is a hiding place I am not aware of.

"That doesn't matter. What is important is that I have been selling wine with every loaf of bread I bake. I am doing it to keep food on our table, Sofia. I hope you understand that."

"Papa doesn't know?" I can't fathom how my father has let something as big as this secret slip past him.

"No, and I pray that he never does. Nonno takes care of the grape sales and he adjusts the numbers, so it looks like the grapes are worth more than they actually are."

The seriousness of Mama's secret hits me. "Papa already thinks the grapes alone are worthless. He said as much today." My thoughts leap to consequences. "What kind of trouble will you get in if you get caught?"

Mama nibbles at her bottom lip. "It's a federal offence to sell wine, Sofia."

"But, what does that mean? Will they take the wine away?" My heart leaps into my throat as another possibility surfaces. "Or the vineyard?"

"The wine, for sure." Mama's head bobs up and down soberly. "They may press charges if I am discovered, then I would be put in jail."

"Mama, no!"

"The risk is worth taking. We need to eat and we cannot

survive on garden carrots and bread alone. With so many families struggling to make ends meet, this is a risk I am willing to take."

"There must be something else we can do instead." I scramble to a standing position and pace the floor. "I could help you bake more bread and we could sell that. Surely, we could make enough."

"I didn't tell you so you could wear the problem as your own." Mama stands, brushing the back of her house dress as she does. "I told you so you could understand that sometimes it's more important to be true to yourself than to anyone else in the world. Do you understand?"

I shake my head no, the worry over Mama's revelation consuming all of my attention.

"Your Papa would never agree to me going against the laws of our country even if the alternative meant disaster for our family. I made the decision myself, to do what is important to me and that is taking care of my family. That is what I am doing by selling the wine."

Mama squeezes my hands in hers. "You see, if you want something different for your life than others see for you, it is up to you to go out and achieve it. I love your father with all my heart, but he does not walk in my shoes. He does not think in my head. I am the only one who can decide what is best for me."

"You want me to help you with your secret?" My brow crinkles in question as I wonder if Mama will cast me aside just as Papa did if I don't agree to help her.

Embracing me in a fierce hug, she whispers into my hair. "No, Sofia, I want you to understand that knowing yourself means being proud of your accomplishments, whether others deem them worthy escapades or not."

. . .

Months later, as the winter chill transforms into a warm spring breeze, Mama's secret continues to cling to me like a shadow in the noonday sun. Too close to ignore the constant threat of its presence, yet barely visible to the naked eye.

"Sofie." Nonno calls me one afternoon from the porch steps. "Come. Help an old man with his chores."

I stuff my arms into my coat and meet him on the porch. "You aren't an old man," I say with a smile. "I've seen you carry more buckets than Papa and Al combined."

Nonno chuckles. "Come anyway. I want to talk to you." He inclines his head toward the farmhouse. "And these walls have ears."

We walk in silence into the vineyard, with the only sound being the birds singing their praise of a spring day.

The white marble bench covered with a layer of winter dust waits patiently in the distance, as it always has. Happy memories wash over me as I recall the moments this bench has been a part of. Mama used to pack a picnic for Al and me as we toddled into the vineyard in search of Papa and Nonno having their mid-day break.

The corners of my mouth lift as I think back to last summer and all the summers before when Papa would gobble his sandwich in a hurry so he could play a rousing game of tag among the vines with us. The bench, of course, has always been home base. I remember how genuine his wide grin was and wonder if I've been mistaken and too hard on him all these months since our tenth birthday. I shake my head in disagreement of my poor attitude toward Papa. Mama is right. He is managing as best he can in difficult times.

Nearing the bench, Nonno pulls out a handkerchief and sets to wiping the grime from the seat, sides, and wide decorative legs that hold the seat stable. Heat rises in my cheeks as I remember the day I attempted to carve my name into the underside of the marble, determined to mark my stamp on the Russo Vineyard.

The cold marble seeps through my overalls as I settle myself on the bench and allow my eyes to be pulled in by the rows of grapevines.

"Did you know I put this bench here, in this exact spot, the year your Nonna and I married?"

"I didn't know that."

"Yes. She loved spending time in the vineyard, just like you do."

"I'm sorry I didn't get to know her." Even at ten years old, I am aware of the place she held in his life. "But I feel like I know her a little. From all the stories you've told me."

"That is what I want to talk to you about, Sofie. The stories. The history of our family. The importance of keeping the Russo Vineyard alive. Your mother tells me you no longer wish to be a winemaker."

A passing cloud blocks out the low-lying sun.

"She also mentioned that she feels you do not approve of our secret."

There is little I can say to dispute what he already knows, so I say nothing and instead clamp my lips tight.

"I understand how you might feel. I am not here to convince you of anything you do not wish to be convinced of."

I resist the urge to burst out in laughter. Nonno is far from subtle and seldom beats about the bush. I am here precisely because he wants to convince me of something. He gets right to the heart of the matter when he has something to impart. I don't expect today to be any different.

Nonno swivels on the bench, lifting a hand to point at the grapevine a few feet away, the one marked with a stake that has a pink ribbon tied around its top. "That is the only surviving vine from my homeland in Sicily."

I turn and follow his gaze. "You planted that?"

"No, your grandmother did." Nonno stands and walks toward the vine and I follow. "She arrived a year after me. We had been

48

promised to one another while we were both still in Italy. I sailed to America first, making my way to the Napa Valley, having heard this was where European wine was seeing success. I knew wine from my father, and his father before him. But I didn't know English, so it took me some time to sort myself out and by the time I did, Phylloxera had destroyed my meagre planting of vines. Here I was, a young grape farmer without a vine to call my own."

"What did you do?" As usual, I am drawn in by his story, even if a lesson will be hidden within its telling.

"I spent my days building a small house, wrote letters home, and then I waited."

"Waited for what?" I take his hand and guide us back to the bench to sit.

"I waited for my angel to arrive." Nonno's eyes become misty and, without warning, so do mine. "She came in on a ship three months later and when I went to embrace her, having missed her dearly, she pushed me away saying *Nella botte piccola c'è il vino buono*, meaning in small barrels, there is good wine."

"I don't understand."

Nonno takes my hands in his. "She pushed me away from an embrace so I did not crush the vines she had hidden under her coat. You see, she was not permitted to smuggle Italian vines onto the ship. She disobeyed the rules to save her family. Your Nonna reminded me that a dream can be reached with small barrels too. Everyone begins somewhere. *This* is where we began and it was your Nonna who made our dreams a reality."

"That is so sweet." I squeeze his hand.

"This bench commemorates the day we planted her vines, the ones that started the Russo Vineyard. Never dismiss the importance of a woman's contribution to beautiful wine, or a beautiful world, Sofia."

The toe of my shoe digs into the soil as I consider Nonno's words.

"Your mother, too, is only doing what is best for her family. I do not agree with what the government has done to grape farmers with this law. It seems, neither does most of the country, given all the disruption it is causing, but you don't have to agree with her actions to appreciate her efforts. She risks herself and her freedom every day for her family. To me, that is a great sacrifice indeed."

I nod in understanding, deciding Nonno is right to remind me of the love that fuels Mama's actions. "I can see your point." I offer an olive branch of sorts. "I will do better by Mama."

"While you are doing better by your mama, I must ask you to reconsider your own contribution to the family. I need your help in the vineyard. You have the talent, love for, and natural instinct when it comes to the vines. I know it lives within you." Nonno points to his chest as he speaks. "Just as it does me and your papa too."

I am about to speak out, to refute him, aware of where his words are taking us when he holds his hands up, gesturing for me to let him speak.

"He may not know it yet, but your papa needs your help. Just like Nonna helped me and how your mama is helping in her own way." Nonno tilts his head and softens his delivery. "Your father is afraid. He feels he is letting his family down with a vineyard he can't earn a living from. You must understand how difficult it must be for him to think of losing the vineyard he loves so dearly."

Unable to hold my tongue any longer, my words tumble out, tinged with sadness. "Papa doesn't love the vines. He is ready to plant plums instead."

"That is where you are wrong, Sofia. He loves them, more than life itself."

I shake my head in dispute but offer an agreeable response. "For the sake of the vineyard, I hope you're right."

Eight

JULY 1932

BEADS OF SWEAT run down the side of my face as the summer heat beats down on me. If it weren't for the welfare of my family, I would consider slipping away to enjoy the shade of an oak tree. But, if Nonno can keep going at his age, surely my twelve-year-old self can too.

Though I continue to pray circumstances will improve, the newspaper headlines are determined to dampen my spirits. Each bringing with it news of more tenant farmers from what they've labelled the dust bowl making their way, by any means possible, to California in search of work. So far, 1932 hasn't offered much relief to those suffering.

Papa hired some of those men last autumn to help him clear a few acres of land when he tried his hand at planting vines that produce grapes more suited to long-distance rail travel. He argued his point over dinner last summer, clearly wrung out over the low prices his less travel resilient grapes were getting and the constant but unreliable chatter that promised an end to Prohibition.

He spouted off about what other wineries were doing while the rest of us sat silent, fearing any sudden movement would have him throwing in the towel entirely. "They've either closed up shop, gone underground, or are pretending to be the solution to Prohibition altogether. Grape bricks," He bellowed at Nonno. "That won't make anything close to good wine." He ran a hand through his dark hair and continued his rant. "Ruining the good name of Zinfandel, I tell you. Even if we do survive this godforsaken law, our wines won't fetch what they're worth going forward."

I shake my head in an attempt to remove Papa's torments from my thoughts.

"Sofie." Nonno calls out to me from farther down the row, waving a hand to signal me closer.

I put my pruning shears on top of the crate growing full with excess leaves I've been trimming from the vines and walk toward him. He is bent on one knee, examining the vine with care. I notice his face, red with the sun's kiss.

"Should I bring the water pail?" I ask, worry coating my words.

"I'm fine. I'll take a break at the end of this row." Nonno stands, stretching his arms overhead before rotating them in large circles, a move he's convinced increases the oxygen to his brain so he can connect with the vines better.

I stifle a giggle and wait for him to tell me why he's interrupted me mid-row.

He sneaks a look over his shoulder and I am instantly curious as to what he is up to, given that Papa spends little to no time with the vines that make Russo Zinfandel anymore.

"Sofia, I need you to help me with something." Nonno's whisper forces me to lean in. "I understand you might not be inclined to help, but we need to move the crates."

"Okay." I stand up straight again, our difference in height becoming smaller as the years pass. "What crates do we need to move?"

"The ones we hid." Nonno raises his eyebrows to convey his meaning. "The ones your mama sells with the bread."

"Where are they now?"

He purses his lips and I wonder if he is questioning whether to tell me or not. "It's okay, Nonno." I place my hand on his forearm, hoping to convey my sincerity. "I know it's taken me some time to get used to the idea of Mama bootlegging our wine, but I understand better now how challenging times truly are. I've seen newspaper photos of those families living in empty fields. Their whole lives whittled down to a tent or a car that won't run anymore. You can trust me. I want to help."

I assume he comes to the realization that he must tell me if he requires my help, but his next words take me by surprise. "They're at the Parisi's."

"The Parisi Vineyard?" The meaning of this awareness causes me to stumble backward a step. "That's brilliant, hiding contraband wine with sacramental wine. But, if Papa ever found out, he'd be furious. Mr. Parisi is his closest friend."

"Yes, it is why Mateo helps us," Nonno says plainly. "Because he cares for your papa and his family so dearly."

"I see. How do you suggest we collect them without Papa noticing? And where do we hide them once they're here?"

Nonno marks his spot on the row with a bright length of red yarn, picks up his crate, and ushers me forward. I follow suit, gathering my crate and tools as we sweep by the spot I had been working on, and I'm thankful a support post is there to remind me of where I am leaving off.

We step out of the row as Mr. Parisi's farm truck rolls into the driveway.

"*Perfetto*," Nonno says as he hurries me toward the truck.

"Where is Giovanni?" Mr. Parisi asks as he steps away from the truck.

"In the field—the far back corner. The one that butts up

against yours," Nonno says, nodding hello to Tino who has slid from the passenger's side and is walking around the front of the truck.

"Tino will help you unload. I'll walk over to him and keep him busy, buy you some time." Mr. Parisi tosses Tino the keys. "You head back as soon as you're finished. I'll cut across the vineyard and meet you back at the house."

Tino nods his understanding and slides into the driver's seat.

"You've done this before?" I ask Nonno as Tino backs the truck up toward the far side of the farmhouse, the side not visible from the road.

Nonno looks at me, surprised. "No, this is our first time. We have never run out of wine before now. Word is getting out that Russo wine is superior to those grape bricks your papa goes on about." His voice embodies the pride of a true vintner, and I can't help but smile at his dedication to his craft, legal or not.

Mama is waiting at the back cellar door, wringing her hands in what I can only guess is concern at being found out, either by the authorities or perhaps worse, Papa.

The weathered wood slat door rests on its edge on the ground beside the dank space yawned open below. I thought the cellar had been locked shut after one of the farm kittens got stuck inside several years ago. When Papa built Mama an indoor pantry, the extra storage space of the cellar wasn't missed and has clearly been forgotten by almost everyone in the Russo household.

With no time to waste, we set to work. Tino and Nonno remove the tarp to uncover the crates and start shuffling them closer to the truck's tailgate. Mama and I carry one crate between us as we descend the few steps into the musty storage room.

My eyes adjust to the darkness, and that's when I see it. A flat square, a little wider than a crate of wine, rests against the wall of the cellar. A makeshift handle sticks out—that is what drew my eye to the area.

Mama follows my gaze, a shy smile gracing her lips. "It's a false door. The other side is painted just like the pantry."

I nod in understanding.

"It's where I retrieve a bottle at a time. That way, I only have to enter the cellar every other week or so." Mama shrugs. "Makes it easier to keep things under wraps."

Tino enters the cellar with another crate, spurring us into action once more.

Less than ten minutes later, the cellar door is secured and Tino is driving down the road back to the Parisi estate.

Mama pours us a glass of lemonade each, its sweetness a treat after a hot afternoon spent in the sun. The three of us lounge on the back porch, recovering from our morality testing adventure and our physical efforts.

"Nonno, do you remember what you told me about Italian wineries?" I don't wait for a response. The idea already percolating inside my head. "You said that at the end of the season, the vine-yards were permitted to sell their wine directly to the townsfolk. They hung a wreath of vine leaves at the farm gate to notify those passing by that the wine was available for sale."

"Yes, that's true." Nonno sips his lemonade.

"Mama, you said you only sell a crate of wine in two or so weeks' time? That's only twelve bottles. What if there was a way to sell more wine without drawing attention?"

"Sofia Russo." Mama's shock is evident in her open-mouthed expression. "We are merely trying to get by, not profit in large sums with this arrangement." Mama shifts uncomfortably in her chair. "Besides, we do not wish to draw any additional attention to ourselves. At all. We sell only to those we know well and can trust."

Nonno's eyes twinkle with mischief. "Sofie may have a point, Angeline. If things don't turn around soon, we may have to examine other options."

Mama looks between Nonno and me, her eyes darting from one to the other, concern growing by the minute. Today's activities have unhinged my bold and brazen mother a touch more than I expected.

Nonno chuckles, slapping his knee with his free hand as he smiles at me. "When did you become such a clever fox?"

I shrug my shoulders. "I'm an accomplice now. In for a penny, in for a pound."

Nine

~~~~

APRIL 1933

WE DANCE IN THE VINEYARD, Nonno and I. He was waiting in the driveway, his face lit by happy news, as Al and I walked up the road from school. More than a week's worth of *Napa Valley Register* headlines is the reason for our celebration. A light spring mist does little to dampen our spirits this afternoon, since thirteen years of Prohibition are about to come to an end.

News, first of the Cullen-Harrison Act signed by President Roosevelt and now the push for the legalization of ten percent alcohol wines to be permitted for sale once more, is music to our ears and a much needed balm to our weary souls.

"Only a matter of time now, Sofia." Nonno shouts at me as he shuffles his seventy-three-year-old body in circles in front of the Zinfandel vines. "*Arrivederci*, Prohibition." Nonno's laughter is contagious, even garnering a smirk from Al staying dry seated under the cover of the porch. He watches us, his only response a shaking head and raised eyebrows, ensuring we are aware he thinks us ridiculous.

"Woohoo!" I join in, clapping my hands at the sheer pleasure of knowing our vineyard is safe. Our future is assured and my family has nothing more to worry about.

A weight has been lifted from my chest, one that didn't allow for easy breathing for more years than I care to count. No more sneaking around for Mama. No more hidden bottles of wine. No more risk of being found out. Papa is sure to be pleased, now that he can return to what Nonno insists is his calling. I'm not foolish enough to think bringing the vineyard back up to pre-prohibition production levels will be easy, but the hope that has been severely lacking has magically reappeared. I squeeze my eyes shut and thank God for the turn of events before us.

Nonno interrupts my thoughts by calling out to Al. "Where are your parents? They should be out here celebrating with us." Nonno raises a finger. "In fact, I have an idea, Alonso, get the glasses, I will find the wine and we will have a toast to the future of the Russo Vineyard."

Nonno turns, heading toward the outbuilding that has, since Papa took over the larger operation for grape transport and juice processing, served as the much smaller, private batched wine production and storage for our personal family allotment. He is halted in his tracks as Papa's pickup truck pulls into the drive, skidding to a stop that sends the little gravel that remains flying.

"There you are." Nonno steps forward. "Where have you been? We are just about to celebrate. It is good news, yes?" Nonno's joyful expression vanishes as Papa storms past him, headed in the direction of the barn.

As Papa retreats from our line of sight, Mama slips from the truck, eyes red and puffy. I take a concerned step forward, but it is Nonno who asks the question. "Angeline, what is the matter?"

Mama shakes her head no, but doesn't say a word. She climbs the porch steps and disappears into the farmhouse.

"Alonso, Sofia, you better stick with me." It isn't as much of a suggestion as it is a command. Nonno's worried expression propels Al toward us and together we venture into the depths of the vineyard, knowing our celebration will have to wait.

Several minutes later, our quiet examination of the vines is interrupted by the clanging of metal on metal. Drawn to the first row of Zinfandel grapes by the commotion, Nonno stops short, arms splayed to prevent Al or me from going past him.

"No." Nonno hurries forward, tugging on Papa's arm as he pushes a sharp ended shovel into the ground in front of the vines. "What do you think you are doing?"

Papa continues digging and I cringe with every slice his shovel makes into the ground where delicate roots live. "The vines have to go."

"But why? Giovanni, please. Listen to me."

"Listen to you?" Papa's shovel hovers mid-air. "Listening to you is what Angeline did, isn't it?"

Papa forces the shovel into the ground. A tear slips down my cheek as the sound of roots being ripped from the vine pierces my heart. I want to call out. I want to protect the vines but I am rooted to the spot, just as the vines before me were, only moments ago.

"Prohibition is over." Nonno tries again. "Don't you see? The end is in sight. We can be a real winery once more."

Papa's laugh is anything but lighthearted. Instead, it's laced with anger and fueled by a layer of disgust that I don't understand.

My world, my family, my vineyard, all of it is falling apart around me. My hands are shaking, balled into fists, and trembling at my sides. What will we be if not winemakers?

I take a step closer, the question burning within, propelling me forward. Who will I be if there are no vines? After everything we have sacrificed to keep the vineyard alive, how can he destroy it now?

Papa returns to his digging, Nonno's words falling on deaf ears.

"If you give it a little more time," Nonno pleads. "Perhaps, you will see, the vines will provide for us. They have always provided for us."

Papa's emotion-filled face is wet with sweat. "How is anyone to afford a bottle of wine when they can barely afford to put food on their table?"

"Things will turn around. They always do." Nonno reaches a hand out to place it on Papa's shoulder.

Papa steps aside, letting Nonno's hand fall. "I used to think so."

I've seen that look before. The one that screams defeat. Usually, the stakes are much smaller and involve Mama convincing him of something he isn't inclined to do, such as repainting the farmhouse when he has a vineyard full of vines to tend. This time, though, his defeat is about to take each one of us down with him.

If he won't listen to Nonno, what else is there to do? A shiver rushes through me and I sense Papa is a breath away from giving up and giving in. My doing nothing is sure to result in disaster at the hands of a defeated man, but standing up to him could be the ruin of our relationship. It's no secret, we've continued to walk on tender ground these past few years. Standing against him might mean losing him forever. I take a lungful of damp air and square my shoulders.

"Wait." My voice is stronger, more assured than I expect it to be. "Papa, please. Wait."

"Sofia, this has nothing to do with you." Papa tosses his shovel to the ground and reaches for the top of the vine, angling his body in preparation for tearing it down.

I take three fast strides and step between him and the vine. "This has everything to do with me." The words growl out of me. "The vineyard is our home and our livelihood. It is not yours alone to destroy." I jut my chin in an effort to still my nerves.

"This is a Russo family vineyard. You may not wish to be a wine-maker anymore, but you cannot stop me from becoming one."

Papa takes a startled step back from the row of grapevines. A sad smile flits across his face. "You know, when you were little you stood in front of a weed, ready to protect it with everything you had in you. You were as stubborn then as you are now."

His eyes search the faces of Al and Nonno before turning back to me. "Back then, you were cute. Now, you're just insolent."

I take the insult like a bullet shot from a gun, stumbling backward into the damaged vine.

The sun has dipped behind the distant hills and the inky blue sky casts no shadows as Papa picks up his shovel and pitchfork and turns his back on the vineyard he used to love.

Ten

SUNDAY, MAY 1960

PAPA WAS ARRESTED! My eyes scan the slightly smudged warrant dated *April 4, 1933*.

How had I not known about this? The realization hits me hard and I slump into the chair with a weighted collapse. The news steals my breath away, and the aged paper falls to my lap. My mind whirs with questions.

My first instinct is to call Al. However, this is not something my brother would have kept secret and only leads me to reason that he, too, is in the dark about this piece of our father's past. We were only thirteen-years-old at the time and though I understand the desire for my parents to keep this information from us, I search my memory for where and what we might have been doing as children that would have occupied us enough to miss the fact that our father had been arrested. My head, heavy with uncertainty, finds a moment's rest in my hands as I consider what else I don't know.

Looking back, I can hardly believe arrests were occurring at the time given that Prohibition was on its way out with the twenty-first amendment coming into effect in December of that same year. I count on my fingers. Seven months shy of ratification and Papa was charged with the crime of—what?

I shake my head in disbelief and lift the yellowed page toward the beam of lamplight to examine the details. *Unlawfully selling intoxicating liquor containing more than one half of one percent alcohol.*

I can hardly comprehend it. Papa, to this day, has a criminal record. One of the more obscure realities of Prohibition is the fact that any charges issued during the law's existence remain a blemish on the lives of bootleggers nationwide, despite the very same laws being repealed thirteen years later.

The word bootlegger jolts me back to reality. Papa has always been steadfast in living by the rules, even if it threatened his livelihood. "This can't be right."

I reread the warrant again. That's when I see it. Through the smudged ink caused by creases and time, there is something typed before Papa's name.

Leaning forward, I yank on the narrow desk drawer that holds a mishmash of stationery supplies. My fingers clamp around the handle of a magnifying glass and I tug it free. Bringing it to the paper and light, my eyes squint as I try to make out what is typed there.

The weighted magnifying glass almost drops from my hand as the struck out letters that spell *Angeline Russo* appear, tilting my world with a whoosh of vertigo.

Mama. It was Mama who was charged. I suck in a sharp breath. Her actions caught up with her in the end. My mind detours to the memory of the cellar beneath the house and the false pantry wall that hid the wine bottles.

Though I don't have all the details, I do my best to fill in the blanks with what I know to be true of my father. He wouldn't let his wife go to jail, even if he disagreed with what she had done. That's the reason his name appears on the warrant after her crossed out one. He sacrificed himself to save her.

My mind flashes back to the afternoon in the vineyard. The one where I stood against Papa and his resolve to tear the vines out. At the time, I told myself I was courageous and bold to have done what needed doing in an attempt to keep the vineyard going, despite the fact that my relationship with my father suffered an irrefutable blow.

"No wonder he was furious. Everything he stood for had been stripped away from him by the person he loved most in the world." The words said out loud cause my heart to plummet toward the floor.

I have no idea how my parent's marriage survived such a devastating blow. All I know now is, I added insult to injury when I chose the vines over Papa that day.

I stand abruptly. The whirring in my brain forcing my body into action. I place the arrest warrant on the desk, next to the photograph of Papa and me, and step away from it, willing it not to exist. The irony is not lost on me. I wanted to know more about my father. I was determined to learn the reason he continues to push me aside when it comes to being the next Russo to take charge of the vineyard. Perhaps I've trodden down a path that is better left alone or maybe I've uncovered the real reason for my father's lack of trust in me.

My stomach gurgles its displeasure at having not been fed. A quick glance at my watch confirms the late hour. I give in to hunger and retrieve the pasta salad from the fridge. Leaning against the kitchen counter, fork in hand, I let my mind sift through all that I've learned this afternoon as I chew. I feel as though I am a few puzzle pieces shy of a complete picture and no further ahead with writing eloquent words for the speech I'm supposed to give next weekend. It's not like I can simply stand in front of our neighbors and friends and tell them all about the day my father was arrested.

Leaving my plate in the sink, I traipse back to the living room, a fresh glass of my latest vintage of Pinot Noir in my hand. I reach into the trunk and pull out two journals at random, switch off the lamp, and head to the bedroom, already knowing the night is about to be a long one.

Settled under the covers with my wineglass an arm's length away on the nightstand, I flip open the burgundy colored journal, its hard cover corners bent from years of use. I skim past notes scrawled in pencil. Bits and pieces of information handed down to me by Nonno. He seldom missed an opportunity to fill my brain or my journals with learning.

Nonno was the one who suggested I record my thoughts and his teachings in a journal, a habit I must admit has stayed with me all these years. Each Christmas after I turned ten, he would proudly present me with a new journal and a fresh pencil. If there was ever something he was imparting to me that he felt was especially important, he would tap a finger to his head and say, "Sofie, you must remember this. Write it in your journal tonight." I smile at the memory and silently thank him for giving me one of the greatest gifts I have ever been given.

These days, my journaling is mostly limited to vineyard activities. Dates, weather, and vine health notes keep me in touch with the vines from year to year. Another journal is filled to the brim with my winemaking experiments, a practice Tino and I started when we began our venture together.

But these journals from days gone by take me back in time, allowing me another glimpse into the mind of my younger self. As I read, I feel the sensation of being on the cusp of understanding something that has, for far too many years, slipped through my fingers.

November 1932

Today, when I was in town with Mama, I overheard a conversation at the drugstore. A man was quietly trying to convince the pharmacist to give him a prescription for a shot of whiskey. The pharmacist declined, stating the man would need to obtain one from his doctor and once he did so, the pharmacist could then issue him his prescription. The man explained he was only traveling through and did not have a doctor in the area. The pharmacist then leaned closer and suggested he look for Bertha's bricks. Not quite whisky, the pharmacist said, but it'll do the trick if you leave it in the cupboard for twenty days or so.

I remember the boxes of concentrated grape juice and how they were apparently purchased in large quantities for home wine-makers to mix and set aside to ferment into wine. In the era of bathtub gin and back country stills, grape bricks were a much simpler solution for a dry nation. It became a well-known fact in later years that Bertha Beringer was the woman behind the idea that kept the Beringer vineyard afloat, with the help of a sacramental wine license during Prohibition.

I savor another sip of wine and flip toward the back of the journal, musing about women and the way they contributed to keeping vineyards alive.

March 1933

I spotted the four sprigs of vine leaves nailed to the farm gate as Al and I came up the road from school. I kept the secret to myself, but I felt a jolt of pride at seeing Mama, or maybe it was Nonno, take my suggestion to increase wine sales. I'll have to wait to get them alone to learn of its success, but for now, I am pleased to be a part of their effort to keep the vineyard on track until all this Prohibition stuff is done with.

"Women and wine," I say out loud in a singsong voice that lifts my spirits.

A sinking feeling causes me to spill my wine on the journal's page, my hand shaking unsteadily as I rush to return the glass to the nightstand.

The dots of my past connect with one another, drawing a discernible path of how the rocky relationship with my father came to be. A sensation that squeezes my heart.

What if Papa's arrest was all my fault?

I blot the journal with the corner of my bedspread, not caring that the bedding will forever be stained red, and reread the date at the top of the entry.

March 1933. What if Mama was discovered because of my suggestion to put the vine leaves out? Why didn't she say anything to me? Does Papa know? Is this the reason he is forever disappointed by me? Why I can't seem to make him proud?

The questions trip over one another in the low light of my bedroom. Now that I see it, I cannot erase it from my mind. Mama, Bertha Beringer, and me.

"Women and wine." My voice wobbles. "Perhaps Papa does have a reason to worry over the fate of a vineyard left in the hands of a woman."

I close the journal and sink into the cocoon of my covers, desperate for a respite from the knowledge I've gained and the future that is now more uncertain than it was a few short hours ago.

Eleven

MONDAY, MAY 1960

I PUSH BACK the covers with a groan. Heavy eyelids from a lack of sleep make the sunlight streaming past my bedroom curtains far less welcoming than usual. I've slept through my alarm and my morning tasks in the vineyard.

I can count on one hand the number of times I've missed morning chores since Mr. Parisi gifted me the use of his land. Rationally, I know nothing will be amiss for my lack of attention of a single day, but I chide myself all the same. I place my feet on the cool wood floor, not wanting to let myself off the hook, though I suspect the self-loathing has more to do with the realization of how I may have contributed to the turbulence with my father rather than the delayed start to my day.

Readying myself for work, I consider the arrest warrant and wonder who placed it there, in the trunk's lid, wedged under the strapping, camouflaged but not entirely hidden from sight. I think back to the day I left home, carting the only item of real value to me, Nonno's trunk. Despite having not made much use of the trunk all these years, it was the only piece of furniture I took from my childhood home. Sentimental, I suppose.

I scoff at myself in the bathroom mirror. On second thought, perhaps I was being just plain stubborn and unwilling to leave my memories of Nonno behind. If I had to guess, it would be that Nonno himself managed to sneak the telling piece of paper into the trunk's lid, his attempt to enlighten me one last time as to the things I don't understand about my father.

My head drops to my chin, hairbrush in hand. "I'm trying Nonno, really I am." I brush my teeth and attempt to coax my mind into the present moment.

Noticing the time, I stuff a day-old croissant and an apple into my bag before returning to the bedroom for the journal I didn't finish reading last night. I'll have my lunch break to scan a few more pages. Maybe then I will have a better understanding of what to say to Papa about the future of the vineyard and my role in it.

Pausing at my desk to gather the rest of my things, I rearrange everything in my hands to add the unread wine books under my arm. Juggling my bag, car keys, and books, a weary exhale catches the dew in a faint cloud when I step onto the gravel. Locking the cottage door, the morning's air, crisp and clean, greets me with a breeze.

I walk to my car, unloading my arms of books by piling them into the passenger seat. I pull the croissant from my bag to eat on the way before starting the car. With breakfast in hand, I do my best to nudge a better disposition into my mood for the day ahead.

The morning at the Vintner's Society offices goes by in a blur of memos, typing, and the scheduling of next month's meetings. I am startled from my thoughts when Mr. Zellerbach steps into the office and makes a beeline to my desk.

"Miss Russo. Good morning."

"Mr. Zellerbach, how lovely to see you." I quickly scan the calendar to the right of my typewriter. "I didn't see you on the schedule today. Have I made a mistake?"

The good-natured man waves his hat-holding hand dismissively. "No, no, not at all. I was in town for another meeting and thought I'd visit. Get a status report and such."

My cheeks blush with a lick of heat. "That's kind of you, sir."

"Well...how did the harvest and crush go? I've been most eager to hear about your progress with the Pinot Noir."

"As it happens, I bottled the second harvest recently." I can't hide the joy that erupts from within me. "I think I've done well for a second harvest, or so I'm told."

"Well done, Miss Russo. I'm very pleased to hear it." Mr. Zellerbach beams at me. "I don't wish to be a bother, but is there a chance I'll be able to sample the fruits of your labor? I would love to compare our vintages given the grape is relatively new to the region."

A laugh escapes my closed lip smile. "Of course, you may. I would have brought you a bottle today had I known you were coming in." I flip the pages of the calendar and locate his name, written in pencil. "I have you down for two weeks from Wednesday. I'll be sure to bring you some then. Given it was your insight and willingness to sell me the vines in the first place, the gift of a bottle is the least I can do."

"Ah, but it is you, Miss Russo, the grape farmer and the vintner who accomplished the feat. You alone."

"Thank you. That's kind of you to say."

"The success of creating a wine others will enjoy should be savored, like a good wine itself." Mr. Zellerbach's eyes twinkle with what I interpret is an appreciation of our mutual love for the vineyard life.

The clock on the wall reads noon as he heads out the door. Thanks to the kind gentleman, my mood has indeed improved and I reach into my bag for what's left of my meagre lunch. Placing the apple on the corner of my desk, my right hand roots around in my bag for the journal I could have sworn I tucked inside.

Several minutes later, after checking the journal hasn't inadvertently been left with the stack of wine books I deposited on the back filing cabinet when I walked in this morning, I return to my desk and dump the entire contents of my bag out. My spirits dip once more—the journal is exactly where I left it. Sitting on the corner of my desk at the cottage.

A sleep deprived headache begins to throb at the edges of my temples. With the rest of the work day still ahead of me, I am destined to make zero progress in my quest to learn how best to connect with Papa over the sensitive topic of the future of the vineyard. Not to mention beginning the looming task of writing the speech I promised Mama I would have ready in time. Thwarted by my own doing once more, I slump into my office chair, biting into my apple only to discover it, too, is rotten.

Tick. Tick. Tick. The office clock intensifies the urgency building within me. I have less than five days to come up with a plan that will convince Papa to reconsider my involvement with the vineyard.

My eyes take in the wide, white face of the clock, its black hands quivering with a steady beat. With everyone away for their mid-day break, it taunts me with a warning. *Running out of time*, it seems to shout at me as I shift nervously under its gaze.

My heart picks up speed as I race through my options. Scanning the surrounding room, my stubborn side asserts itself.

I am stronger than this.

My disgruntled thoughts are of little use to me. I push them aside, choosing instead to use my lunch hour productively. The journal, forgotten at home, can't be helped. I will simply have to turn my attention to the other time-sensitive task before me, the speech.

Needing a new perspective and a breath of fresh air, I grab a notepad and pencil, turn on the office's latest acquisition, the answering machine, and slip out the office door. I flip the open sign to closed and lock the door from the outside.

Seeking out a bench to soak in the warm May sun, I wander the sidewalks, dodging shoppers as they go about their daily errands. I settle myself on an empty bench, the scent of Napa blooms and citrus trees distinct in the air. The combination of sweet and spicy lingers and I wonder, not for the first time, if this is what makes Napa wine so unique and appealing.

A young man, about twenty-years-old, draws my attention from across the street. He is leaning against a new sedan, its fresh polish gleaming in the sunlight. A breath catches in my throat. Whether it's the way he's standing or his build and hair color alone, I am caught off guard by his presence, one that reminds me of Tino.

What a pair we would have made, I think to myself, unable to pull my eyes off this man, at least twenty years my junior. I watch him, following every move as he opens the passenger door for a woman with a grocery bag. My eyes remain on the car until it disappears from sight. Some people stay with you forever, even if they are no longer in your life. That is Tino Parisi for me.

The moisture in my eyes dissipates in the warm breeze, allowing me to turn my attention to the notepad in my lap. If I can write the speech, perhaps that will spur my thoughts on how to make amends with my father. Maybe then, he will see me as the right Russo for the job. I write down the number one, determined to make a start. If I can get my thoughts organized I will have better success. The place to begin, I tell myself, is at the beginning, of course.

1) Papa is an avid reader and lover of Dickens' stories. When we became old enough, he used to tell Al and me about the story of our arrival into the world before tucking us in on Saturday evenings. Referencing the opening line from A Tale of Two Cities.

"It was the best of times, it was the worst of times, it was the age of wisdom, it was the age of foolishness, it was the epoch of belief, it was the epoch of incredulity, it was the season of Light, it was the season of Darkness, it was the spring of hope, it was the winter of despair..."

My twin brother and I were born on January 16, 1920, the same day the Russo Vineyard and every other vineyard in the country was threatened with extinction due to the enactment of Prohibition.

I reread my words, letting the weight of them settle over me. If I'm being honest, I can't even begin to imagine the burden of a new family, two for the price of one in Papa's case, on the same day your future livelihood is stolen out from under you.

The life of a grape farmer is far from easy. Luck and Mother Nature dictate much of one's success, but not before taking every waking hour, every breath, and every aching muscle in payment.

When I think about Prohibition now, I waffle between the absurdity of it all and a visceral anger that makes my blood boil. Destroying countless industries, families, and farms is one thing, but the Volstead Act managed to cost the government over ten billion dollars in lost tax revenue. Not to mention the speed with which organized crime rose up when the opportunity to bootleg was handed to them on a silver platter. All this meant an additional $300 million tax dollars spent trying to enforce the Act.

I shake my head in disagreement of the facts. Knowing now that Papa was one of those casualties in more ways than one due to the criminal record that follows him to this day, I find myself humbled, unable to truly comprehend what his life might have been like.

I think back on the insensitive cold shoulder I gave him most of my teenage years. Some of them, likely undeserved, I imagine. The disagreements because I thought I knew better. The entitlement to his legacy that I've assumed was mine for the past forty years washes over me with a wave of shame. With the recent discovery about my father, I can't blame him for finding me wanting of the values he holds dear. Mama has always said Papa and I are more alike than either one of us realizes, but this time, it seems only our differences are rising to the top and getting in our way.

I tear the piece of paper from my notepad, disappointed with my lack of progress, and crumple it into a ball. The closer I come to reconciling the past and my part in it, the more the question of whether I am worthy of the role of Russo winemaker pokes at me. The awareness of my previous youth-driven behavior is doing a good job of making me flinch inwardly while giving me reason to pause.

I let the thought sift through my mind, wondering how I will ever convince Papa that I have grown into someone he can trust with his vineyard. I have worked hard to gain the skills of a vintner. The proof is bottled and ready to savor. I have the passion for all aspects of the job. Now, all I need is to persuade Papa that I have grown beyond his expectations of me and that I am capable of making him proud.

Getting nowhere fast by sitting on this bench, I stand, deciding to pick up a sandwich from the deli on my way back to the office. A girl needs to eat, after all. A less hungry stomach would allow a clearer thinking brain to prevail.

I wander back toward the office, soaking in the flashes of colorful blooms while trying to match the scents in the air with each flower along my route. Napa is prettiest in springtime. Wisps of white clouds paint the blue sky, finishing off the picture perfect painting in front of me as if all I needed was a little Napa spring to remind me that an answer to my dilemma exists, somewhere, I just haven't found it yet.

Twelve

DRIVING HOME FROM WORK, I let my mind wander. The distraction of the Napa Valley hills blooming with the colors of spring serves me well, finally allowing my thoughts to land on something useful as I turn my car into the back driveway closest to the cottage.

Wine, I think as I close the car door and move toward the cottage. What better way to convince Papa of how ready I am to take on the vineyard than to show him how far I've come? For the past fifteen years, I have been quiet with regards to my efforts with wine, assuming he wasn't interested in hearing about them. Or, maybe I've simply kept them hidden in an attempt to protect myself from what I've always believed was his disappointment in me.

But now? Now is the time to speak with him in the language we both understand. The language of wine. I drop my bag inside the cottage, noting the half-read journal is, as I expected, sitting on the corner of my desk. Shaking my head at my muddled brain, I change clothes, pull on my rubber boots, and head out into the vineyard, eager to see my vines before the sun disappears from the sky.

Feeling like a caged bird let free to soar, I wander the rows. Turning a leaf here, checking the progress of flowering there, I allow myself to relax. I breathe in the scent of the fields and am reminded of the hope that exists in a vineyard in springtime. The same hope I desperately need to carry me through if I am to connect with Papa in a meaningful way. The task feels daunting. Too many years of rocky soil between us have left boulders instead of pebbles in our way.

I near the Parisi home at the far end of my vine's rows. I glance toward their kitchen window and consider stopping. A warm embrace and a home baked Italian treat from Olivia Parisi would certainly be welcomed, but would, in the end, delay me from tending to tonight's purpose. Instead, I turn around and soldier on, knowing the task that needs doing is waiting for me at the cottage.

Dinner is cheese and crackers and a glass of Parisi Zinfandel. Though I promise Mama I am eating well enough, I'll seldom mention dinners like tonight where food takes a backseat to a more pressing matter.

I settle myself on the floor, in front of Nonno's trunk and pull several notebooks from inside. Being dedicated to journaling, it doesn't take long for a stack to pile up around me. From a young age, my grandfather taught me well and most of those teachings have stayed with me, if only in the pages of my journals. I smile at the thought.

What would he think of how my life has turned out? I know he wanted more for me. He asked—no—he begged me to carry on the tradition of Russo wine.

He also would have insisted I put more effort into my relationship with my father. As of now, I see Papa once every few weeks, despite living a stone's throw away from my childhood home.

Even those visits, the ones that have all seven of us including Al's wife and their two kids, sitting around the farmhouse table for a traditional Italian meal, have felt shaded by words left unsaid and hurts left unhealed.

Digging through my journals, I am looking for reminders of what brought me to this point in my life, with wine at the center of it all. It's a funny thing, really. I've spent my entire life tending to, learning about, and embracing the vines and the gift they provide but the years and lessons blend within my mind until they remain as a solitary lifelong lesson, one I have difficulty articulating.

Though, communicate my journey I must, if I am to use our shared experience in wine to meet Papa where he stands. I reach for another journal from the trunk, determination asserting itself once more. Now is not the time to shy away from a difficult conversation, not when my future in Russo wine is at stake.

My hand tugs out a small brown journal. I open the front cover and find Nonno's sharp, straight script on the first page. "Gold." My mouth stretches into a wide grin. "Pure Russo gold."

I lean forward on my knees and peer deeper into the trunk. The bottom of the trunk is lined with more little, square journals. Nonno's journals.

My palm strokes the leather cover of a journal, and like a time machine, his journal takes me back to a childhood spent in Nonno's company. He always preferred the small, square notebooks, the kind he could carry in the back pocket of his work pants. Together with a tiny pencil, he could be found sitting on an upturned bucket while he wrote his observations about the vines, wine, and even life on occasion. I scan the first page and laugh out loud.

He wrote his observations in English and Italian, it seems. I may need Mama's help to translate some of this.

His lessons and wisdom have imprinted my past. I wonder if

my father realizes how much Nonno taught me about grape farming. Does he remember Nonno saying that Russo wine runs through my veins? My grandfather used to tell me of Papa's love of the vines. How, if given the chance, Papa would become a renowned winemaker. Part of me questions the truth of his words, not the heart from which they came, but the truth of them, all the same. I recognize Papa was fighting an uphill battle with Prohibition and then The Great Depression but, he has had twenty years since then. If he was going to make his mark in wine, wouldn't he have done so by now?

Maybe that is the reason he refuses me when it comes to the vineyard. What if Papa's concern is that I will eclipse him? I instantly cringe at my ego-infused thought and take a sip of wine in an attempt to put distance between me and my self-important musings. My hackles rise in unbecoming fashion, so I tamp down the conflicting emotions gathering inside me, reminding myself of the purpose and importance of my trip down memory lane.

My knee jerk response to preventing the vineyard from failing lies at the core of who I am. Al is capable, but he isn't likely to reach any sort of recognition status in Napa on his own. Too many times, I have stood by as Russo Wines faced challenges that could have pulled us under. I've spent a lifetime willing the success of a continually struggling vineyard.

Even after the country got back on its feet, the wine industry limped along with everything from farmhand shortages to bottle shortages and distribution delays. For a commodity that is in great demand, especially during the years it was illegal, things certainly don't seem to get easier.

Bracing a hand against the trunk, I hoist myself to a standing position. I take my glass of wine and three of Nonno's journals and sit down at the desk, determined to, at the very least, draft some words for Saturday's speech, even if I have to borrow them from my grandfather.

With pen in hand, I get to work, deciding the introduction, though basic, will hopefully help create some much needed momentum.

Welcome to the Russo Vineyard. Thank you for joining us as we celebrate the grand opening of the first tasting room our little winery has ever seen. I see most of you have a glass in hand and if you don't, be sure to see my sister-in-law, Eva, as we will be raising our glasses in toast shortly.

As my Nonno used to say, in jest, of course, Chi non beve in compagnia o è un ladro o è una spia. *People who do not drink with others are either thieves or spies. We don't wish to call anyone out, so be sure to have a glass in hand as we recognize my father, Giovanni Russo, for his lifetime achievement as Russo vintner.*

"Finally." The words whoosh from my lips. I have a start, complete with a little humor and a nod to my grandfather who is truly the reason we are all here to face the challenges before us and celebrate the winery as it exists today.

An hour later, I find myself lost in Nonno's musings. He details the health of the vines from top to bottom, the soil conditions, and even the general mood of the vineyard. This is something I don't recall him sharing with me, but clearly, he considered the idea that those who tend the vines and their state of mind, have an effect on the grapes. I am wondering if he was a visionary or simply an eccentric old man when I see a familiar Italian phrase.

In vino veritas. I know this one. Nonno recited the proverb as a cheers of sorts. He would raise his glass and proclaim, *In vino veritas.* To which the rest of us would raise our glasses and reply back to him. *In wine, there is truth.*

A thought rolls around my head and I try not to give it too much encouragement, fearing it will grow legs and walk to the Russo Vineyard all on its own. Al is convinced I must share my wine with Papa. He said Papa wouldn't be able to refute a good bottle of wine on its merits alone, but the worry of a little girl crawls up my spine, whispering into my ear. What if he shuts you down again? What if there is no coming back from our tumultuous past?

I shake my head in an effort to loosen the grip of my dwindling rumination. "No, this is my last chance to show him I am capable."

I stand, grasping for an infusion of strength to propel me on to what I must do. The short distance between the trunk and the cottage's entry way isn't much of a runway, but I pace the path anyway, my mind racing ahead. "I will bring Papa a bottle. Convince him to taste my wine."

Tapping a finger to my chin, I take another lap back and forth. I am contemplating my delivery, questioning whether it is best to approach Papa alone or if I should bring a bottle to dinner with everyone there to bear witness. The thought of being judged by my wine rattles my confidence. With my future as a vintner at stake, I need to be more than certain. My wine must be perfect.

I dash to the kitchen and pour a glass of my Pinot Noir. Swirling and sipping. Swishing and spitting. I come up for air in a fluster, reminding myself I am neither a sommelier nor an unbiased observer. But is my wine enough to convince my father that the future of Russo winemaking is safe in my hands? A quieter, more apprehensive voice whispers in the back of my mind. Am I worthy enough?

Determination rises within me. I will never know the answer if I don't ask the question. I return to my desk, reasoning the speech isn't my most pressing concern. I shuffle the papers before me and tell myself the speech I write will likely change, if I can convince Papa of my abilities as a winemaker. The first thing I must do is connect with him over the love of a good wine.

Thirteen

WITH TWO HANDS, I push the contents of my desk to one side and out of my way. I need all the space I can get to map out my plan. I place the beginnings of my speech gingerly on top of the pile, promising to return to it once I've spoken with my father.

Hesitant to rely solely on the virtue of a freshly bottled Pinot Noir to persuade Papa into anointing me the next Russo winemaker, I turn my attention to showing him the process that brought me to this point. His guard may be up when it comes to his daughter taking over his winery, but if I can draw him into a conversation, vintner to vintner, I am hopeful he will begin to understand the work, thought, and time I've put in to being the best winemaker I can be. Surely, my father will appreciate my efforts, if nothing else.

I push my feet back into my rubber boots and dash out the cottage door. The outbuilding, the one Tino and I used as our hideout, stores most of my rudimentary viticulture supplies. A roll of butcher paper that I used for mapping out the plot of land that holds my Pinot Noir vines hangs on twine dangling from the ceiling. I pull a sheaf of paper down and slice it with a utility knife.

Back inside the cottage, I lay the paper flat on the desk and riffle through the shallow drawer for the only marker I own. I work quickly, detailing the process of how I arrived at the end result of my latest vintage. I draw boxes and arrows while creating a map of my thought processes from beginning to end. Using a red pen, I draw stars where more detail is needed, writing notes at the side of the page as a reminder to myself.

The hours pass quickly as I transition from drawing the map to the written word. I tape the oversized diagram to the short entryway wall beside my desk and delve into the details. If there is anyone who would appreciate the methodical way I approached the designing and planting of my own vines, it would be Nonno. But since he doesn't hold the keys to my future, all I can hope is that Papa will be open to what I have to say.

"Nonno." His name elicits a mental picture of the instructions I discovered years ago. I hurry toward my bedroom, seeking the copy of *A Tale of Two Cities,* from the bookshelf. The place where I keep Nonno's recipe tucked for safe keeping. Returning to the living room, book in hand, it occurs to me that I chose a copy of Papa's favorite novel as the place to secure the information that inspired the Pinot Noir I have today.

Some things come full circle. I tug the folded piece of cardstock from the confines of the novel's pages.

The clock on the wall tells me I have worked past midnight. I lean back in my chair and stretch my arms overhead. Pleased with my efforts, I read through the pages once more, making a few more notes before deciding to pack it in for the day.

Marker and pen in hand, I pull on the desk drawer's handle. The sliding mechanism is far from smooth, given its age. A loud creak erupts from the desk and the drawer lurches open, sending the contents of the drawer backward then forward as I halt its abrupt momentum with the palms of my hands. I deposit the items into the drawer, but my attention is lured to the small scrapbook, the one where I paste Al's drawings whenever he shares his artwork with me.

Lifting the scrapbook from the drawer, I slide a little closer to the lamplight. Al has continued to choose a small square canvas for his art since as far back as I can remember. My eyes travel from Al's art to the rudimentary diagram I've mapped out on the butcher's paper. A laugh rises in my throat at the difference between the two. Clearly, there is little talent my twin brother and I share, as is evident from my lackluster drawing.

I remember the first time he cut the paper into squares. Not understanding the reason for the size and shape of the paper, I teased him, telling him he was making extra work for himself.

He shrugged, saying he didn't mind, as the small squares reminded him of the comic strip boxes he was so fond of. Al was happy, as always, to be left on his own to create his pictures. I can't recall a time when he wasn't drawing something. First, it was characters from his beloved comic strips, everything from Bozo the Clown to Popeye the Sailor Man captured his attention. Then it was landscapes. Eventually, he started focusing on abstract images, even creating a few logos for businesses throughout the Napa Valley on the side.

Thinking about Al's love of art stirs the prospect of our mutual aspirations within me. Both of us have been striving to follow our dreams for what feels like an eternity. The same eternity that Papa has been pushing us away from them. I've thought long and often about our situation, yet I continue to find myself unable to make sense of it.

I am all for respecting one's elders. Heeding the voice that comes from wisdom and appreciating the efforts and sacrifices made on children's behalves by their parents. However, I wonder if parents, too, have a responsibility to allow their children to become who they are meant to be. True, a parent's dreams for their children might not be met, but maybe those same children will shine brighter than their parents could have ever imagined. I'm holding out for the latter.

I sift through Al's drawings once more, pausing on a particularly detailed image of a grape cluster. My brother, the artist, shouldn't be forced into the life of a grape farmer. He should be allowed to shine as the talented man he is. I can't even imagine how he might flourish if given the chance to breathe. "I've got you, Al." I say to the drawings in my hand. "I'll find a way to make this right."

Given the late hour and tomorrow's early wake up, I consider skipping over the nightly task of writing in my journal. The struggle between my responsibility toward the task at hand and the desire to fall straight into bed brings a frown to my face.

Sighing an exasperated sigh, I am annoyed at myself for the compulsion to do as I said I would do. I sit up in bed, reaching for my journal and pen. Writing the date at the top of the page, I detail my impression of the vineyard from this afternoon. Once immersed in the task, I am easily lost as I walk past the vines in my head. I make a few notes on the day's weather and the status of the vines as they begin the flowering process. With the new insight gained from Nonno's journal, I add an extra line, reporting on how I was feeling as I spent time in the field. Who knows if there is anything to it, but it certainly won't hurt to be more aware of my own emotions.

Thumbing a few pages back, I assess the information in full, ensuring I don't miss anything of importance. Mr. Parisi used to chuckle softly when he saw me coming, journal in hand, lips lined with a host of questions ready to fire his way. "Sofia," he would say. "You don't have to record every insect that lands on your vines." I laugh at the thought of his wide friendly smile, knowing he, too, has made notes of Nonno's and my ways and now keeps a much more detailed journal all his own.

Placing the journal and pen on my bedside table, I switch off the lamp, sink into the pillow, and give thanks for how my years of dedication to recording my insights is about to pay off. I finally have all the information Papa needs for him to understand how capable I truly am. He won't be able to discredit my abilities now. I can't believe how foolish I've been, thinking years of pleading and arguing was the way to convince him of my suitability to become the next Russo winemaker.

All this time, I have been trying to sway him as his daughter, his own flesh and blood, with more than a passing interest in the family vineyard. Perhaps that should have been enough, but my emotions often got the better of me, usually resulting in both of us storming off angry. Now, though, I can see the day when I meet him as a winemaker, with mind-changing evidence in my hand and also in my bottle of Pinot Noir.

Fourteen

APRIL 1933

"HOW CAN he just walk away like that?" My dismay at Papa's intent to destroy the vines makes my voice wobble. I turn toward Nonno, fists clenched and teardrops streaming down my face, desperate for an answer.

"Sofia," Nonno's emotion-filled voice whispers my name. He is torn, taking a step toward Papa and then one back in my direction. "These are hard times. Your father is upset. Everything will be fine. You will see." He offers me a sad smile before gesturing in the direction Papa went. "I must see about your father."

Rapid Italian bounces off the outbuildings as Nonno traipses after Papa, his voice rising along with his concern.

Al shuffles his feet behind me. I cast an exasperated look over my shoulder at him, the fury still loaded in my gut like a cannon. Sensing my unease, Al takes a wide berth on his way back toward the farmhouse. He reaches the end of the row and turns, exhaling a long, slow breath.

"You really want to be a winemaker?" He asks tentatively, though I imagine he is ready to run at the slightest hint of my wrath being directed at him.

I shrug my shoulders, wrought emotion and uncertainty swirling around me. "I've always wanted to be a winemaker." I suck in a breath to hold my emotions at bay. "I thought I'd be just like him." I jut my chin in the direction of the outbuildings but given both Nonno and Papa set out that way, I am thankful not to give away the truth of who I am referring to, even to Al.

"Good. You can have it." Al kicks at the dirt, creating dust clouds with the toe of his shoe. "I don't want nothing to do with it."

I nod once at his resolute confession, and he nods his confirmation. We both understand one another perfectly, my brother and me.

Moments later, the back door to the farmhouse closes with a soft thud and I imagine Al taking a direct route to our bedroom in search of a sliver of peace and solitude. Everyone has vacated to their respective corners and yet here I remain, standing beneath a darkening sky among the rows of vines I can only hope holds the promise of our future.

The headlights bounce up and down as Mr. Parisi's truck bumps over the divots in the drive. I don't know if Mama called him for reinforcement or if he's come for another reason. I step out of the vineyard as the truck comes to a lurching stop.

Tino steps out from the driver's side and lifts a hand in greeting to me. I wipe my cheeks with the back of my hand and walk to meet him.

"I thought you were your father," I call out as I close the gap between us.

"He said your father needed my help with something." Tino scans the yard, squinting into the darker corners. "I came as soon as I could, but I suppose it is too late to accomplish anything more today."

I nod in agreement. "I don't think you'll be needed anyway."

"Why's that?" Tino rounds the front of the truck and leans against its hood.

"Papa is just having a bad day." I pivot slightly to take in the vineyard.

"Well, we've all had those. Anything I can help with?"

I shake my head no. "Not unless you can convince a stubborn man with a bucketful of frustration that plowing our vineyard under is a bad idea."

"I see." Tino dips his head up and down, my comment providing him understanding of some fashion.

I take in his usual relaxed posture. Has Tino ever had anything to fret over? In all these years, I've never seen his feathers ruffled, and honestly, I can't imagine him being anything but contemplative and respectful.

"What do you see?"

"Earlier." Tino pauses. "Your father was going on about—well, I figured he was simply ranting, but I understand now, he's feeling the pressures of life upon his head."

"Earlier?" I lift my eyebrows in question. "When did you see him earlier?"

"He came to our vineyard, needed my father to drive him somewhere." Tino's eyes drop to the ground, signaling to me he is holding something back.

I step closer, gesturing with my hand, indicating for him to continue. "And?"

"I overheard him tell my father that he needed to go get your mother from somewhere she shouldn't have been."

"Mama?" The new information swirls like a dust devil in my head. "But they came back in the truck... together." I let my words peter out as my brain attempts to understand.

"Do you think your father will really plow the vineyard under?"

My head snaps up at Tino's question. "Not if I have anything to say about it."

He nods in understanding, "I know it's been tough and he's planted more than grapes in the back acreage. So—I thought perhaps he might be done with wine altogether."

"What?" I take another step closer, gaining a clearer view of Tino's face in the glow of the porch light. "What did you say?"

"I thought you knew." Tino's voice wavers. "I didn't think it was possible to hide a good planting of plum trees."

"Plum trees. So, that's what he's been up to." My head shakes defiantly from side to side. I should have known that while Nonno and I worked on our own, happily tending the vineyard, Papa was busying himself otherwise. "I haven't been out to the back acres for some time now." I bite my bottom lip, deciding Mama wouldn't want me telling Tino of my displeasure with my father. "I didn't realize he had given up on us already."

"Given up on who?" Tino's relaxed posture stiffens as he stands, his face contorting with concern at having said something out of turn.

"Me. The vineyard. All of it, I suppose." My raw emotions threaten to spill again.

"I'm sorry." Tino steps forward, placing a warm hand on my shoulder. "I know how much you want the vineyard to succeed."

Crossing my arms across my chest, the anger that has settled in my belly licks upward like an out-of-control flame. "The vineyard will succeed." The words roar out of me not heeding my awareness that Tino, though on the receiving end of my fury, is not to blame.

Undisturbed by my discontent, Tino remains directly in front of me. "But how? How can you ensure the vineyard's success? You're only thirteen, Sofie."

Without knowing so, Tino has added fuel to the fire within me. "Only thirteen?" I holler back at him. "I take care of the vineyard every day, I'll have you know."

"I didn't mean—"

Tino's words are cut off abruptly by my own much louder ones. "I am telling you, just like I told Papa. I will be the next Russo winemaker and nothing he does will stop me."

Both of Tino's hands go up, palms facing me as he assumes the stance of surrender. "I have no doubt you will."

Thankful for the shadows of descending darkness, I tuck my chin in embarrassment over my outburst. "Sorry," I mumble before quickly adding, "I didn't mean to yell at you. I'm just…" I pause, taking a moment to assess how I'm feeling.

"Determined. Stubborn. Bullheaded." Tino's soft chuckle lightens the tension in the air. Lifting my chin with his finger, he continues. "Or maybe you're a visionary who has a passion for the vineyard life."

Our eyes meet and I sense his understanding of me, something I have never noticed before now. How is it this boy I've known all my life, but paid little mind to, can see into the deepest part of me when my own father seems unable to catch even the slightest glimmer of who I am?

"Well, I should head home." Tino drops his hand, retreating to the truck's cab. "I am quite sure I don't want to be here when your father returns."

I stifle a laugh. "You are probably right about that."

Rolling down the driver's side window, Tino leans out. "If you find yourself losing hold of your dream, Sofie, please find me. I'll be happy to remind you of what you're fighting for." He waves a final goodbye as he backs the truck out of the drive.

I consider Tino's words. He is going to make someone a fine husband someday. Not me, but someone.

Fifteen

THE BEDSPREAD IS TENTED over my head, hiding the beam of my flashlight, as I lie on my stomach, notebook splayed open in front of me. Al has been snoring for the better part of an hour, leaving me to ruminate on the boldness of my announcement this afternoon. When Papa turned his frustration toward the vines, I felt compelled to save them.

I meant what I said. I do want to be the next winemaker in the family. But, the weight of such a responsibility that I know less about than I admitted to, is heavy on my mind. In my defense, Papa was to be the one who taught me everything he knows. He was my guiding light until—he wasn't. How am I supposed to learn it all now?

Panic continues to grip my chest whenever I allow the memory of my tenth birthday to creep in. It's been three years and I still don't know what I did to fall out of favor with Papa. Mama and Nonno say it's the hard times and Prohibition putting a strain on my father. I've been told not to worry myself and that it will all work out in the end.

Their words offer little comfort though, and I can't let go of the notion that somehow I disappointed him, and the others are simply trying to spare my feelings. Even when all we had were grapes and juice to see us through, I felt Papa's pride in me each time he turned around and found me working, right alongside him. It didn't matter if we were repairing a fence, painting a barn, or working in the vineyard, a flash of his smile was all the motivation I needed to keep on going.

Of course, if I think back on it now, Papa's smiles became fewer and fewer in the months leading up to our tenth birthday. I hadn't thought much of it given Al's and my school schedule, and the shorter working hours available during winter. Still, nothing significant comes to mind when I think of how I may have misstepped.

I tug my attention back to the concern at hand. There is more to running a vineyard than planting vines and watching them grow. Decisions about grape variety, spacing of vines, the type of pruning to be used, when to harvest, and more, are things I've never had to consider on my own. I haven't even taken to memory the many growing conditions that different sections of our land offers. Not to mention taking into consideration the lengthy and detailed process of making wine. The pressure of the immense undertaking rises within me, and I know I am done in for.

No wonder Papa thought me impertinent. Perhaps he was right. Maybe I'm just a girl who doesn't have the right to say such things to her father. Despite his willingness to walk away from it all, I have no authority over his household or the vineyard. Heck, at thirteen-years-old, I don't even decide when I am to be afforded a new pair of shoes. Which is less often than I prefer, if I am being honest, since my current shoes pinch my toes and their heels are almost worn through. All of it, the decisions, the money, the power, lies with Papa.

My forehead drops, bumping against my open journal. The burden of the task ahead of me leaves my head and my heart heavy.

Mama's words about the lengthy process of making a traditional Italian dinner comes back to me as I hide from the world in the warm seclusion of my bed's covers. "Any endeavor with many tasks requires only a plan and a willingness to take the first step."

Lifting my head, I grab the pencil tucked within my notebook and write.

Step one: Learn everything I can about the vineyard.

Step two: Learn everything I can about making wine.

Step three: Wait for Prohibition to end and figure out how to sell wine.

Step four: Show Papa I am capable and willing to work hard to accomplish my goal.

Step five: Become the next Russo winemaker and make Papa proud.

I am examining my list, pleased and feeling a little bit better to have gotten it down on paper when raised voices from somewhere else in the house startle me from thought.

"You must understand, Giovanni. My intention was to help our family."

Papa's voice is gruff, exhaustion laced through his words. "Against my wishes. You knew my thoughts on all of this."

The sound of closing cupboard doors and chairs being pulled out muffles the argument coming from the kitchen. All I can guess is that Papa finally came in from the barn and Mama is now reheating a dinner that likely turned cold waiting for him.

I was relieved when Papa didn't return in time for dinner tonight. More than a little worried that one look at me might anger him enough to make him turn around and walk straight out the door. I'm not sure I could have handled that. Disagreeing with Papa has become a mainstay these past few years. How did we veer from the path of the man who could do anything and the little girl who believed it to be true? He may be angry with me but I'm angry with him too.

I flip through my notebook, reading over what I've recorded since January. Looking for insight into where I should begin with the plan before me.

"We've been over this, Angeline. You've put a target on our backs with your actions."

"The authorities have been by on occasion. They visit all the remaining vineyards as a regular course of action. It isn't as though you haven't had words with the man in the brown suit before."

A half hour later, the voices rise again. Not because they're shouting, but because they are much closer. I scramble back into place with my head on my pillow, flashlight switched off, and the covers pulled tight up to my chin.

The door to our bedroom opens with a faint creak and I squeeze my eyes shut. I feel Mama's presence as she moves first toward Al, then around the strung up bed sheet that separates his space from mine. Her hand brushes the hair from my face. Her scent surrounds me when her lips brush my forehead.

The floorboards groan under Papa's footsteps. Mama's voice is barely a sigh. "All I'm asking is for you to carry on with the plum trees, but let your father and Sofia work the vineyard. Even if they can't sell the wine, think of the bond they're building."

Immense love for my mother flows through me. Her quiet words are often far more persuasive than any angry ones she might be able to muster. I open my eyes a sliver, taking in their shadows in the darkness. Mama turns to face Papa, pressing her hand against his chest. "I know in your heart, Giovanni, you value tradition and connection with your family. The law can't keep us from growing grapes. Besides, this senseless law is coming to a close, my love. None of it will be cause for concern in a year's time."

Mama leaves the room first, and I try to fill in the blanks of their discussion. So, Papa and Mama had some sort of disagreement with the man in the brown suit. I remember him from that day last month. He was here in the driveway when Al and I arrived home from school. He was some sort of official, but clearly, according to Mama, nothing to worry about.

Though my eyes are closed, Papa's presence lingers. A creak in the floorboards announces his arrival at my bedside. His weathered hand is warm against my head as he strokes my hair a few times before turning to leave. A sigh of relief slips past my lips. Perhaps Papa isn't as angry with me as I thought.

I let several minutes pass, listening to the sounds of the farmhouse as it makes its way into slumber.

Burying my head under the covers once more, I fish the journal from the foot of my bed and flick on my flashlight. I have a plan, and if Mama's request of Papa holds water, then I've just gained some time to accomplish my list of tasks.

But how? I tap the pencil against my bottom lip. I consider asking Tino for assistance. He appeared to understand why the vineyard is important to me, and he did offer to help.

No, I don't want to give him the wrong impression since Papa so embarrassingly pointed out what a match we would be. I wouldn't want to muddy the waters of our mutual awareness of one another. I like Tino. He is helpful and kind and a hard worker too. But maybe he comes with too many strings attached and those are strings I am not at all interested in.

Nonno is the one who shows me what to do whenever I ask. He gives the instruction, often providing a demonstration if needed, then I go about the vines and do as I am told. He is a good teacher and I enjoy spending time with my grandfather in the vineyard. He tells the best stories and is easy to share a laugh with. I don't know what any of us would do without him.

Nonno has a vested interest in seeing the vineyard he built from scratch succeed too. Surely, there is plenty more he can teach me. If I promise to take the lessons seriously, like I do at school, then maybe he will agree to such a plan.

I turn off my flashlight and slide my legs out of bed. Placing my journal and pencil on top of my chest of drawers, I tiptoe from the room in search of the man who can help make my dreams come true.

A soft knock on his bedroom door is all it takes to be invited in.

"Sofia, what are you doing out of bed at this hour?" Nonno sits up, his hand outstretched to test the temperature on my forehead. "Are you ill?" Before I have a chance to answer, he pulls his hand away from my cool head and tugs my arm to sit beside him. "Or, is it your heart that is in need of healing?"

The words do not come as easily as I had hoped and instead are replaced with an unresponsive shrug of my shoulders.

"Come child. Something got you out of bed." Nonno's wrinkled hand squeezes mine in encouragement.

"I was wondering if you would teach me about the vineyard?"

"I do teach you about the vineyard. Every day we work together after school, I teach you something new." Nonno eyes me suspiciously. "Have you not been writing in your journals?"

I nod my head vigorously, not wanting to disappoint him. "I have. Every night before bed, I write what you have instructed me to put down."

Nonno's eyebrows converge in question. "Then what seems to be the trouble? You are learning and you will continue to learn."

"I suppose—well, I guess, I just want to make sure I'm learning the things I need to know, so I'm prepared to take over the vineyard one day."

"Oh Sofie." Nonno chuckles softly. "You have many years ahead of you before you need to worry about such things.

My eyes shift to examine the bed's quilt. I find myself torn in my allegiance between my love of the vineyard and my love for my father. "I want to know everything in case Papa decides to take it away."

"Ah, I see." Nonno pats my hand, a gesture I've learned to

interpret as a mutual understanding between us. "You will have to leave the matter of your Papa to me and time." Nonno tilts my chin, lifting my eyes to meet his. "Do you understand? Some situations take years to settle and wanting to rush them doesn't mean it is possible to do so."

I nod, a little disappointed that my involvement is once again being set aside.

"As the saying goes, *Roma non è stata costruita in un giorno.*"

My questioning expression nudges him to translate.

"It means, Rome wasn't built in a day." Nonno cocks his head to the side and smiles. "Neither was a master vintner. Rest assured, Sofia, I will teach you everything I can with the time I have left on this earth. I promise you that. Now, come and give me a hug and get back into bed before your mama catches you."

I tiptoe back to my bed, feeling my way in the darkness in both body and mind, with an outstretched hand.

Sixteen

JULY 1936

I AM thankful every day that our vineyard still remains. I ready myself for the day by dressing in a long sleeve shirt, shorts, and the wide-brimmed hat Mama passed down to me last season. Two months of long summer days in the fields are before me and I couldn't be more excited.

Nonno and I have maintained our afterschool and weekend routine in and around the vineyard but I'd be lying if I said I wasn't more than a little annoyed that Al has been permitted to stay home from school and work alongside Papa since the summer of 1933.

When the topic arose on the heels of Papa's outburst in the vineyard, Mama agreed to Al working the plum trees in an effort to grow the family's stability. The first crop is coming to maturity now and its bounty has lifted Papa's spirits after three long years of planting and care. The first harvest of European plums has been delivered to a farmer over in Yountsville for dehydrating.

I grab a plum from the bowl on the kitchen table and step onto the back porch. The sweet juice threatens to run down my chin as I bite into it. Nonno is waiting for me in the rocking chair that points out over the vineyard.

"Are you done making a mess of yourself?" he teases as he hoists himself from the rocker.

"Just getting started." I grin back at him.

"Your Papa will be joining us today." I catch the warning glance from my grandfather and wait for the admonishment. "You'll be on your best behavior?"

"Of course." I deliver an innocent bat of my eyelashes. When he doesn't respond to my attempt at humor, I assure him of my sincerity. "I will. I promise."

Nonno leads the way into the vineyard, and I dutifully follow. Papa has been reappearing among the vines since his anger dissipated after the end of Prohibition in December of 1933. Not every day, but often enough that it has been interesting to watch him reconcile his emotions with the vines that caused him much angst for far too many years.

Having walked on egg shells around Papa for several years now, I am accustomed to knowing when to hold my tongue, which is far more often than seems fair. But nobody is asking my opinion on this particular matter.

Mama says I've transformed from a stubborn little girl into a tenacious sixteen-year-old. Though her delivery is serious, I am convinced she finds some amount of pride in my ability to know my own mind. But when it comes to Papa, I've learned that some scars aren't as easily healed.

The sun is high in the sky when Papa finds us in the farthest corner of the vineyard. He and Nonno go over the work scheduled for the afternoon while I maintain the dance of ducking comments, eye contact, and more from my father. I am already hoping the afternoon will send us in separate directions down the rows, but I am reluctant to miss out on any bit of Russo wisdom that is sure to reveal itself as Nonno and Papa discuss their detailed approach for this year's canopy management.

Once a plan is decided upon, Nonno directs me to the far end of the first row, walking me through the steps he wants me to take. Having explained to me that thinning the leaves is a crucial element to our role in producing the desired flavor for our wine, I pay close attention to the how and the why of the task I've been given. I think back to last year's vintage as I work and contemplate how, due to a less rainy spring, we took a more modest approach and still the wine tasted different from the year prior.

How the end result changes from year to year is what compels me to learn more. My bookshelf is growing full of books on wine, and since Nonno has yet to trust me with actual winemaking, I take what he has taught me in the field and try to understand the effect his practices will have by reading everything I can get my hands on.

Working in solitude allows me the time to think. The more I ponder my lack of winemaking skills, the more anxious I become of running out of time to master all aspects of vineyard life. I've asked again, but still Nonno has determined I am not yet ready to make a wine of my own. Even with his assistance and his presence at every step of the process, he has refused my annual request.

"Not this year, Sofia," he said with as much patience as he could muster. "You have lots to learn yet. That learning must take place in the vineyard and in here." Nonno pointed to his chest and not for the first time I wondered if it is not my lack of knowledge of the vines that gives him pause, but instead it is perhaps my heart where the problem lies.

Movement from across the way draws my attention. Tino and his father are working their back rows, the ones that butt up against ours with a dirt road separating the two vineyards. Moments later, I hear Mr. Parisi's cheerful greeting. Nonno and Papa stop what they're doing to join in a neighborly chat. I keep my head down and continue moving up my row, my thoughts now tugged to Tino and his winemaking experience.

Last summer as Al, Tino, and I sat in the shade of the porch after a particularly hot afternoon, he had talked of his first venture into making his own vintage. Being a few years older than us, Tino's time in his father's vineyard has progressed to one of a partnership rather than adhering to the stagnant rules of parent and child. Though part of me wonders if that is down to Mr. Parisi's generous nature.

My hands itch as a thought emerges. Excitement gathers steam and I steal a glance in Tino's direction. Would he teach me what he knows about winemaking? He has grown into a handsome young man, I notice as his shirt stretches over lean muscles while he works. The heat of a blush warms my cheeks, and I'm thankful the sun can be blamed if the whirring of my inner mind was ever discovered.

As far as I am aware, he doesn't have a girl in his life, though from the rumor mill, I can count at least six who would jump at the chance to call Valentino Parisi theirs. Maybe Al was right in his assessment last summer. I punched him in the arm for saying so, but Al is often observant where I am not. Suggesting Tino was waiting for me to notice him was at the heart of our discussion that particular day.

It couldn't hurt to ask. I sneak another glimpse in his direction and ponder the best way to request such an immense favor. I've never been one to be coy, or for that matter, bold, when it comes to interacting with a boy. Honestly, I've never been interested more than a passing glance. I suspect my inexperience has more to do with the hours I spend in the vineyard than anything else, but given what is before me, I will need to think more about how best to proceed.

Spending the rest of the afternoon in thought serves me well. By the time the sun is sinking into the horizon, I have worked several rows and gathered my courage to speak with Tino. I am fearless as I bathe off the day's grime and slip into my favorite floral print sundress. Though it's a few years and inches shorter since I wore it last, I can't imagine a shorter hemline being a disadvantage for the plan I've set in place.

Declining dinner, I sneak out the back door, grabbing a light sweater as I go. The scent of hot earth cooling is a comfort as I skip down the porch steps, daring to be brave. Tino mentioned an outbuilding his father lets him use. The outbuilding, behind the old winemaker's cottage, is my first destination. If he isn't there, I'll have no choice but to check the main house. Knocking on the Parisi door with hardly a reason to visit, makes my stomach tie itself in knots. I cross my fingers and hope for him to be at the outbuilding instead.

The bare lightbulb hanging from the roof's overhang gives him away.

"Hi." I do my best not to startle him, but given the surprised look on his face, I haven't succeeded.

"Sofie, you made me jump." Tino's voice turns into a light laugh.

"Sorry, I didn't mean to." I step closer, the plan filtering through my mind. "I was hoping we could spend some time together." My fingers twist into a clenched grip that I hide behind my back.

"Sure. You are always welcome to join me." Tino's invitation is sincere, confirming Al's assessment of the situation.

"What are you working on?" I move to stand beside him, brushing my arm against his.

He doesn't retreat or even hesitate in his response. "I've been thinking about the flavors I want to introduce in my vintage this year." Tino points to a book laid out before him on the wooden shelf. "All day trimming and evaluating the rows got me thinking ahead."

"That's funny. I was thinking the same thing today." I summon a slight pout while adding. "Of course, I don't have a vintage to plan for." I let the sentiment hang between us.

Tino turns toward me, his features kind and full of compassion. Our bodies are inches away from one another. The heat from the day emanates off him.

"Sofie." My name spoken with tenderness is all I hear. Taking the cue, I lift my heels and rest on the balls of my feet while leaning toward Tino's chest.

I bite my bottom lip, holding it between my teeth for a split second then take the plunge. My lips meet his in a rush of nerves and excitement.

"Sofie!" Alarm lifts his voice. Tino's hands are on my arms, pushing me away with haste. His expression screams mortified, which is precisely how I now feel.

Seventeen

OCTOBER 1938

I STEP into the shelter of the winemaker's cottage outbuilding, the one where Tino and I have spent more hours than I can count over the past two years. "Hey you."

"I wondered how long it would take you to escape." Tino smiles mischievously before wrapping me in a bear hug.

Breathing in, I am comforted by the smell of him. A mix of pure joy and vineyard life is what I inhale each time we meet. "You know, you should really bottle that scent of yours. The girls would go wild for it."

Without missing a beat, he murmurs into my hair, "Too bad I'm not inclined to concern myself with what girls would go wild over."

"Don't I know it?" I pull away and search his eyes. "But oh, how they dream." I give him a cheeky wink before continuing on. "I don't think us spending time together is much of a secret anymore, at least not at my house."

"Nah, my parents are comfortable with you and me." Tino gives me a lighthearted slug to the shoulder. "I am still certain, my mother would like to adopt you, but she seems to have found a way to hold her tongue when it comes to questions about the chance of future wedding bells."

"Do you think they know?" I feel myself spin as vertigo sets in at the thought.

"What, that I'm not the marrying kind?" He rolls his eyes at me. "Not a chance. The only person I've ever told is you."

"Your secret is safe with me." A bite of autumn breeze whips between us, eliciting a full body shiver down my spine.

Tino wraps a protective arm around me, kissing my forehead as he does. "I love you even more because of it. Speaking of secrets, shall we get back to work on yours?"

"I can hardly wait." Excitement bubbles up inside me. Together, we move farther into the outbuilding and survey the rows of wine bottles that line the makeshift shelf. A small vintage, but a huge step forward for me and my goals.

Tino pulls two glasses from a bag he has brought from home, clinking them together as he sets them on top of a wine barrel.

"Your pick." Tino inclines his head toward the bottles.

I move closer to the wall of wine, relishing in the existence of it. Together, Tino and I harvested and crushed a small batch of grapes several months ago. We followed Mr. Parisi's very basic instructions, aiming for a passable vintage, and not necessarily stellar, in our first attempt at making wine together. Though Tino has seen some results in the past few years, he let me make all the decisions, guiding me through each stage.

I pull a bottle from the top shelf and deliver it to Tino, waiting at the upturned barrel with the corkscrew.

The most beautiful sound, *pop*, fills the room and I giggle in anticipation.

Tino pours two glasses of wine, then places one in front of me.

I learned more than I ever imagined I could in one season of winemaking with someone who has become my best friend. Knowing I owe it all to Tino, I raise my glass in his direction. Gratitude for his existence in my life spills out of me in the form of happy tears.

"Don't cry Sofia, you'll water down the wine."

I laugh and swipe at the moisture with the sleeve of my sweater. Taking a few deep breaths, I lift the glass to my nose. Not the best wine I've ever smelled. I am not concerned, since my expectations are fairly low anyway.

After watching me for a moment, Tino lifts his own glass, crinkling his nose slightly at the aroma.

"Together," I say.

We clink glasses. "*Salute.*"

Taking a small sip, I am prepared to let the wine sit and linger on my tongue. Ready to savor and taste the notes I've intended to be present.

Without warning, we are spitting our first sip of wine onto the floor. Complaints coming in the shape of groans and gasps are quick to erupt from both of us. Tino reaches for a bottle of water he brought with him from home. Scrubbing the taste from our mouths, we pass the bottle back and forth until we find the words to say.

"That is nothing like wine." Tino snickers before taking another sip of water.

"What do you think happened?" I lift the glass, peering at its crimson contents.

Tino is shaking his head, trying to stop himself from a full out belly laugh. "I have no idea. I'm just glad it was only a small batch."

"Thank heavens for small mercies," I try, but I can't hold back my own laughter and within moments we are laughing so hard we can no longer speak.

A few hours later, my mind is still busy going over what might have gone wrong with the wine. The clock reads well past ten by the time I return home. Aware the rest of the household is fast asleep, I close the back door quietly behind me and step into the kitchen. I jump, clutching a hand to my chest when he calls out to me.

"Where have you been?" Nonno sits at the table, arms crossed, as he assesses me before I can utter a word.

"Nonno, you startled me."

"I expect you thought you could simply sneak in and not be noticed?"

Gauging his mood, I choose my approach. "Perhaps I was being quiet so as not to disturb anyone."

"You may fool your mama, Sofia, but I am not as easily convinced."

"Nonno, I am eighteen-years-old."

"That still does not tell me where you've been." Nonno tilts his head in question.

"I was with a friend." Moving farther into the kitchen, I retrieve two glasses from the cupboard and fill them with water, already knowing he is going to want more than what I've provided.

Placing a glass before him, I settle myself in a chair and meet his eyes. "I was with Tino."

"Ah, I see." Nonno sips his water with slow, contemplative movements. "So, not just a friend, but a friend who is a boy." His bushy eyebrows lift then converge, making a statement all their own. "What do you think your Papa would say about you being out with a boy at this hour of night?"

An ironic laugh slips through my lips. "Tino is a friend. Nothing more than that. Honestly, that's the reason I didn't say anything. Papa would be more than eager to push Tino and I together and that isn't what we want."

Nonno nods in agreement. "Yes, that is true."

I may be off the hook. I wait a moment for permission to be granted before placing my palms on the table and pushing myself to a standing position, ready to escape his interrogation.

"But there is something you aren't telling me." Nonno leans back in his chair. "What is it, Sofia? What are you keeping secret?"

I slump back into my seat. "Fine." Sneaking a glance over my shoulder to ensure we are in fact, alone. "I will tell you, but you must promise to keep it a secret. Even from Mama." I extend my hand, inviting him to shake on my proposed deal.

He waits a moment before accepting my hand. "I presume since you've been with Valentino that you are not in any danger."

I shake my head sullenly. "The only danger I am in is the danger of not having the skills necessary to be a real vintner." Emotion lodges in my throat as disappointment from tonight's tasting catches up with me.

"So, you and Tino have been making wine?" Nonno's eyes twinkle as he comes to understand.

"Not very well, apparently." My thumb runs up and down the water glass, wiping the condensation away with each swipe. "Tonight was the first time we tasted our wine. Well, my wine, really. Tino let me make the decisions along the way. Clearly, I have no instincts as a winemaker."

Nonno laughs. "You think you are the only one to fail at making wine?"

I shrug my shoulders in response.

"Do you know the reason I said you weren't ready to learn how to make wine?"

My face flushes with color, embarrassment over having gone behind his back making itself known.

"Intelligence and skill are important aspects of making good wine. It is true." Nonno shakes his head back and forth. "But what lies in the winemaker's heart cannot be ignored."

"What do you mean?"

"Sofia, why did you set out on your own, without your family's support or awareness, to experiment with making wine?"

My face grows hot under his pointed comment.

"One cannot make wine worthy of acclaim if the heart of the winemaker is not a pure one."

"Are you saying my heart is..." My words falter, unable to be spoken from my own lips.

"Did you or did you not want to prove your Papa wrong?"

My shame knows no bounds. I incline my head once in agreement while shifting my eyes away from his.

He isn't done making his point. "Did you also presume that because you wanted it so much, making a great vintage would come easily?"

"But I only wanted a place to start. To get my feet wet. If I don't begin learning now, I fear I never will." My arguments are futile, but I feel compelled to defend my actions.

"A winemaker who holds vinegar in his heart will taste vinegar in his wine, Sofia. That is what I'm trying to say. You must get your heart right first, then you will be ready for the wine."

"Get my heart right? How do you suggest I do that?" An exasperated sigh whooshes past my lips. "I live in the home of a man who doesn't believe I should have any dreams when it comes to making wine and would rather see me married and tied down in an existence I don't desire."

"Do you remember when you were a little girl and we would walk through the vineyard? I would point out the vines that were doing well and flourishing. But I would also point out those that were struggling."

"Yes." I have no idea where Nonno is going with his story, but his ability to draw me in has yet to fail him.

"One day, you were about seven-years-old at the time. You

asked me why I bothered showing you the vines that were struggling. Do you remember what I said?"

My head shakes back and forth. "No. What did you say?"

"No vine grows into greatness without first struggling. Some
come out stronger and produce sweeter grapes once they've had to
rise above their challenges. Do you understand? You too, Sofia, are
growing into greatness right before our eyes."

Eighteen

TUESDAY, MAY 1960

THE SUN HAS BARELY RISEN over the vineyard, but the happy chirp of the birds beyond the cottage window coaxes me awake. With only a few hours of sleep behind me, my eagerness to speak with my father has multiplied. Placing my feet on the cool wood floor, I hesitate.

Is it excitement or apprehension that I'm feeling? I have no desire to rush toward a mis-step, especially one with Papa, but as I tug my robe over my shoulders and trundle to the kitchen to make a pot of coffee, I feel that time to set things right is slipping through my fingers.

Once showered and dressed, I slip out the cottage door with a steaming cup in hand. The dark brew takes the chill from my hands as I cradle the cup, while its aroma promises a jolt of energy for the day ahead. I walk the property with speed, my footsteps fueled by my racing mind and a gathering bundle of nerves that has settled in my chest like butterflies.

Thirty minutes later, I am back at the cottage. I drop my mug in the kitchen and stop at my desk to make a few notes about this morning's walk through the vineyard before heading to the bedroom to finish readying myself for the day.

Papa is sure to be well into his morning chores at the Russo Vineyard. I gather my bag, last night's notes, and a bottle of my unlabeled Pinot Noir. I dash out the door, hoping to catch him before I leave for the office.

Deciding to avoid a lengthy welcoming by the whole family, I pull into the back driveway, the one that leads directly to the cellar and the back acres of vineyard land. My little car rumbles along, bouncing and dipping with each pot hole carved out by spring rain.

Parking on a small section of grass, I see Papa's head as it pops out from the cellar's wide barn door entrance. He disappears again by the time I make my way around my car and toward the cellar. With my bottle of Pinot Noir in hand, I step into the darkness of the cellar's interior.

"Papa." My voice bounces off the brick walls, their thickness providing the consistent year-round temperature that benefits the wine well.

"Sofia? Is that you?" Papa leans over the upper balcony railing, a second addition that was built as a compromise between my father and Nonno when our fields were producing both grapes and plums and extra storage space was needed. "I was expecting your brother."

I resist the urge to mumble *of course you were* and instead offer a more suitable greeting. "Good morning," I call up to him. "I was wondering if you have a few minutes to talk?"

"Today is busy." Papa sighs and I wonder if he will forever be exasperated by me or if I will be able to win him over in the end. "I'll be right down. I have to head over to the new tasting room, anyway."

Papa's work boots clomp down the stairs, the reverberating sound echoing ahead of his arrival.

He kisses my cheek in greeting. "What have you got there?" A weathered finger points at the bottle tucked under my arm.

"Ah, this is for you." The words hesitate, reluctant to leave my lips. "I thought you might want to—well, Al suggested."

Papa shoots me a questioning look.

"I made it." I cringe at the five-year-old sounding boastfulness of my words. "I mean, this is my second vintage of Pinot Noir and I thought, maybe, you would like to taste it. Then we can talk about the vineyard."

"Sofia, what is there to talk about? Your brother is about to open the tasting room. He will take over the vineyard. We have been over this more times than I can count. Everything is decided." Papa accepts the bottle from me. "But, thank you for the wine. Pinot Noir, that is bold of you. I am sure your mama will be happy to taste what you've made."

My heart sinks at his words, wearing the word *bold* as a rebuke instead of a compliment. I did not come here to be talked down to. I bolster my courage and square my shoulders. "I would like to discuss all the options. I have more experience now." I point to the bottle in his hand. "I've even brought you a map of what I've learned and how this wine came to be. Maybe we can talk vintner to vintner and..."

Papa's expression softens around his eyes, though I cannot discern if he feels sorry or concern for me. "Sofia, I do not wish for you to bear the weight of the vineyard. Besides, you have a job." Papa checks his watch. "One, I imagine you will be late for if you don't get going."

"But, Papa. Will you please just taste the wine and then we can talk more?"

"Alonso, there you are." Papa, having spotted his chosen one, places my bottle of wine on top of an upturned barrel and waves my brother closer. "We have much to do today. I expected you earlier."

"Hey Sof." Al bumps my arm with his in a welcoming gesture. "Mama made fresh biscotti this morning. She caught me as I was coming in. You know I can't resist Mama's biscotti." Al winks at me before pulling out a cloth napkin and handing it to Papa. "I even brought some for you."

Papa wraps an arm across Al's shoulders. "A very good reason for lateness. I agree." Without even a goodbye to me, Papa is off, heading toward the new tasting room, biscotti in hand.

Al turns to me. "So, what'd he say?"

"He won't even listen. I gave him a bottle, but—" I point to the cast aside bottle sitting on the barrel. "He thought Mama might want to try it." The words are strangled as they lift from my throat. "I thought I could come to him as a winemaker and he might respect that, but clearly he isn't about to change his mind."

"This is Papa we are talking about. He doesn't see you as a winemaker. He sees you as his daughter."

I shake my head in disagreement. "I'm not quite sure he even thinks of me as his daughter some days."

"Alonso, are you coming?" Papa, a hundred feet away, hollers back over his shoulder.

"Don't give up yet, Sof. There must be some way to reach him. To make him listen."

I nod, but my enthusiasm for convincing my father has been lost, at least for today. "You better go." I jut my chin in Papa's direction. "I have to get to work, anyway."

Dismissed by my father, I slide into the driver's seat and give my mood permission to fall.

I see Papa's apathetic expression as it plays on repeat in my mind. Thankful for a job I am more than a little familiar with, I manage to go through the motions at the office as I contemplate if there is a way to get through to my father. If only he wasn't so fixed on the one path as the future of the family vineyard.

By eleven o'clock, I am in a meeting taking notes on the state of the current wine season. The numbers fly from the tip of my pencil as I record the details from the roundtable discussion. I am stopped in my note-taking by the mention of Josephine Tychson, one of Napa's first women to run a vineyard successfully.

The conversation shifts, as it usually does, to the demise of Mrs. Tychson's vineyard. Phylloxera is a word with the power to give any winemaker worth his salt the shivers. All vintners know that everything they've worked for, everything they've sacrificed, could disappear in rapid succession should a pest or disease decide to strike the region.

Grape farming is not for the faint of heart, I remind myself as I am excused from the meeting, the men transitioning into casual chatter, all business having been completed. I set straight to work on typing up the meeting minutes. The keys clack happily as my fingers move with speed. Shorthand is a skill, for certain, but my memory of a recent meeting is far more reliable, so whenever possible, I aim to have the minutes complete while the conversations remain fresh in my mind.

As I reread my typed notes, I am caught once more by the mention of Mrs. Tychson. She was the woman I sought to follow when a librarian helped me with a school project. Though the resources were few, given the era and the fact that she was female and thus was hardly considered worthy of commenting on, the librarian found an article about Josephine and her winery, complete with a photograph. That photograph drew me in. Not because she was exceptionally beautiful, but because she represented a truth. Women are just as capable of running a successful vineyard as men are.

My thoughts shift back to Papa. Al is convinced his resistance to my involvement with Russo Wine has nothing to do with my gender. Something is amiss. Even I, who have been on the receiving end of more than one of my father's disapproving looks, can't quite believe him to be a cold-hearted man whose only desire is to keep women in their place. No, Al is right, gender has nothing to do with my father's decision as to which one of us inherits the vineyard.

Thinking of strong women leads me directly to thinking of Mama. She is the one person who may very well know what this is all about. Mama knows Papa better than anyone else, but will she confide in me now? Would she be an ally if I told her of how I continue to dream of being the next winemaker in our family?

Decades have passed since Mama and I last spoke of my being involved in the vineyard. Once I moved from my childhood home, I forged my own path of wine education. It became clear early on that avoiding the topic that all too often turned the dinner table into a battleground, was not only necessary but prudent if I wanted to maintain any semblance of a relationship with my family.

So, for the past fifteen years, I have kept the few discussions I've had with Papa about the future of the vineyard on neutral ground, away from Mama's listening ears and the farmhouse walls. Nonno's words about family being everything must have imbedded themselves in my skin long ago as no matter how frustrated or disappointed I become with my father's inflexible position on the subject, I can't bring myself to walk away entirely.

I busy my hands by filing papers, thankful for my memorization of what goes where in the tall cabinet with the sliding drawers. My thoughts drift back to Mama who was bold and determined herself once upon a time. To this day, I remember her telling me quite plainly to be a winemaker, if that was what I wanted to be. *Be true to yourself, Sofia,* she would say, infusing me with the belief that all I had to do was want something bad enough, then work to achieve it.

Her advice, in this regard, will only take me so far though since that which I seek is in the hands of another. Though I am certain Papa would object, speaking with Mama may be the only way I can put right whatever wrong I've caused between my father and me. Her guidance could very well be my last hope. With only four days before the vineyard is officially handed over to Al, time is running out. I would be remiss if I didn't do everything possible to prove to Papa I am worthy of both the Russo title and his praise.

When she handed me the article on Josephine Tychson, the kind librarian shared her own insight regarding the topic of my school paper. Her words stuck with me and tumble through my mind, giving me a much-needed boost of encouragement. "We may do things in a quiet way, my dear, but a woman should never be underestimated when she gets her teeth into something, even if that something is grapes."

Nineteen

AUGUST 1941

THE HOT SUMMER sun sketches ripples in the space between the vines and the clear blue sky. The heat, a constant presence over the past week, has done in any semblance of a pleasant mood within me. Adding insult to injury, Mama made me responsible for shelling the peas this afternoon, a task I have never taken a shine to. As a child, she would have scolded me into submission. Now, at twenty-one-years-old, all she has to say is, *we all have a part to play in the running of this farm. Don't disappoint me now, Sofia, and take that bowl with you out onto the porch.*

My eyes follow Al and my father, back and forth from the barn to the field, while my disgruntled frame of mind simmers from my vantage point under the shade of the porch's roof. Every now and again, I catch Al's eye though I am certain he would rather ignore me entirely. My brother knows me well and even from a distance he is aware I am furious about the lack of attention being paid to the vineyard.

Nonno is in bed, recovering from a bout of heatstroke. At his age, Mama has every right to be concerned, but I still can't fathom how I, too, must be forced to remain out of the vineyard today. I should be grateful for the reprieve from the heat, but all I can think of is the vines. They need constant attention at this stage of the season and as evidence before me, Nonno and I are the only ones to worry about them, or so it seems.

A bucketful of peas later, Papa and Al approach the porch, shirts soaked through with sweat. Reclining in a slice of shade with a cool glass of water in hand, Papa tells Mama about the progress they've made.

"All of them watered well." Papa nods in Al's direction. "He's a hard worker. I'm proud to see it."

Mama takes a seat in the rocker, positioning it to catch a breeze should one come our way. "The heat won't affect the harvest?"

Papa gulps his water down in two swallows before shaking his head. "Our plums are a hearty bunch now. If the weather persists, we'll water again, but I think we'll be fine."

I toss another pea shell into the discard bucket. Despite knowing better, I can't bite back the comment. "Good to know the plums are safe. Heaven knows the vines—"

"Those plums are safe," Papa cuts me off. Whether out of a desire to save me from myself or a lesson in humility, I am not sure. "And that's just the way we need them. Let me remind you they saw us through the thick of hard times. If taking care of the crop that keeps a roof over your head needs to be prioritized, then so be it."

Al shakes his head at me, a warning to let it go. If only he knew how deep my discontent runs.

Without another word, Papa wipes the sweat from his brow and heads in the direction of the barn.

Standing, Mama scolds me with a disapproving look. "You shouldn't goad him like that. And in this heat, especially. You don't have to start an argument at every turn."

Another peek in Al's direction and his eyes plead with me to keep quiet.

When I don't respond, Mama returns to the farmhouse. I imagine her questioning why she was blessed with such an obstinate child.

"You've heard the expression, you'll catch more flies with honey?" Al stares at me pointedly. "You should give it a try sometime."

"Better than being a do-gooder." I can feel Al's hackles rise before I look his way.

"Sofie, you can be incredibly difficult. Do you know that?"

"So I've been told." I shell another pea into the bowl, discarding its shell.

"Does it take a lot of effort to be so infuriating? Cause let me tell you, not everything has to revolve around the vineyard."

I couldn't conceal the huff if I wanted to. "We live on a vineyard. That's precisely the point of this land. Why doesn't anyone see that?"

Al stands, scanning the vineyard before us. "Not today, Sof. I can't do this with you today. It's way too hot out here to be wasting any time on an argument with no end." Without another word, he stomps down the porch steps, retracing Papa's path toward the barn.

I am left to my own company, the only sound coming from the pop and slice of the peas as I make my way through the lot of them.

* * *

"I thought I'd find you here." Al's voice startles me from my thoughts. "Hiding or sulking?"

He is teasing, but I don't answer either way.

He sits beside me on the bench, the scent of earth and vines permeating the air around us as the heat of the day recedes toward a moonlit sky.

Al jostles my arm with his elbow. "You didn't say much at dinner."

"Wasn't much to say." My shoulders drop, exhaustion from the heat, the emotions of the day, or perhaps both, ushering me into restraint.

"I know you're disappointed that we didn't see to the vines today." Al makes a show of turning and looking around. "But hey, they're still standing. No harm done."

"Today is merely a symptom of the disease that is eating away at the vineyard, bite by bite."

"That seems rather harsh. I know you disagree, Sof, but Papa isn't wrong to make sure the plum trees are secure. They were responsible for keeping us afloat all those years. They still are."

"I—it's just. I feel it all slipping away."

Al pivots to face me, his knees knocking into mine on the slender bench. "What's slipping away?"

"My dreams. My future. I don't know, maybe my sanity." My lips twist as I grapple with how to explain myself. "I am old enough to know what I want. The only path for me is in the vineyard. This isn't the fairytale dreams of an eight-year-old. This is me, wanting to carry on the family legacy."

Al nods in understanding, the solidarity between us found once more.

"I see it every minute of every day. So, honestly, it scares me sometimes. I dream about the vineyard and then I wake to give my life to it. I guess it sounds a bit fanciful." A sigh escapes from my lips. "But, every day that passes, it's slipping through my fingers. After surviving Prohibition and the depression, I figured we had a real shot at success."

I turn to meet Al's eyes. "Did you know there were only twelve vineyards remaining when Prohibition ended? Twelve, Al, and

Russo Vineyards was one of them. I'm not sure I can walk away from it without a fight."

"Didn't think anyone was asking you to."

"I am surprised you haven't noticed. For better or worse, you, my brother are the chosen one. All I ask is that you do good things with it." Another sigh sneaks past my lips. "I don't blame you. Nothing like that. But I do envy you."

A strangled laugh bursts from Al's lips. "Well, I guess he has chosen wrong then."

Wiping my face, I do my best to control the emotion sure to be laced through my words. "What do you mean?"

Al pulls out a square of paper and a short pencil from his pocket and begins to draw. With the paper balanced on his knee, I listen to the scratches as the pencil hits the paper, waiting for him to elaborate.

"It's quite simple, really. I don't have the mind for the numbers." Al's head snaps up as he looks at me, incredulity written all over his face. "Do you know how many calculations are required every day in a vineyard?"

A shrug of my shoulders tells him I know very well what is required for vineyard math.

Al shakes his head in what I interpret as disagreement. "I had no idea Papa was so skilled at math."

"Surely, Papa will teach you the math over time. Or, you could ask Nonno. He taught me. Though, to be honest, I did write the calculations down so I could check my numbers, not that anyone is looking for numbers from me, but if they did, I want to make sure they're correct."

"I don't have the head for it, Sof. I just don't." Al's defeat is mirrored in the slump of his shoulders.

I do my utmost to rally his spirits. If this vineyard is to be left in his hands, Al needs all the support I can grant him. "But Papa seemed delighted with your efforts. He's always boasting about what a hard worker you are. You can't let the vineyard fail, Al. You just can't."

Al returns to his drawing as a silence falls between us, both of us contemplating what our futures hold. A light breeze tickles the back of my neck. After the heat of the past few days, I expect the breeze to be refreshing. Instead, it seems to carry an omen of dread with it, and I sense the potential failure of our vineyard to settle within me once more. What more must we endure? If wine is life, like Nonno says, we are nothing without it.

Al's pencil stills. He reaches for my hand and squeezes it gently. "I just want you to know, you aren't alone. You aren't the only one disappointing our father these days."

Understanding all too keenly the sting of Papa's disappointment, my heart sinks. No words can remedy what Al is feeling and so we sit, together, in silence, on the bench placed here by Nonno in a vineyard whose true potential, like our own, is waiting to be realized.

Twenty

OCTOBER 1941

SUMMER IS LONG GONE NOW and any hope of a good mood, it seems, has vacated along with it. Cooler October days have given way to fog, drizzle, and a slight hush in the vine-yard, now that the vines are picked clean. Earlier in the week, Nonno, Papa, Al, and a team of twenty laborers ventured into the vineyard in the cool of the early morning to harvest the grapes.

By evening they were done and we celebrated with an Italian feast, all of us gathering on and around the farmhouse porch to eat, drink, and sing old Italian songs. Papa informed me the day before the harvest that Mama needed me in the kitchen to help prepare the feast. Touting what he felt was the first real harvest since Prohibition, his spirits were lifted at the same time he was dashing mine.

I watched the merriment from the porch railing with a glass of Russo Zinfandel in hand. Mama, stunning in her new dress and heels, danced with Papa to the lively beat until a slow song lured them into one another's arms. Papa spun her once, his eyes shining with adoration, before leaning her into a deep dip which ended in a stolen kiss.

Embarrassment at having watched the romantic moment between my parents, I turned my attention to the vineyard beyond the porch. With its vines stripped clean, the vineyard holds a subtle sense of melancholy within its rows. Perhaps it is merely settling into the resting season, or maybe this is how it feels when you've been left exposed and vulnerable to the elements. A shiver runs down my spine with a slight gust of autumn breeze.

I, too, had felt the energy of the growing season as it drew to a close. The vines literally vibrate with a readiness that only happens once a year. Being in tune with the vineyard only adds to my endearment of the land. I equate the connection to that of an ongoing conversation, one where I listen and the vineyard talks. Papa, though, seems not to notice my connection to our land or worse, he simply does not care.

The Russo men moved on to sorting and crushing yesterday. This season, Al is being guided through his first official crush. Another step toward taking up his position at the vineyard, I suppose. He came in tired and grape-stained at the end of the day, barely saying two words during dinner.

Papa, however, caught his second wind and was full of stories and banter about the day as he beamed widely between mouthfuls. I didn't think I'd ever see the day, but his passion for making wine, apparently no longer cloaked by ridiculous laws and economic disappointments, was on full display. This is what Nonno had spoken of over the years. I catch my grandfather's eye and in turn receive a knowing smile and a wink from the man whose relief at the end of a good times drought, is evident within the wrinkled creases of his expression.

I think back to last night's dinner as I do my best not to appear put out by the hive of activity taking place in the cellar without me. I tug the biggest book on winemaking I can find from the living room bookcase and settle myself at the kitchen table with a warm drink, determined to immerse myself in the process, if only through the pages of a book.

Mama, having completed her mending, moves into the kitchen with the suggestion of needed assistance. "I suspect they'll be in earlier tonight."

Nudged into helping her by her comment, I close the book and join her at the counter. Wrapping an apron around my waist, together we shape pasta dough into gnocchi in preparation for tonight's meal.

We work in silence for several minutes before Mama inclines her head toward the book I've left on the kitchen table. "Your time will come, Sofia. Your time will come."

"I am not so sure." I keep my eyes glued to the pasta dough before me.

"Your Papa. He was happy yesterday."

"Yes," I agree, though I've no idea what she is trying to say.

"You'll see. Once he can relax again and not worry so much, then he'll be ready to discuss the vineyard with you."

Mama knows him best. I am certain of that. However, I can't help but wonder if what she says is true. I keep my thoughts to myself, aware that Mama, too, has a bit of a spring in her step today.

"He was certainly pleased with the day." I add a conciliatory offering along with another shaped pasta to the plate.

Mama wraps an arm around my shoulders, her flour coated hand sprinkling remnants onto my shirt like falling snow. "Yes, he was. Happier days are ahead of us now." Mama squeezes me close with her enthusiasm before turning toward the oven to start on the sauce.

All through dinner, Papa grills Al about his accomplishments from the day. The conversation is friendly and full of pride, but I feel Al's resistance beside me as the hour wears on.

Nonno finally interjects, the only one besides me to notice Al's disintegrating patience. "Enough. Let the boy eat in peace."

Papa looks at Nonno, a question forming on his lips.

"You've been talking his ear off all day, Giovanni." Nonno offers a warm smile. "Let the teaching settle into his bones for now."

Clearly thankful for the reprieve, Al excuses himself from the table, beckoning me with a covert wave of his hand. A slight nod of my head tells him I'll be in soon.

Mama and I clear and wash the dishes as Papa and Nonno retreat to the living room for a game of checkers. I help deliver glasses of wine to the living room before withdrawing to Al's and my shared bedroom. Feigning tiredness due to the earlier darkening sky, I slip from the room with no objection from the others.

I yank back the sheet that separates my space from Al's and sit on my bed to face him. "That bad?"

"You have no idea." Al plumps his pillow and lies down, his gaze fixed on the ceiling. "The man who has barely spoken a word for the better part of our lives has somehow discovered how to speak."

I stifle a laugh and move to sit cross-legged.

Al continues. "But, now that he knows how to communicate, he can't seem to stop." An exasperated sigh leaves Al's body. "I am telling you, Sof, Papa talks incessantly about wine and what to do and what not to do. He talks about vintages past and how we might do this to create a similar vintage. I honestly can't imagine how he expects me to remember it all."

"He's happy. Mama said so today." I dip my chin in understanding. "Maybe he needs a few days and then he'll find a rhythm that's more sustainable for both of you."

"I'm telling you, I would trade places with you in a heartbeat." Al swivels his head against the pillow, finding my eyes in the low light of the bedroom.

"I'm sure you would rather do more than cook meals for the men as they go about doing all the important things." I keep my tone light in jest, but the quirk of Al's lips tells me I haven't succeeded.

"Sof, you might be onto something." Al lifts himself up on one elbow. "I have an idea and one where we both get to do what we enjoy doing."

I offer him an *I don't believe you* look and wait for more information before agreeing to anything.

"Seriously, you would say no to an offer of making wine? I underestimated your desire, it seems." Al teases me with bait he knows very well I am unlikely to refuse. "Well, I suppose if you want to keep up the count of the number of days spent sulking, you could do that."

"I haven't been sulking." The hair on the back of my neck rises in response to his insinuation.

Sitting up, Al inches forward and lowers his voice. "What if I told you everything Papa has been telling me and then..."

"Then what?"

"Then you do my chores, which is what you want to do, anyway." Al smiles mischievously.

"And what, pray tell, will you be doing?" I flutter my eyes at him with mock innocence.

"Besides keeping watch?" Al lifts both eyebrows. "I will have my paper and pencil with me."

"Let me get this straight." I stand and pace the small space the length of our beds. "I will do your chores and you will spend the time drawing. Have I got that correct?"

Al nods enthusiastically. "All we have to do is wait for Papa to let me work on my own for a while, then we'll be in the clear. He's already drafting a list of daily tables and recordings that he intends me to take charge of. Math, Sof. He wants to leave the calculations to me. I mean, does he even realize how horribly I failed math in school? Come on. What do you say? This is exactly what you've been waiting for. A real chance to have a hand in making Russo wine."

"I don't know." I bite my bottom lip in contemplation. "What if Papa finds out? He'll skin me alive."

Al is about to interject when I add in. "No. Not you. You'll be fine, oh chosen one. I, on the other hand, will be served for dinner."

Rolling his eyes at my exaggeration, Al laughs.

Though I don't voice my true concern, worry creases on my forehead. What if Papa finds out we've swindled him, then as punishment he refuses to let me set foot in the cellar again? Any hope of learning all that he has to teach me would vanish in an instant. This is his vineyard, after all. How hard would it be for him to ban me from the very thing that gives my life purpose?

"I don't know, Al. I am not sure it is worth the risk."

"Come on, Sof, isn't taking the next step toward becoming a winemaker worth a little risk?"

I waver, mulling over the idea as Al eyes me expectantly. Being a winemaker is a lifelong dream of mine, one that comes with a lifetime commitment to learning, experimenting, and dealing with whatever Mother Nature, and possibly our father, throws my way.

But what if we succeed? Imagining my name on a vintage of Russo wine takes only moments to conjure, given the repetition with which I've dreamed of the scenario throughout the years. A vision of vineyard life with me at the helm flashes in my mind's eye and I feel myself leaning into my brother's scheme.

"Do you really think we can do this?" A nervous bubble rises in my stomach.

Al stands and lifts his hand for me to shake. "Do we have a deal, Sof?"

I stare at his outstretched hand for a moment before squeezing it tight within my own. "We have a deal. But, don't you dare make me regret this, Al."

Twenty-One

NOVEMBER 1941

I SLIDE the oversized cellar door closed behind me, hiding both my presence and the goings-on within, in one swift motion. The smell of wine permeates the air and I breathe in deeply. Al is seated in what has become his usual place. I can see the younger version of my brother each time I spot his six-foot frame tucked in a corner, beneath a window for light. With an upturned wine barrel as his drawing desk, his head is bent toward the paper before him.

"What took you so long? It's nearly three o'clock." Al looks up from his latest sketch.

"Mama decided today was a good time to polish the silver." I cock an eyebrow. "You know, in time for *La Vigilia*."

"Last I checked, we were still in November." Al shakes his head. "I swear she starts preparing earlier each year."

I move toward the equipment. "December is only a few days away. Besides, she mentioned something about inviting others to join the Christmas Eve feast. I suppose they're feeling rather grateful, given how everyone has been getting by and making do for so long. I imagine they're looking forward to a celebration this year. Maybe she's right. It is time to put away the past and step toward better times." I lift the notebook and pencil from the shelf and read through the previous recordings detailed within.

Al's pencil scratchings filter through the expansive space. "Yeah, well, I guess it would be as good a time as any to invite Eva to meet the family."

Turning slowly, I examine my brother's expression with raised eyebrows of my own. "Eva?"

The back of Al's neck turns red. "I wasn't keeping it a secret." His coloring gives him away as his face deepens with embarrassment. "I wanted to make sure she was worth the inquisition. Why put her through it if she isn't going to stick?"

"How thoughtful of you." I offer dryly. "And romantic too. Maybe keep those kinds of thoughts to yourself or you'll be sure to scare the poor girl away."

"I didn't mean..." Al looks up but stops when he sees me smiling.

"I'm only teasing. When will I ever have the chance again?" I wink in his direction and turn my attention back to the notebook. "If she's the one, that is."

All he can do is let out an exasperated sigh. A little light teasing from me is nothing compared to how the rest of our family will react to Al settling down. I am happy for my brother, I truly am, but I wonder how the family dynamics will shift with the addition of someone new.

With Al focused on his drawing, I pull out the equipment and set up the hydrometer. I have barely begun when the sound of the cellar door opening startles me. Panic grips me as Mama steps in and closes the door behind her.

I hear Al's movement as he shuffles closer to me, an attempt, I presume, to demonstrate his involvement in the work being done with the wine.

Mama, though, is wiser than her years give her credit for.

"What have we here? I was looking for your Papa but now I've found you."

"I can explain." Al steps forward, prepared to take the brunt of the blame.

"An explanation is not necessary, Alonso." I cringe at Mama's use of his full name. She, understanding a young man's desire to shorten his very Italian name into something more American, acquiesced on the topic years ago. "Though perhaps I can give you something to consider."

Despite knowing we are about to have our almost twenty-two-year-old heads handed to us on a silver platter by our mother, I can't help but marvel at her ability to transform a potential argument into a contemplative musing.

"Keeping a secret from someone you love and respect is a dangerous game to play." Mama's eyes scan the expansive room before landing on us again. "There is no guarantee they will find it in their heart to forgive you. I assume you both know that what you're doing behind your father's back is not the path he would have chosen for you. Are you willing to risk his adoration of you?"

She waits as we both shake our heads no, shame weighing heavily on our shoulders.

"Good. I didn't think so." Mama steps forward and takes the pencil from my fingers and hands it to Al, meeting my eyes as she continues. "I admire your spirit. Truly, I do. I only suggest that if you wish to be successful in your venture that you tell your father what you've been up to."

Mama turns to leave. "If you're dishonest in your heart, I know for certain, you will never find the kind of success you're looking for." At the door, Mama turns one last time. "If you see your Papa, be sure to tell him I am looking for him. I'd like him to invite the Parisis for *La Vigilia*."

Closing the door behind her, I feel Al's whoosh of relief as he exhales it. "That was close." He glances sideways at me.

"Close? That's what most people refer to as caught. Not close, Al." I shake my head at my brother's lack of understanding of the situation. "This means, you go back to winemaking and I go back to the kitchen."

"She didn't say that." Al looks at me, a hopeful expression in his eyes.

"Yes, she did." I roll my eyes at him and put the notebook back on the shelf. "That was classic parenting by guilt. Haven't you picked up on that yet?"

"Maybe I am immune to guilt."

"Lucky you." My sarcasm is hardly contained.

"Hear me out, Sof." Al returns the pencil to me. "What if we continued on?"

I shoot him a look that begs the, *are you crazy,* question.

"We continue as we are doing. She didn't say she would tell Papa. I suspect she will wait for us to do that. But what if Papa likes the end result? Then we can tell him it was all your influence, with his strict instructions, of course."

"Of course," I say, haughtiness lacing my words. "This would be so much simpler if Papa would let me help."

"That's why we're here, sneaking around." Al's voice drops, the seriousness of his words sobering the situation. "Convincing Papa to reverse our roles isn't a likely solution with words alone. We must prove to him what you're capable of. Then he won't be able to refute the evidence when it is right under his nose."

"I have a bad feeling about this, Al."

"We'll be smarter this time. I'll move myself closer to the door and be ready to stop anyone who tries to enter. You'll have time to sit down and get settled, so it will look as though you're hanging out while I work." Al nudges my shoulder with a light punch. "We can do this, Sof."

My chin drops to my chest. "Fine, but if I get caught up in trouble..."

"You'll what?" Al mocks me with pretend punches, dancing around me like a champion boxer.

"I don't know, but I'll think of something." Al chuckles then repositions his drawing table closer to the cellar door and I return to the work. Focusing on the task at hand, it is easy to push my disgruntled emotions aside, replacing them with the headiness of making wine.

* * *

Days later, Sunday's radio program is cut short by an urgent announcement.

We interrupt this broadcast to bring you this important bulletin. On this day, December 7, 1941, the White House announces Japanese attack on Pearl Harbor. In a telegram posted at two twenty-five p.m., Washington time, President Roosevelt issued the following statement. "The Japanese have attacked Pearl Harbor from the air and all naval and military activities on the Island of Oahu, the principal American base in the Hawaiian Islands."

All five of us gather around the wooden box radio, alternating between leaning in to hear better and recoiling at the reality of the events coming through the airwaves. President Roosevelt's message left little room to imagine an outcome save for the one where America enters the European war.

We barely move from our positions, breath held as the radio announcer speculates and informs. Four hours later, we lean in once more to listen intently to Eleanor Roosevelt's Sunday evening program.

As the news ends, Papa raises his voice in concern. "I was Italian American, but at least both of my countries fought on the same side during the war to end all wars." His sarcasm is not lost on me. The slogan being tarnished the moment the second war began. "I can't imagine what will happen now that Italy has joined forces with Germany."

Nonno stands to address the room. "We will fight as Americans. We have no other option or else we will be seen as traitors in our own country."

Al stands in unity with Nonno. "Yes. We will fight as Americans."

"No!" Mama cries out, fear for her only son brimming in her lower lids.

Papa's voice wavers as he scrambles to stand, but his direction is clear. "Alonso, don't worry your mother with such boastfulness. We will go to the doctor and get an exemption. You're needed on the vineyard."

Al pivots, standing toe to toe with Papa. "I will go. If I am called upon. I will defend our country to the death if I must."

Mama's silent tears turn into inconsolable sobs. Papa pats her shoulder with one hand while asserting his presence as head of the household with his posture. "I will see that you do not go. Young men will be needed at home too. Someone must work the fields and the farms. We will pull together, but you will not go. We will visit the doctor next week and it will be settled." Having said his piece, Papa returns his attention to Mama.

I watch as the fire in Al's belly licks its way into his eyes. I want nothing more than to keep my brother safe and at home, but asking him to do so is not what he needs in this moment.

"Papa," I say the words quickly in an effort to get all of them out before he has a chance to respond. "If Alonso wishes to fight for his country, surely you cannot dismiss his desires. He will be twenty-two next month. Wouldn't you rather he goes on good terms with your support than spiteful ones?"

"Sofia." Papa's voice is an octave below a roar, but I feel the sentiment all the same. "This does not concern you. Your brother is needed here, at the vineyard."

"I disagree." I feel the energy in the room shift. I avoid Nonno's eyes for fear that he might convince me to hold my tongue. "Having my brother stay or go does concern me." I soften my words, hopeful to soothe him with a touch of sweetness. "Besides, you will have me. I will stay and help with the vines and the other crops. You know I—"

"No. We will go to the doctor and get an exemption." Papa cuts me off, an attempt at closing the discussion entirely.

Even when I use honey, my words invoke a sour response from my father. I stand to leave the room, not interested in going five rounds with a man who more often than not, resembles a mule. Lingering in the space between the living room and the kitchen, I do my utmost to bring my father into a new era. "I think you'll be surprised, Papa, by what women can do. They will surely take up the tasks of men as the war continues and they'll do so while baking bread and nursing babies too. We are stronger than you give us credit for."

I let my words linger in the air, willing them to settle in the hearts of those in need of hearing them. Seeking some quiet to think through the events of the day, I turn on my heel and move toward the kitchen. Grabbing my coat off the hook, I am almost out the back door when Papa's voice halts me in my tracks.

"Someday, Sofia, you will understand that what I do, I do out of love, not spite."

I nod once, indicating I've heard him. I keep my disagreement of his words to myself and step out the door, heading toward the vineyard, without a single glance back.

Twenty-Two

WEDNESDAY, MAY 1960

A VISIT to my childhood home is first on my agenda this morning. I remind myself of the sensitive task at hand while prodding aside the weariness brought on by yet another fitful night of sleep. I push the bedcovers off me and let the cool morning air coax me into motion. Hesitant about the conversation with Mama, I need all the encouragement I can get this morning.

At forty-years-old, I've run out of ways to express myself on the topic of the vineyard with Papa. I have argued, pleaded, and more, but I suspect I've known, even as young as ten-years-old, where I stood with my father. Yet, here I am, still trying to convince him that I'm the right Russo for the job. My head begins to pound, the weary side of me wondering if it's because I continue to bang it against a wall on a regular basis where my father is concerned.

If it wasn't for Al and his clearly stated disinterest in being the head of the Russo vineyard, I might let things stand as they are. Before the thought is even fully formed, deceit creeps up my spine at the lack of truth to my musings. Even I don't believe I would give up without at least trying to persuade Papa otherwise.

I have tried not to care. To let go of my hopes and dreams for the vineyard. Not concerning myself with worry over how the vineyard will succeed is a battle I have yet to win. Russo wine runs through my veins, Nonno used to say. I wonder, not for the first time, if his words were meant as a blessing or a curse.

Weary of my own rumination, I run a hand through my tangled hair. "Coffee, vineyard, Mama." I say the words out loud, hoping to infuse a sense of purpose to them as I begin the task of readying myself for the day ahead.

Coffee cup in hand, I head out the cottage door to spend time in my favorite place. My rubber boots squish into the soft ground, making a slurp-slap sound as the morning mist sends a chill down my spine. The vines welcome me with their leaves turned upward in anticipation of the rising sun.

In these early morning moments, my thoughts often turn to those who have steered me on my way. Nonno, Tino, and now Mr. Parisi are the pillars that hold me upright against the challenges faced in a vineyard full of dreams and disappointments. The only thing missing from the equation is Papa. What I wouldn't give to see his face light up with delight at one of my accomplishments.

With only three days left to persuade my father, my thoughts turn to what my future will hold should he stay true to his decision. I could continue living at the cottage. Mr. Parisi has said as much. And, he is pleased with the progress I've made. I suppose I could inquire if he would consider hiring me on to help take care of the Parisi vineyard full time. On cue, my memory calls up an image of Tino's smiling face. He would be pleased, or perhaps I only hope so.

Turning at the end of the row, I see the land before me in a different light. One of the most magical moments in a vineyard is sunrise and sunset. The light changes by the minute and if one pays close attention, the vineyard comes to life in a display of color and life. Waking up to the day ahead in the vineyard, it's easy to muse about the touch of magic the vines hold within them, and I swear part of what draws me back again and again is pure magic.

I contemplate my work at the vintner's office and ask myself if I see myself there for another twenty years. Though working in an environment that is predominantly vineyards and wine all day long has been fantastic for both my bank balance and my soul, the simple answer is no. The more complicated one is yet to be determined. Relocating to another town in California, where distance can be put between me and the sting of the Russo Vineyard is another option but if I am honest, not one I am quite willing to embrace just yet.

Back at the cottage, I turn my attention to making a proper breakfast. A diet of coffee and lack of sleep are hardly the answer to a level-headed conversation. Dressed and ready for the day, I reach for the telephone to give Mama a few minutes' notice. Not that I am unwelcome at my childhood home. Quite the opposite. Mama would open her door to me at any time, day or night. But courtesy is something she instilled in us from a young age, and with that in mind, I make the call.

Knowing she will expect a draft of the speech I've yet to finish, I tuck the page, with its lonely few paragraphs into my bag and lock the door behind me.

The drive is less than two minutes long, not even enough time for my car's heater to spew warm air. Pulling into the driveway is like stepping back in time. I am keenly aware of how each of us resumes our roles within the family the moment we are all together again. Hindsight has made me wish, on more than one occasion, that I hadn't taken up the role of stubborn, single-minded daughter. But here we are with few perceptions of me having changed in forty years.

Mama is at the back porch door, waving before I even step out of the car. "Hi, Mama." I wave back at her before closing the driver's side door and climbing the steps to greet her properly with an embrace.

"Sofia, how nice to see you, and on a Wednesday no less." Mama's eyes sparkle with anticipation in the morning sun. She is, as always, ready for whatever I have come to bring her.

"I only have a few minutes." I pull my sleeve back and glance at my watch. "But I was hoping to talk to you about the vineyard."

The movement is slight, but her chin juts forward a touch, an indication that this wasn't what she was hoping to hear. Scanning the space between the house and the barns, likely gauging Papa's whereabouts, she hurries me through the door with an arm wrapped around my shoulders. "You'd better come inside then."

Mama places a warm biscuit and a cup of coffee on the table, the scent of fresh baked bread permeating the air. "Sit. Eat. You're shrinking away to nothing these days."

I do as I am told and wait for her to join me. Instead, she busies herself at the kitchen counter, forcing me to swivel my chair to see her.

"What is it you want to talk about?" Her tone is clipped and guarded.

Clearing my throat, I dive in, not wishing to waste time or words. "I have spoken with Al and he has convinced me to try again with Papa. To ask him to allow me to take part in the running of the vineyard." I hesitate before adding. "As the winemaker."

"But your father is set to hand the vineyard over to Al. This week," Mama adds for emphasis.

"And he still can. I'm only asking that Papa allow me to be the next Russo winemaker. You know all I've ever wanted was to make Russo wine. Why can't Papa see that?" My tone detours from pragmatic to pleading without warning.

"The one thing you have never understood, Sofia, is that the vineyard belongs to your Papa. It is up to him to decide who he hands it over to."

"Even if the recipient doesn't want anything to do with it?" The question, a knee-jerk reaction to being put in my place, flies from my lips.

Mama gives me a warning glance but lets me continue.

"You know Nonno wanted me to be next in line. He knew Al had little interest in the vineyard. He encouraged Al's drawing, even when Papa disapproved."

"Why must you continually poke the bear?" Mama's reprimand slices through the air between us.

"I am not trying to upset anyone, truly, I'm not." My gaze drops to my hands as my mind spins in an effort to find the right words. "I can make him proud, Mama, if he would just give me the chance."

"Why do you assume he's not proud of you now?"

Mama's question is a valid one and when presented with it, I am at a loss of how to respond. Papa certainly hasn't shown any indication of pride in me thus far. Being a thorn in his side? Yes, that I am aware of, but pride, I don't think so. "I'm looking to find a way to talk to him. I'm not asking you to defend me or my wishes. Only that you help me speak with him so he hears me. I'm not a little girl anymore."

Mama nods in agreement.

"Did you try the wine I left?" I'd like to quench it in self-protection, but hope rises in my chest despite my best efforts to tamp it down.

"Wine?" Mama's head tilts to one side in question.

My heart sinks. "It's probably still sitting on the barrel in the cellar. I brought it to him yesterday morning. He said he was sure you would want to see what I made. Not him, of course, but he was quite sure you might appreciate my efforts."

"You made wine? By yourself, Sofia?" Mama, with her questions, confirms my secret has been more than safe with Mr. Parisi. "I am assuming it is good, if you brought it to your Papa to taste." Though she doesn't divulge anything, I can see her mind whirring, trying to make sense of what she hasn't been made aware of.

My head bobs slowly up and down, but all enthusiasm is lost from my response. "I have worked hard to learn the skills required to be a winemaker. Mr. Parisi allowed me use of a small section of land. I planted vines and have been tending them for several years. This is only my second vintage and I am still learning but, honestly Mama, even Al thinks I might be on to something. You know, I always dreamed Papa would be the one who taught me." A tear slips down my cheek before I can tuck it out of sight. "I wanted him to be as invested in me as I was in the vines. You told me two things that have stayed with me all these years. Your words have kept me working toward my goals."

"What did I say?" Mama moves around the counter toward me, emotion glistening in her eyes.

"The first thing you told me was that if I wanted to be a winemaker, then I only had to decide to be one and not let anyone else stand in my way."

"I should have known you would hold me to that one day." Mama's voice edges on wary. "What else did I say?"

I smile at her, a deep appreciation for her ability to truly listen to others when they speak. "You also told me, my time would come." I stand and step toward her. Grasping her hands in mine, I look directly into her eyes. "Well, Mama, it's been twenty years since you uttered those words. All I'm asking is for you to place a finger on my side of the scale this time."

A shuffle of movement draws our attention in the direction of the front porch, its door open wide to the morning spring air. Papa stands there, hat in hand, with only a screen separating the kitchen from the outside. His face is twisted with emotion in what I interpret as disappointment at our overheard conversation, stealing years from his life right before my very eyes.

Twenty-Three

DECEMBER 1941

TINO WRAPS his mother in a fierce embrace, her sobs muffled by the folds of his winter jacket. The smell of diesel fills the chilled December air as I attempt to keep my emotions in check by scanning the train platform. Our small group of Tino and my family are not the only ones saying farewell to our brave men. War has a habit of bringing out the patriotism along with the handkerchiefs. I pinch the inside of my arm to prevent the sorrow that is swimming around me from taking me under.

When Tino broke the news that he was enlisting prior to being called up, I wanted to ask him to reconsider. He, like Al, is far more in tune with sentiments toward Italians who don't pick up arms on their own. I was being selfish at the time, not wanting to say goodbye to my best friend, confidant, and fellow wine-maker, so now I remain quiet, allowing the best man I know to do what he needs to do.

With reality setting in around me, I cling to the words he shared with me last evening as we sipped a bottle of Parisi red and reminisced about our adventures shared over the past few years.

When he spoke of his desire to ensure his parents continued to have good standing in the town they called home, I felt his immense love for them. He is willing to sacrifice himself so they never have to be condemned for having an inconvenient ancestry in a world at war.

Mr. Parisi pulls his wife free as she clings to her only son, wrapping her in a one-handed embrace as he extends the other to shake Tino's hand. "We are always proud of you, Valentino, always."

My raw emotions climb into my throat as Mr. Parisi pulls Tino in and the three of them become one, a family cemented together with love, respect, and generosity. If Tino weren't immediately departing for war, I'd be inclined to feel the stab of jealousy at seeing a family so supportive of one another.

The train's departure is announced, startling Tino into action. He hugs my mother then shakes Papa's and then Al's hands, offering a quiet, "see you over there" to Al. With a final farewell to his parents, Tino takes my hand and tugs me away from the group.

A few feet of privacy is all we are afforded, but I am thankful for a moment to ourselves. "I'll miss you terribly." I say, the sniffles barely held at bay.

"You won't have time to miss me." Tino brushes the hair off my forehead. "You'll be too busy making wine."

"I'm not so sure about that."

"Listen, Sof. I spoke with my father this morning. He's given you permission to continue working in the shed. He said he would welcome the company, something to remind him of me and my love of wine while I'm away."

"Oh, Tino. I don't know."

"You have to Sofie. Do it for me." Tino tilts my chin up with his finger. "I believe in you. As you discover who you are inside, you will find what is missing from your wine."

Unable to utter a word for fear of falling apart completely, I nod in response.

"I expect a great vintage by the time I come home, so no slacking. You hear me?"

Nodding once more, I search his eyes, trying to embed the look of them in my memory.

"Now, come over here and give me a kiss." Tino sneaks a glance over my shoulder. "It's what they're waiting for." He whispers the words before leaning in. With a hand behind my head, Tino bends forward, touching his lips to mine with a tender kiss. It isn't a romantic coming together. My heart doesn't flutter or leap, but it is the kiss of true love. The kind that others would climb mountains and cross rivers for. Friendship, understanding, and acceptance have always been at the heart of our connection and even though he isn't the marrying kind, I would happily spend the rest of my life in his presence.

"I love you, Sofia Russo, now and for always." Tino's forehead rests against mine.

"I'll love you forever and always, Valentino Parisi." I squeeze his hand in mine. "I expect letters, though, and lots of them."

Tino laughs, his head tilting backwards with amusement. "Yes, ma'am." He mock salutes me and without a glance back, he climbs the steps to the train, and he is gone.

I stand, unmoving, as the train departs, watching as it trundles into the distance, until there is nothing left to see. People move around me, jostling and bumping as they leave the platform, hearts heavy with the weight of their farewells.

* * *

"Did you find it?"

"Not yet." I holler over my shoulder as I shift Nonno's journals to one side of his trunk, searching for the requested green leatherback one. Dust motes circle in the air around me while the scent of old books makes my nose itch. "Did he really think there would be only one green journal?" I mutter to myself as I dig a little further, setting books on the floor as I go.

I am sure in what is an effort to take my mind off of Tino's departure earlier today, Nonno has demanded an impromptu study of vines in hibernation. A study, which apparently requires a small, green, leatherback journal from I don't know how long ago. My hand touches a dark olive green journal wedged under a larger blue one. I tug it free, only to have several pages come loose and scatter to the floor. "What year did you say I'm looking for?" I gather the pages, searching for a date scrawled at the top. August 12, 1918, is written in Nonno's hand.

"Nineteen ten," Nonno calls from the living room, where he is in the throes of drawing vines in the hibernation stage from memory.

"Not it." I set the journal aside and continue my search.

Fifteen minutes later, the sought for journal is discovered under a pile of those dated as 1924. I deliver the book to the living room before returning to Nonno's bedroom to organize the mess I've created during the search. I consider sorting by date as I place the books back into the trunk, but think better of it and make a note to ask Nonno if there is a better way to catalog his notes.

I shove the trunk back to its position against the wall and stand, a trickle of sweat dripping down my back as I move. A piece of paper catches my attention as I turn to leave the room.

"Shoot." I bend to pick it up and look behind me at the closed trunk, wondering how difficult it will be to find the journal this page fell from. I examine the page again, noticing it is of heavier weight than the rest of the journal pages I rummaged through. Turning the paper over, I am met with what I assume are instructions for making Zinfandel. From what I know of winemaking thus far, these instructions are different. Every winemaker tweaks and influences the wine during the process but this is not like what I have seen as general rules of practice from the books I have read.

For starters, the instructions indicate the use of new French Oak barrels in a much smaller size that seems cost prohibitive or even useful for Zinfandel. The Russo cellar is filled with old French Oak barrels in a size that remains too big for me to move by myself once filled with wine. The other recommendations are more technical in nature and will require further research if I am to learn more.

I sit on the edge of Nonno's bed and reread the instructions. Tino's words come back to me. *I believe in you. As soon as you discover who you are inside, you will find what is missing from your wine.*

Maybe Tino is only half right. I know who I am, at least I think I do. But what if it's what is missing from my wine that matters? I examine the instructions again, my brain thinking ahead to next year's harvest. This could be the answer. A Russo recipe is sure to have a successful outcome. I fold the paper and tuck it into my back pocket.

The recipe burns a hole in my pocket for the rest of the afternoon, making me twitch with nervous energy. Two hours into Nonno's lesson, I excuse myself to remove the offending page.

In my bedroom with the door closed, I pull the paper from my pocket and stare at it some more. This could very well be the solution to my winemaking dilemma, but I can't. Not without Tino by my side. He is the steadying hand, the guiding force, the one who makes me slow down and breathe before every step. "No, not without Tino." The words arrive in a breath of air. I think about my promise to him, to keep trying and working. Perhaps a little time will help. He hasn't been gone even a full day yet. Surely, I can allow myself grace to sort out my next steps.

I tuck the instructions in-between the pages of my current

journal and promise myself I will revisit the option at a later date. Until then, I lay down on my bed and close my eyes. The memories of Tino filter through my heart and wash over me, making him feel not so far away at all.

Twenty-Four

THIS MORNING'S trip into town is absurd. Papa's position on Al visiting the doctor for an exemption from the war has not altered in the months since he first proclaimed it. As such, I am here as moral support for Al, though I've told Papa I'd like to visit the stationery store for some much-needed letter writing supplies.

With the dreariness of February matching my mood, I slide into the middle section of the truck's bench seat and wait for Al and Papa to join me. Yesterday's newspaper shouted out bold headlines above a smattering of society news, including Ronald Regan's marriage to Jane Wyman. The updates about the war, the draft, and what Americans can expect going forward, are far from happy tidings.

Al's expression is smug as he climbs into the truck, having informed me last night that he would need a physical examination before signing up, anyway. Papa, unaware that Al plans to use his iron-fisted moral high ground against him, is pleased by the ease with which Al has agreed to the appointment.

The radio plays quietly as Papa navigates the country roads and then the streets of Napa before pulling up in front of the low-rise office building. I shoot Al an encouraging smile and walk in the direction of the stationery store, a short two blocks away. I purchase new stationery for my letters to Tino and add in a sketch pad from the bargain bin for Al before retracing my steps to the doctor's office.

The bell tinkles as I open the door, the air unmistakably ripe with disinfectant. The receptionist, who has known us since I was a small child with a poison oak rash that gave away my adventurous nature, smiles at me. I take a seat in the narrow space opposite her desk, the door to the doctor's office beside me, slightly ajar.

The inner door to the examination room squeaks open then shut, the doctor telling Al he can get dressed as he moves into the space where his expansive desk sits against a windowless wall.

Papa's voice is filled with what I imagine is anxious energy. "Well, can you do it then? Will you write Alonso an exemption from military service?"

"Giovanni, I do not take your request lightly. It is an offence to falsify medical records." I can hear the patronizing lilt in the doctor's voice, but I keep my expression plain, not wanting to give myself away.

"But, the boy. I need him at the vineyard. With the war on, I am hearing rumors about planting crops that can feed the men. I am not as young as I used to be. I will require Alonso's help to do whatever the government says we must."

"Surely the war office will see right through a false assessment of a healthy young man." The doctor continues to reason with Papa. "Besides, you'll have Sofia to help you out on the farm."

"Sofia?" The confusion in Papa's voice in unmistakable. "She's just a girl."

The doctor lets out a light chuckle. "I wouldn't let her hear you say that, Giovanni. You underestimate that girl of yours."

I try to hold it back, but a smile emerges on my lips at the doctor's words. "At least somebody recognizes I am capable," I mutter under my breath, catching the eye of the secretary, who returns my smile with a knowing wink.

"Anyway," the doctor, clearly understanding he is not getting through to my father, continues. "You've nothing to worry over. Alonso won't be going to war."

A chair squeals as it is pushed back. "That's great news. Thank you, doctor." I imagine Papa vigorously shaking the doctor's hand until the realization pokes at him. "Wait, is there a problem? Is Alonso ill?"

"You haven't noticed?" The doctor's words grip my heart.

"No, nothing. What is it? Please tell me Alonso will be okay." Papa goes from elated to sick with worry in the beat of a heart.

"Please, sit Giovanni." I hear the creak of the chair as Papa resumes his seat. "I haven't seen it often, but then again, he's a clever young man. Clever enough to hide it, even from his family, it seems."

"He is clever, doctor. All the way through to seventh grade. His mama insisted on it."

"Yes, well. I am sorry to say Alonso suffers from a condition known as dyslexia."

I gasp from my position in the hall, right along with Papa.

"There is nothing to worry about, really. The condition is severe, but Alonso can make do quite well in life, just not in the army where they require you to read, write, and do math, double time."

A laugh, forced out with what I imagine is a heap of relief, erupts from within Papa. "I think you're mistaken doctor, Alonso does all the figures. He keeps good records for the wine. He's an intelligent young man, always with his nose in one of those comic books he favors."

"Dyslexia has nothing to do with intelligence, I assure you. But Alonso suffers from it all the same. When he sees numbers and letters, they don't look the same as how you or I see them.

The message gets jumbled up inside his brain, making it more difficult for him to read, write, and do mathematics. Doing these tasks quickly is near impossible for him. You don't have to worry, though. He has complete comprehension, and it seems, memorization of the information around him. He has been fooling me for years."

"I don't understand." Papa's voice is humbled now.

"Alonso must have memorized the eye chart years ago. Come to think of it, I imagine he encouraged Sofia to go first at their annual appointment so he could repeat her answers." The doctor chuckles, finding humor in the lengths Al would go to keep his condition a secret. "He's motivated to learn, but he doesn't do so easily."

I think back to our yearly visits to the doctor, Al always insisting he would take his turn after me, telling me he knew I couldn't wait for the lollipop that awaited me at the end of the examination. I shake my head in disbelief. My brother truly is clever, but perhaps a tad tortured as well.

The squeal of the exam room door creaks open. "Alonso, this is the form you will need should a request for active duty arrive." The rustling of paper being exchanged signals the end of the appointment. The doctor opens the office door closest to where I am seated. "Please let me know if you need anything further. I don't want you to worry, son. You'll do just fine in life."

I stand abruptly as they move into the small reception area. Al's eyes remain focused on the floor while Papa's dart in every direction, his mind trying to reconcile the information he's just been given.

"Thank you, doctor." Papa exhales the words before leading us out of the office.

Following obediently behind him, Al and I climb into the truck without a word.

After a few moments of staring into nothingness through the

truck's windshield, Papa slams his foot against the gas pedal, causing us to lurch forward onto the quiet street. Al and I exchange a look but remain silent. We pass by the post office, the letters Papa was supposed to mail for Mama bouncing lightly on the dash.

The town of Napa fades into the distance as Papa drives, his silence becoming more awkward with every passing mile. I can't help but feel his thoughts are punctuated with more brooding than concern over his son's diagnosis, though I hope I am wrong.

I am about to mention the errands Mama asked for as we near the turn that will take us down country roads toward home, but think better of it when Papa lets out a low, slow, grumbly, exhale. I sneak a sideways glance in Al's direction. Instead of finding sibling camaraderie there, I see a young man's face, cold as stone as the decision he had made to enter the war is yanked from his grasp.

I had assumed Al was eager to enlist, partly to carve a different path for his life. The army was his chance to escape vineyard life and Papa's insistence that he carry on the family business. I can't blame him for having those kinds of thoughts, especially now when I understand a little better how hard daily tasks in the cellar are for my brother.

I marvel at his ability to hide his condition. Even I, who know him best, had little understanding of the challenges he faced growing up. Going to school must have been torture for him. I think back to all the times I was envious of his being allowed to stay home and work alongside Papa while I continued my studies. How uninformed I was.

Al's drawings pop into my head as though they are the key to everything. I remember commenting once about how his sketches of the characters in his comic books were always reversed. Instead of facing the right, they would face the left. He explained how that was his challenge to himself to ensure he had mastered the skill of drawing the character if he could recreate them facing the opposite direction. His response was so effortless and smooth, I believed him in an instant. I suppose it is true. Confidence, real or imagined, can sell anyone, anything, if they are already inclined to believe it.

Papa takes a sharp right turn into our driveway, jarring me from my thoughts. His foot is once again heavy as it hits the brake, jostling us on the bench seat enough for me to reach out a hand to brace myself against the truck's dash.

Putting the truck in park, Papa turns off the engine. Being sandwiched between them, my escape from the awkward silence is impossible. Papa places both hands on the oversized steering wheel, bracing himself against it before he swivels his head in my direction.

"How long have you been doing your brother's work, Sofia?"

Twenty-Five

"GIOVANNI, I didn't see you there. There is no need to lurk." Mama, completely unflappable, steps forward and pushes the screen door open. "Perhaps you should come in and join the conversation."

Papa steps through the door and I instantly shrink backward.

"Come, I will get you a cup of coffee. Yes?" Mama acts as though I haven't just asked her to side with me on a matter of utmost importance to the future of our family's vineyard. Instead, she moves between the kitchen and Papa as if all we are guilty of is swapping recipes.

"Sofia." Papa dips his chin in greeting. The frosty tone he uses to address me does not go unnoticed.

"Hi, Papa." Shame washes over me at the words he has borne witness to. I check the time on my watch, readying an excuse to vacate sooner rather than later.

Mama sets his coffee and a warm biscuit on the table. "Sofia tells me she brought a bottle of wine yesterday." Subtle as a freight train, she is.

Papa's eyes flash up, assessing Mama's motives.

"A nice bottle of wine would have been a pleasant accompaniment to last night's stew." A look I don't understand passes between them before Mama tosses him a bone. "I imagine the day got away from you and you forgot it in the cellar."

Reading Mama's cue as if it were written on the kitchen wall behind her, Papa concedes the point. "Yes, I forgot it in the cellar."

"I figured as much." Mama smiles sweetly. "I look forward to enjoying Sofia's wine tonight, then."

Papa nods, knowing he's been beaten, if only on this particular point.

"What brings you back again so soon? We don't see you for weeks and now twice in two days." Papa bites into his biscuit.

Feeling the rebuke as he intended, I hold my tongue, determined not to make this situation any more uncomfortable than it already is.

"I wanted to speak with Mama." I attempt to keep my tone even, despite the gnawing feeling growing in my stomach. "She asked me to write the speech for the grand opening and I haven't yet found the words I need to complete it."

"I find that hard to believe." Papa's steely gaze lands on me. "You seem to have plenty of words to say, Sofia. More than plenty, if I'm being honest."

I take a step forward, not wishing to cause additional harm but unable to shrink away any longer. "I never meant to hurt you, Papa. Or disappoint you. I only came to Mama to try to understand you better. All this time, I have never known what I did wrong to make you push me away. But you did, Papa. You pushed me away and I've spent too many years trying to figure out how to make things better between us." A strangled sob leaps from my throat closely followed by a cascade of unrestrained emotion.

Mama moves to my side, squeezing an arm around my shoulders, showing me with her presence that in this moment, I have her support.

I wipe my cheeks with the back of my hand, certain I will have erased all existence of make-up by the time I leave this conversation. "We can spend the rest of our lives walking on eggshells around one another or we can embrace and accept each other as we are. Of course, like the vineyard, Papa. The decision is yours to make."

I offer Mama a sad smile and slip from her protective embrace. "I should go. I don't want to be late for work." I inch my way toward the back door, not wishing to pass too near Papa while he licks the wounds I've inflicted on him.

"Sofia." Papa's voice is gruff, ripe with emotion, stopping me as I reach for the doorknob. "I'm invested in you."

The relief of hearing those words shakes my shoulders free of the noose they've been restricted by, issuing a fresh downpour of tears.

"But a family vineyard is about family, not just one member of it. My decision has been made. Your brother will carry the tradition of Russo wine into the future. You are not to be burdened with the weight of the vineyard."

My head dropping once is all I can offer as the defeat of losing everything I ever dreamed of slips through my fingers for the last time.

Twenty-Six

APRIL 1942

I BOLT UPRIGHT IN BED. Panic grips my racing heart.

"Sof, what's the matter?" Al pushes back the bedsheet that separates our individual spaces, and stares at me with a bleary expression.

"I don't know. I just... must have had a bad dream." I offer a sheepish smile in the dimly lit room. "I'm sorry. I didn't mean to wake you. What time is it, anyway?"

Al rolls toward his bedside table and lifts the small clock that resides there. "One fifteen, or thereabouts. Do you think you can fall back asleep?"

"I think so. I need to change first. I'm soaked through."

"Must have been some dream." Al lets the sheet drop to provide me the privacy I need to change into a fresh pair of pajamas.

I change the bedding before settling back under the covers, the early morning April air not quite warm enough for me to find comfort in damp sheets. My head buries into the softness of my pillow and I am pulled under toward sleep once more.

"Tino!" I scream his name as my body is once again propelled from my bed. My scream turns to sobs as the dream's images flash through my mind like the tail end of a strip of film at the movie theater.

Al stands beside my bed in the pre-dawn light. "Sofie, what is it?"

"He's gone, Al. Tino is gone."

"Shhhh, it's a bad dream, that's all." The bed sinks as Al's tall, lanky frame sits beside me. He wraps an arm around my shaking shoulders, and my sobs make it difficult for me to breathe.

Our bedroom door opens with a whoosh of air as Papa, Mama, and Nonno, concern coating their faces, peer into the room at Al and I huddled on my bed.

Mama is the first to act. "What is the matter? Is she ill?" Mama directs her questions to Al, given my emotional state.

"Sofie had a bad dream." Al turns his head to the side, muffling the rest for my benefit. "She dreamed Tino died."

"Oh, Sofia." Nonno is beside me in a few strides. "Your heart is hurting. When a heart hurts, the mind tries to make sense of it all through our dreams. Come, your mama will warm some milk and we will settle it out."

Mama hands me my robe and the five of us, now fully awake, trudge to the kitchen for warm milk.

My head shakes in disbelief. "It felt real." Fresh tears threaten to spill. "I could hear him calling to me."

Without asking her to, Mama mixes the batter for pancakes, my favorite breakfast. Papa sits silently in a chair in the living room, wanting to be present, I presume, but not knowing what to do with an emotionally wrought daughter.

Nonno pats my hand and tells me everything will be alright. I would like nothing more than to believe him, but the reality is, Tino is in the middle of a war and nothing about that sits as *all right* with me.

Al, quietly reserved since the visit to the doctor a few months ago, delivers the warm milk around the table while Mama flips pancakes. The scent of the sweet batter grilling makes my stomach rumble in anticipation.

Nonno teases me. "Perhaps it was a hungry stomach that woke you. You must listen to your mama and eat better. You hardly touched your pasta last night." He wriggles his eyebrows at me, telling me he notices far more than he often says.

Placing the pancakes on the table, Mama calls for Papa to join us. The conversation shifts to the day ahead. Plans are made, chores are handed out, and pancakes are eaten, all of it taking place under the dark cloud that war has a tendency to deliver.

Nonno suggests I join him in the vineyard, and Papa acquiesces with a subtle nod of his head.

"The vines will breathe life back into you, Sofie." Nonno's eager expression tells me he believes deeply in his words. "They're the answer to all that ails us. You will see. The vines always have the answer. You only need to ask the right questions."

Pancakes and the musings of my grandfather are enough to lift my spirits. The sharp edges of my dream become fuzzy as it begins to fade into the recesses of my mind.

Between our conversation and the clinking and clanging of cutlery on plates, we don't hear the truck pull into the drive. The knock at the door, however, startles us into silence.

Mama's eyes grow wide as she glances toward the clock on the wall. The time has yet to reach six o'clock. Anyone knocking at this hour either saw a fragment of our lights beyond the blackout curtains from the road or has nothing but bad omens to offer.

Papa rises from the table, tossing his napkin onto his chair. The air stirs as he walks past me, eliciting a slew of goosebumps the length of my body. Nonno, seeing what is likely a stricken expression on my face, places his warm palm overtop my hand, squeezing reassurance into it.

Papa's muffled voice reaches us at the table. "Mateo. What is it my friend?"

Mr. Parisi's sobs reverberate through the farmhouse like a hurricane.

Tears spring to my eyes at the realization that Tino's father has come to deliver the dreadful news. My body begins to rock back and forth in my chair. "No. Please, dear God, no."

Mama is out of her chair and kneeling beside me, both hands on my thighs, rubbing life vigorously into me when all I want to feel is nothing at all. I want to go back to the moment I didn't know. The moment I believed it was only a dream.

Hours, days, and weeks blur into one another as I try to come to terms with the news of Tino's death. I barely sleep and do little more than pick at any food placed before me. I spend most of my days curled up in my bed, staring at the wall, begging for a different ending to our story. The pain of remembering what could have been is too sharp, yet the existence of living in a world without him is even more unbearable.

My family gives me a wide berth, letting me grieve while managing their own sadness along with springtime duties on both the Parisi vineyard and ours. Together we attend the memorial service. Without a body to lay to rest, the service seems unfinished, at best. I wonder if we all will continue to grieve without pause until Tino is once again home and laid to rest in the Napa cemetery. The official word from the war office is that all funds are required for fighting and not for the return of fallen soldiers. This is the reason for his physical absence, though the explanation does nothing to bring me any comfort.

* * *

A month into my life without Tino, I steal away to the Parisi shed. A broken heart propels me there when courage isn't enough to carry me. The shed is exactly the way we left it. Bottles of my terrible vintage still line the makeshift shelf Tino built. Our notebooks and measuring tools are neatly stacked on top of the round table. A shiver runs through me as my fingers grace the sweater he kept here for chillier nights. Lifting the sweater to my face, I inhale deeply. Everything he was washes over me in a flood of emotions. If only my love was enough to bring him back. If only.

I am startled by a knock at the open door. "I didn't mean to intrude." Mr. Parisi stands in the doorway, a shrunken, deflated version of himself that now fits beneath the low slung door frame. "I saw you coming up the lane."

"I'm sorry." I bite back the moisture rimming my lower lids. "I should have come sooner."

"No need to apologize, Sofia. I only wanted to bring you this." Mr. Parisi holds out a key. "Valentino wanted you to have it."

I take the key from his hand. "I don't understand."

"It is the key to this shed. He meant for you to continue on as you would have together."

A sob escapes the confines of my throat. "I'm not sure I can."

"When the time comes, you will find the strength and the way." Mr. Parisi embraces me in a brief hug before holding me at arm's length, forcing me to meet his eyes. "I'm certain of it, Sofia." He turns to walk out the shed door. Turning once more, his shoulders drop, the weight of his grief too heavy for his body to carry. "Actually, I think I might be counting on it."

Mr. Parisi leaves me alone in the shed. The cozy space is filled to the rafters with both his grief and mine. I climb into the lone padded chair, the other hard and less comfortable stools being put there for purpose, not relaxation. The empty bottle and cork of Parisi wine Tino and I shared on his final night at home, sits as a reminder of him on the small table next to me.

I finger the cork, rolling it through my hands before tucking it in my pocket for safekeeping. I never imagined there would be a moment when making wine might feel like a chore instead of the gift I know it to be. Since Tino left this world, I find myself unable to care much about wine or vineyards. For the first time, I wonder how else I might spend the rest of my life. The life I must spend without him by my side.

Grief has a habit of sucking all the strength from one's body. I rest my head against the chair's tall back, telling myself it will only be for a minute. Several hours later I wake to a darkened sky with only the moonlight to guide me back home again.

After locking the shed door, I walk to the end of the Parisi's back driveway. I am startled by the figure of a man, leaning against the fence post, his head tilted back as he gazes at the sky. My foot stops mid stride when I see him. I scarcely have a chance to turn back when he looks my way.

Twenty-Seven

"SOF," Al calls out to me.

"You scared me." I curse under my breath and walk in his direction. "What are you doing out here?"

"I could ask you the same thing." Al's swagger is fully intact, and I wonder how he found the means to recover from the unfortunate incident at the doctors. "I was out with Eva and when I got home Mama said you had been gone for hours and she was worried about you."

"How did you know where to find me?" We walk in the middle of the country road, letting the moonlight and the stars guide us home.

"You aren't very good at keeping secrets. I've known about this place for years. I took a chance and peeked through the window. Saw you sleeping and thought I'd wait for you to come out." Al launches a soft punch to my shoulder. "I figured you'd come back here when you were ready to."

"I'm not sure I'm ready for anything."

"Sofie, you are stronger than you think." Al stuffs his hand into his pants pocket and pulls out a small box. "So, I have this." He hands me the square, velvet box. "Open it."

I stop walking and do as I'm told, lifting the top off the box. "Al, are you..." The question goes unfinished as my head swivels from the small diamond, catching the light of the moon, back to my brother.

"I'm going to ask her tomorrow." Al takes the engagement ring and box back and returns them to the safety of his pants pocket. "I wanted you to be the first to know, but I felt it was only proper to ask Eva's father for his permission."

"And, I presume he gave it to you." I grab my brother by both arms. "I am happy for you."

Al shuffles his feet. "I sold a few of my sketches, so I was able to afford the ring and I'm looking at a small apartment in town."

"This is really happening? You're getting married?" I pull him close, wrapping my arms around his neck, partly in congratulations and partly because I can feel the emotions brewing within me and I am determined not to ruin this moment for him.

Al whispers into my hair. "If Tino taught me anything, it's that life is short. I love her, Sof, and I want to spend the rest of my life making her proud of me."

I pull back and search his eyes. "I know you will."

"Tino said something to me once that stayed with me. He said he'd never seen someone as fiercely driven as you are when it comes to being a winemaker. He said he wanted to be there to see you succeed even if it meant he only had a view from the passenger seat." Al uses his thumb to wipe the drops streaming down my face. "I know it is hard, Sof, but you have to go on without him."

I shake my head in disagreement. "I don't think I can."

Al chuckles softly as he pulls me close, a protective arm around my shoulders. "Then don't think too much about it and just get to work." Al holds me at arm's length, his eyes imploring me to look at him. "For Tino, Sof. Do it for Tino, if you can't do it for yourself right now."

"Okay." I sniffle. "For Tino."

* * *

Al's words have been rumbling through my mind for weeks, though I have yet to act on them due to the fanfare that came with the announcement of his impending nuptials. I put on my excitement for the formal announcement of his engagement like I put on a summer hat, firmly squishing it in place until it is forced to stay put. Delighted doesn't even come close to how I expect I will feel once the veil of my grief decides to allow me a moment to breathe.

Until then, I do what I expect most others who are living with loss do. I pretend. In an effort to halt any well-meaning gestures of *poor dear*, while abating other's discomfort at my sense of grief, I paste on a suitable subdued expression and carry on.

There is comfort in knowing that most people assume Tino was to be my future husband. I have neither the strength nor the words to explain how he was not that and yet he was infinitely more. A sigh slips out with my unraveling thoughts, garnering a glance from Mama. I remind myself to tuck my wayward thoughts away and busy myself with the pastry dough before me.

Papa, having retrieved the mail, sits down at the table for his mid-day meal. Mama bustles around him, setting his place as he slices the envelopes open with a hand stained with grape juice.

"Would you look at this?" Papa hands a letter to Mama. "The government is calling on us to help with the war effort."

Wiping her hands on her apron, Mama reaches for the letter, scanning its contents. "Raisins. They want to commandeer the vineyard to plant grapes suitable for raisins? Why would we ever do such a thing?"

"Angeline, this is our chance to support our country." Papa lowers his voice in what I assume is an attempt to not draw too much attention to his comment. "Since we have nothing else to offer the war effort, this is what we will do."

"Giovanni, we can't. We don't have the manpower or the resources to replant the vineyard." Mama's voice rises as she protests Papa's decision.

"Wine grapes are worth less now since every farm with table grapes is producing bad wine. They're lowering expectations and prices." Papa argues back. "The government is offering us the chance to keep the land and vines, just not Zinfandel vines."

"I don't know about this." Mama, not convinced reads the letter again.

"You must trust me on this, Angeline. We can survive with the government's request. We will not be looked down upon because of our heritage. We will be contributing members of the fight."

Watching the scene play out, I am stunned into silence. Will our vineyard ever have a chance? I can't fathom another loss, another disappointment, with Papa all too willing to give up on wine for a war that has done nothing but take. I can't even bring myself to say the words. Grief has made sure of that.

I place the pie crust in the dish, remove my apron, and walk out the door. The solution is clear. I must do as Al suggested, and Tino believed I was capable of. I must find a way to continue making Russo wine. My frustration prods me toward the cellar while my broken heart buffers me from what others might think.

Once inside, the cool damp air washes over me and I am instantly comforted by being immersed in the aroma. Barrels, used again and again, cling to each vintage's essence like a moth to a porch light. I move toward the bookshelf, searching for the year I remember as being exceptional. Engrossed in my search, I do not hear the scrape of the wood door on its metal slide.

"Sofia, what are you doing in here?" Nonno's question makes

me jump, causing me to bump the shelf, which results in a cascade of books tumbling to the floor.

"Must you sneak up on me like that?" The accusation is tinged heavier with annoyance than I intend it to be, causing me to blush at my mis-step. "I'm sorry. I didn't mean to snap at you."

Nonno arrives at my side, bending to pick up the fallen journals. Coming up with a purple covered notebook, his smile widens. "This was a very good year."

My heart melts watching him talk about vintages like they are family members he is proud to have known.

"I love how you remember them all." I take the book from his hand and flip through its pages.

"How can I forget? They are a part of me. Together, we toiled and flourished." Nonno's distant look tells me he is thinking back in time. "Good wine cannot be made by the vines alone, nor can it be made solely by the winemaker." Nonno interlaces his fingers. "Good wine is the result of a wonderful partnership."

He places the rest of the journals, the ever evolving map of Russo Wines, back on the shelf. "So, tell me. What brings you to the cellar?"

My lips twist in contemplation, not wanting to give myself away, but understanding Nonno is an ally and not the enemy. "Papa has decided to take more of the vines and replace them with whatever the government is suggesting. I came to—"

"Ah, I see." Nonno's head bobs up and down in understanding. "You came to take something that is not yours to take."

Unable to conceal my thoughts on the topic, a huff rushes out of me as though it is on fire. "How can you stand by and let him destroy the vineyard at every turn?"

"I do not stand by. I watch. I listen. Then I provide him counsel if he asks for it." Nonno's patience and understanding is exasperating at times.

"Well, he won't be asking for it now. He seemed pretty

convinced and to be honest, a little too enthusiastic for a man who apparently is one with his vines." The sarcasm is unnecessary and a tad unbecoming, but I can't stop the freight train once it is moving at full speed.

Nonno chuckles, and my shoulders drop in relief.

"Oh Sofia, you have grown into a fierce woman. I'm very proud of your gumption." Nonno's delight fades from his face. "However, wine is to be celebrated, but only when a vintner has been bold and brave and honest. How can you appreciate a wine you have stolen from someone else?"

"I didn't mean to steal. I mean, I was only going to take inspiration." The words, said out loud, hold far less weight than I imagined they would. Realizing I have made a crucial mistake in judgement, I do what he has always taught me to do and I ask the difficult question, the one that's certain to include me doing something I'm not keen to do. "What would you have me do?"

"Now then, we can get to work and sort that out." Nonno pulls up a stool for each of us. "But first." He disappears from sight, returning a few moments later with a bottle of wine and two glasses. "We celebrate wine."

Oh, Nonno, I think. *What ever would I do without you?*

Twenty-Eight

JUNE 1942

"*IN VINO VERITAS*. Here's to living your truth, Sofia."

I lift my eyebrows in question at Nonno's proclamation.

He inclines his head toward my glass, urging me to raise it in a toast. "In wine there is truth." I echo in English.

We clink glasses and soak in the aroma of the Zinfandel before each taking a sip.

"Mmmm." The flavors of candied fruit with a hint of black liquorice roll across my tongue. "This is lovely," I say.

Nonno moves the bottle closer to me, rotating its label in my direction. "You have good instincts. This is from the vintage you were searching for in the journals."

I pick up the bottle and read the simple Russo wine label. "How did you know I was looking for this one?"

A shrug of his shoulders lets me know he isn't likely to reveal all of his secrets. "A grandfather always knows."

"I wish Papa had that ability."

"What makes you think he doesn't?" Nonno eyes me quizzically before finishing his glass and reaching for a piece of paper and pencil. "Now, let's consider what is ahead of us."

I am still ruminating on Nonno's words as he draws a rough map of our vineyard. He uses the side of the pencil to shade in the land Papa has already taken over with plums and other crops he has tried his hand at over the past two decades. There is about two-thirds of Russo land still planted with Zinfandel grapes according to Nonno's map.

Pressing my hands together on the table's top, I brace myself for the emotions that are sure to accompany my words. "Tino wanted me to continue."

Nonno looks up from his drawing, giving me his full attention.

"He knew how important it was to me to become a wine-maker and carry on the Russo tradition. I got that from you, I think." My lips lift in a small smile. "I'm not sure I can battle the elements and Papa's disapproval of me at the same time." Moisture gathers in my eyes. "It's just—and, I may have no right to my opinion, but I can't sit idly by and watch the vineyard slowly disappear. If what you say is true, I suspect Papa would be devastated to see it go too. I don't know. Maybe I'm being selfish and trying to hold on to something because of my own desires. I've been told I have a stubborn streak a mile long, you know."

Nonno chuckles but doesn't confirm or deny my self-depre-cating comment.

"But what if the real reason I'm compelled to keep pushing on is so Papa doesn't ever have to know what it is to be a vintner without any grapes? If he loves the vines as you've said he does, we must do everything we can to convince him to keep them."

Examining Nonno's map closer, I take in the expanse of land with the grapevines still intact. "I can't imagine Papa will have the manpower to plow and replant the entire vineyard." My fingers grace the map, seeing a glimmer of hope within the amount of land currently still available for wine production.

"Now you're thinking like a grape farmer, Sofie." Nonno taps his pencil on the area of land closest to Papa's plum trees. "It will make the most sense for him to work the land closest to where his other crops are. He will save time and effort if he keeps the equipment on this half of the land."

"That makes sense. Do you think you can convince him, though?"

"We, Sofie. Together, we will convince your Papa with a plan that offers the best outcome for him and also for the vineyard."

Walking to the bookshelf, I retrieve a blank notebook and settle myself once more at the table, across from my grandfather. "Where do we begin?"

Nonno's face lights up with genuine satisfaction. "This. This maturity in you is what I have been waiting for. Now, you are ready to become a winemaker, Sofia."

His words ignite a fire within me and though the loss of my best friend shadows me as I move through each day, a new sensation saddles up beside my grief. There is a push to go forward, once more.

Taking a pencil in hand, I meet Nonno's watchful gaze and nod for him to continue.

Twenty-Nine

THURSDAY, MAY 1960

THE WORK DAY passes at a turtle's crawl, with several moments of anguish forcing me to run to the restroom in an effort to conceal my state of mind from those I work with. The cottage never looked quite so welcoming as it does this afternoon.

Thankful I've been granted a day off from the office tomorrow with the upcoming grand opening, I pull into the driveway, eagerly anticipating climbing into my bed and tuning out the world. Even the call of duties in the vineyard can't nudge the foul mood from its grip within my caged heart.

Once again, I've pushed too far, unintentionally disrupting the meagre semblance of a relationship with my father. I can't help but scold myself. I should know better by now and yet, somehow, I continue to manage to be his greatest disappointment.

Slamming the car door, a little harder than is necessary, I blink the moisture gathering on my lower lids away. My steps are heavy, resembling something akin to a long death march rather than the few short strides it takes to get to the cottage door.

Turning at the corner of the cottage's exterior wall, gravel crunching beneath my feet, I sense my brother's presence before I spot him. Hidden by the rosebush that climbs the lattice, Al leans against the brick of my little home, presumably waiting for me to arrive.

"Not today, Al." My sour mood ensures my words are delivered without a sliver of irony.

"I came to see how you are." Al steps forward, taking my bag from my shoulder. "Mama told me what happened."

"Then you already know everything you need to." I slide my key into the door and push my way in.

"Sof, this can't be the end of it." Placing my bag on the floor next to my desk, Al closes the door behind him. "You know how he can be."

"That's the point. I know all too well how he can be and still here I am, trying to force a square peg into a round hole. Honestly, it's worse than that. I've hurt him. I wasn't intending to but..."

"You might have hurt his pride." Al interrupts me.

"Either way, I've put distance between us again." I move toward Nonno's trunk, close the lid, and sit down. "I'm thinking of making a change. This isn't a rash decision, I've been considering the options for a while now."

"What kind of change?" Al steps forward into the small living room before leaning against the wall for support.

"This might be a good time for me to move away. You know, start fresh, without all the baggage."

"Running away won't solve anything." Al crosses his arms over his chest, his body language informing me he isn't happy with my announcement.

"I'm not running away." The defensive scoff in my voice says otherwise, but I continue anyway. "Maybe things would be better if I wasn't here as a constant reminder."

"Mama is going to have a fit. Not to mention Eva and the kids." Al begins to pace. "Have you even considered the Parisis? I'm not sure they can lose you as well."

All I can do is watch my brother as he absorbs the words I've said. I'd be lying if I said I hadn't considered all of them. I can hardly keep the emotions at bay when I think of having to break such news to Mr. Parisi.

"Wait. What constant reminder are you, anyway?" Al stops, turning to face me. "Maybe that's where you need to start. He isn't listening to you, but why?"

"Probably because he rarely listens to me. This isn't new, Al."

"What if we've been going about this the wrong way?"

"I'm not sure there is a right way." I slap my hands on my knees and stand. "I'm getting something to eat. Do you want anything?"

Al shakes his head no, but then changes his mind before I've even reached the kitchen. "I'll take a glass of that wine if you have any to spare. On second thought, I'll take a bottle too."

I peek my head out of the kitchen entranceway. "Did you drink the bottle I gave you already?"

"I shared it with Eva. She said you've elevated yourself to master." Al shoots me an *I told you so*, grin.

"Eva, as in the woman you married who couldn't tell a Zinfandel from a Merlot not that many years ago?"

Al laughs. "I'll give you that, but she's trying, and she is getting better. Most days, I'm thankful she thinks everything I make is wonderful, even when it isn't."

"You romantic, you." I hand him a small glass of wine, placing the requested bottle by the door as I pass by with a plate of crackers topped with a scoop of Mama's antipasto preserves.

Al sneaks a cracker and dips despite my admonishing glance. "I can get you something if you want."

"No, I'm good eating off your plate." Without pausing for breath, he continues. "We can figure this out together if we rethink all that has happened. When did Papa first show signs of resistance to you working in the vineyard?"

"He doesn't have a condition, Al. He has a steadfast belief. I've wracked my brain for years and I've never come up with what I might have done to cause him such grief. Don't you remember our tenth birthday?"

Al shakes his head and reaches for another cracker.

"It was supposed to be a big deal. Us having Russo wine for the first time. Officially old enough to take part in the family tradition. You don't remember that?"

"I remember something. We had chocolate cake, I think. But honestly, Sof, what ten-year-old likes wine?"

"I did." My eye roll does not go unnoticed by him.

"Oh, sorry." He sheepishly takes a sip of wine. "Good thing I grew to like the stuff."

Stuck in the image of that day, my mind turns over the remembrance. "That was the first time Papa cast me aside." I dab at the corner of my eye, determined not to cry over a thirty-year-old memory.

"Did you ever wonder if maybe it wasn't you that caused his reaction? What if there is something we don't know? Something he has kept from us all these years that would explain his vigorous persistence in excluding you from the vineyard."

"Al, it's Thursday afternoon. There is only one day between now and you being crowned Russo prince of the vineyard. We can safely drop all notions that we'll be able to somehow sway Papa into seeing what each of us wants in our lives. If he hasn't conceded by now, I don't think he ever will."

"Oh, come on, Sof. We can't give up yet."

"I'm sorry. Really, I am. I would love nothing more than to release you from the shackles of Russo obligation. There is nothing more for me to do. I've caused enough distress in our family. The time has come for me to let it go. I suggest you do the same." I give him a minute to let the words settle in.

He won't want to hear it, so I soften my delivery and wish my brother luck with his new venture. "Things will be easier if I go. You will have a real shot at making the vineyard a success if I'm not here to get in your way. It isn't as though we will never see one another. I promise. I'll be there for every milestone the kids have. I'll still be your sister, their aunt. Things will work out. You'll see."

My brother is seldom viewed as the stubborn one, a title generally reserved for me alone. He is quiet and contemplative, often lost in his own creative thoughts. Rarely does he speak out in anger or with haste. He's a thinker. Some might say a brooder but either way, he isn't likely to find the gumption or the words required to go head-to-head with our father in the next twenty-four hours. So, I reiterate. "The die is cast, Al. This is the life we have to live."

Al gulps the rest of his wine in one swallow. "I'm not taking no for an answer." The empty wineglass hits the hard surface of my desk with a thud.

My back stiffens in response. "Well." I stride to the door in three steps and pull it open with more force than is necessary. "I've got a speech to write."

Al picks up the bottle of Pinot Noir and steps past the threshold. The afternoon light is painting pastel strokes of color into a blue sky. "This isn't the end, Sof. I'm telling you, this isn't over."

I shrug my shoulders in response, neither agreeing nor disagreeing, and close the door behind him.

Al's words come back to haunt me only moments after his departure. What if I am not the reason for Papa's disappointment in life? My eyes are drawn to Nonno's closed trunk, the stacks of journals inside whispering, calling to me. The gears inside my mind begin to turn. What might I learn about my father if I look at his past from a different perspective, one that doesn't pit him against me?

I shake the question from my mind and sit down at my desk. Time is ticking, and I still owe Mama a speech.

JULY 1942

STEPPING INTO THE WINE CELLAR, I allow myself a moment to still the racing of my heart.

Mama looks up as I enter, a request forming on her lips. "Sofia, please bring those holders over here."

I lay the crystal candlestick holders carefully into my arms, cradling them like a newborn as I make my way toward the large table in the center of the room. Mama, hoping to turn the wine cellar into a suitable location for Al and Eva's wedding reception, is busy removing anything she deems an eyesore. Looking around, I'd say she has accomplished that and more.

"It will work." Mama examines the space.

Understanding reassurance is needed here, I say, "Saturday will be beautiful, in all the ways that matter." I give her arm a squeeze to ensure my message is received.

"Well, now that you're here, you can help me sort out where the flowers will go. I was thinking we could—"

"Actually," I interrupt, having recently become well-acquainted with Mama's unending list of expectations when it comes to Al's nuptials. "I'm hoping to speak with Papa." I lean my head to the left and peer behind her. "Nonno and I have something we'd like to discuss with him."

"Please tell me you aren't going to upset him. There is more than enough to do without adding a brooding mood from your father into the mix."

"That's not our intention." I smile sweetly, restraining the eye roll that is ready to be let loose.

Mama's lips purse. "You know what they say about good intentions."

"Ah, yes, I do. The road to hell is paved with them. Is that what you're referring to?"

Mama swats me with a freshly pressed napkin. "You get cheekier with each passing birthday."

Wrapping an arm around her shoulders, I hug her toward me. "I will help you for the remainder of the day, just as soon as I've spoken with Papa."

She eyes me warily.

"I promise, I will, but this is important."

"Very well. He has gone to ask Mateo to borrow an arbor from the Parisi garden. He should be back any minute."

We are rolling a wine barrel into position to serve as a tabletop for the guest book when Papa and Nonno return carrying a well-weathered arched trellis.

"Here you are." Papa and Nonno deposit the arbor at the cellar's entrance, the door of the cellar flung fully open to catch the summer breeze. "Mateo said it will need a coat of paint, but it is sturdy enough to stand on its own at the edge of the vineyard."

"Perfect. Absolutely perfect." Mama turns to me for my approval. "Don't you think, Sofia? Once we paint it, then maybe we can weave vines and flowers through it." She stands on tiptoe and kisses Papa on the cheek. "Thank you, Giovanni. Al and Eva will have a most beautiful wedding."

Nonno winks at me from his position behind Papa, an indication that the time has come.

"Papa, we were wondering if we could have a few moments of your time?"

His expression reads cautious, kicking my nervous heart into a flutter again. "Who is *we*?"

"Please. Sit, Giovanni. Sofia and I have a proposition for you." Nonno strides to a stack of folding chairs, three dozen of them borrowed from the local church for Saturday's celebration. He unfolds two chairs and places them side by side. Taking Mama's hand, Nonno gallantly guides her to a seat. Papa, taking the cue, follows suit.

"Sofia, go ahead." Nonno encourages me to begin with a twinkle in his eyes. I clear my throat and clasp my hands in front of me while he retrieves a bottle of wine and glasses from the office in the back.

"If not for wine, how would we celebrate? The daily victories, the life milestones, and yes, even the joining of two families when a young couple marries." With wedding plans taking over much of the Russo homestead, Nonno and I agreed the timing to be advantageous for our vineyard proposal, to tie itself to the sentiment of hope and devotion.

The cork pops as Nonno opens the bottle, garnering a questioning look from Papa, given the day is barely past eleven o'clock.

"Russo Vineyards has been making superior Zinfandel for decades." I sneak a sideways glance in Papa's direction. "Something, in its own right, to be celebrated. The vineyard and its stewards have seen challenging times, and yet the wine produced remains exceptional in quality."

The gurgle of wine escaping the bottle and being poured into glasses reverberates against the hard surfaces of the cellar.

"Prohibition could have destroyed the Russo Vineyard, as it did so many others." I pivot and pace with measured steps, noticing Al has joined us and is leaning against the cellar's door, listening to my rehearsed presentation.

"Hard economic times proved even more that the Russo Vineyard and its custodians would not give up hope." Nonno and I decided it was best to appeal to Papa's sense of ownership and care of the vineyard. My grandfather coached me for days, challenging me to remove any remnants of spite or anger I might have toward Papa's lack of action when it came to preserving the vineyard. He finally achieved this task when he reminded me that our effort would be for naught, and I would remain unable to make quality wine, if my heart and mind had not forgiven any past hurts.

I steady my breathing and clench my fists, determined not to fall apart as Tino comes to mind. "The war has already cost us too much." Moisture gathers at the edges of my eyes. I look up at the thick wood beams of the ceiling to stop the teardrops from falling. "I am hopeful—" My voice cracks with emotion. "We will not let it take the vineyard too."

Nonno passes a glass of wine to Mama and Papa before delivering one to Al, then to me. I step to the side as he outlines the details of our proposal.

"Sofia and I have studied the government's request, along with a map of the vineyard." Nonno meets Papa's eyes, letting him know we have done our research. "The government is only requesting half the land be used for war crops."

My eyes drop to the floor at the mention of this fact, a key piece of information Papa neglected to tell any of us and one that continues to leave a bad taste in my mouth.

"We would like to propose that Sofia and I manage the vineyard, that is half of our land." Nonno's delivery ensures Papa is reminded of the use of *our*. "Together, we will hire day laborers when necessary. We will manage the expenses and the sales with all revenue going into the family fund."

Papa opens his mouth to speak, but Nonno cuts him off with

a wave of his hand. "In addition, we agree to assist you and Alonso with the other crops." Nonno lifts a finger to ensure his point is heard. "If you agree to help with the harvest while being available to consult on the making of the wine."

My head snaps up at Nonno's last words. *Consult on the making of the wine.* What? Why is he inviting Papa to be included in the very process I am supposed to be learning, especially when we are committing to doing all the work? I have long given up the idea that Papa will ever take me under his wing when it comes to winemaking. I had assumed I would be learning everything I need to from Nonno himself. Then it occurs to me, Nonno may be giving me the very thing I've always wanted. The chance to learn side by side with my father. I spot Nonno's hand, discreetly pumping in the direction of the floor, cautioning me to remain calm.

"This is our proposal to you, Giovanni."

We have done what we can. The decision is now in Papa's hands. I can barely breathe—all the air has been sucked from the cellar. If it weren't for the wide-open door, I might believe I am suffocating. A trickle of sweat slips beneath my collar and slides its way down my back.

Nonno moves to stand beside me, his arm brushing mine in a display of solidarity. Time stalls as Papa sits quietly, his eyes finding something of interest on the floor in front of his chair. After several minutes pass, Mama places a hand on his arm and whispers something only he can hear.

"What half of the vineyard are you suggesting remains?" Papa's question isn't angry or even tinged with the slightest bit of angst. As far as I can tell, he is merely gathering all the facts. I can hardly blame him there.

Nonno steps forward, pulling his hand-drawn map of the vineyard out of his back pocket and unfolding it. "I have it for you here."

Papa and Nonno discuss the land, each of their hands moving over the map as imaginary lines are drawn and discussed. There is the mention of plums and an expansion to the family garden, a necessity during wartime.

I feel Al's presence as he moves to stand beside me. Part of me wonders if he is here in case I collapse at Papa's refusal. My throat is parched, the wine in my hand imploring me to bring it to my lips for a small sip.

"Alright then." Papa stands with his glass of wine raised to Nonno. "You have a deal."

Relief rushes through me as their glasses clink. My knees wobble, causing me to spill a few drops of wine. Al braces me with a hand on my elbow. My brother is here for me, no matter what the outcome.

Nonno trots toward us, glass lifted in celebration. "*Cin cin.*" I touch my glass to his, my smile growing wider by the second. "Oh Sofie, you should be proud of yourself. Your Papa is convinced. Just think of the day when the vineyard is thriving and Russo wine is flowing. How proud he will be then. How proud he will be."

I translate Nonno's words into my own understanding. *How proud Papa will be of me.* Unable to speak, I sip my wine and think about all the work ahead of us. I couldn't be more pleased.

Thirty-One

OCTOBER 1942

"SOFIA, WHAT IS THE MATTER?" Nonno is leaning over me. A concerned expression lines his well-creased face.

"I'm fine." I struggle to my feet only to sway as the vineyard shifts and blurs in front of me.

"You are not fine." Nonno's words are stern, but even in my unwell state, I can tell they are spoken with care. He lifts my arm over his shoulders, pulling my feverish body close to his so he can support me back toward the farmhouse.

Mama greets us on the porch, wiping her hands on a towel before feeling my forehead and ushering us through to my bedroom. The two of them exchange murmurings while I do my best to remain upright.

The room feels large and airy with only my single bed to anchor the space. Despite spending the past three months without Al sleeping an arm's length away from me, I miss the companionship of my twin. I have come to suspect that I always will.

I fall onto my bed and immediately begin to shiver. Mama pulls the boots from my feet and instructs Nonno to get a cool, damp cloth.

The cloth's temperature against my forehead forces me to a sitting position. Mama pushes me gently back down, cooing comforting instructions to me as she repositions the cloth over my forehead. The scent of her lavender perfume wafts in the air as I drift into sleep.

When I wake again, darkness has filled the room. My head moves and I groan in response.

"Try not to move too much. The fever still has a grip on you." Mama is beside me in an instant, her hand cool against the fire burning within me. "You've worked yourself into illness, I'm afraid."

Though I imagine there is an element of scolding, Mama's words also contain pride.

"How long have I been sleeping?" My voice is hoarse, dry from an internal heat. I lick my lips, the taste of a metal spoon lining my mouth.

Mama tsks my question away. "Don't worry about that now. The doctor has visited and says there is nothing to do but rest. Soon, you will be back up and running. But, first, let's see if we can get some water into you."

With her help, I slant my body forward and sip from a glass. The water cuts like a knife being tossed down my throat and I realize I have been in bed longer than I originally thought. "Mama," I croak the question out. "How long have I been sleeping?"

"You've been here since Wednesday."

If I had the energy, I would come up with something clever to say. "What day is it now?"

Mama pauses and a chill, the existence of which I sense is not due to the fever, runs the length of my spine.

"Today is Saturday." In the dim light of the bedroom lamp, Mama twists the cloth between both hands.

A rush of adrenaline pushes me to sit up. "I missed it?"

"It couldn't be helped." She offers the explanation as though it is an apology.

"But... I worked so hard." A sob that burns my parched throat rises from within me. "And, I missed the harvest."

"Sofia, I know this is disappointing news. The harvest couldn't be delayed. The men were hired, and the grapes were ready." Mama brushes the hair off my forehead and coaxes me back into a reclining position. "Papa and Al were on hand, so you can trust that everything went as it should."

"I can't believe I missed my first real harvest." Deflated, I roll away from Mama, signaling my desire to be left alone.

A week after waking to learn I had missed one of the biggest days in vineyard life, I remain slow to recover. Though I can't confirm my delayed restoration is due to the fever and not the disappointment of being absent from a crucial moment of my education, I concede that my displeasure might be somewhat at fault. Sequestered to remain within the perimeter of the porch's railing, I am left with the less than delighted company of my own contemplations.

I sip tea with honey as the others sort and crush, making the decisions I was eager to make this year with guidance from Nonno. After months of backbreaking, up at dawn work, I am no closer to becoming the winemaker I desire to be.

"A sour disposition is not a good look on you." Mama joins me on the porch with another cup of medicinal tea.

I scrunch my nose in distaste at both her observation and the tea in her hand. "When can I get back to work?"

Mama scans the horizon, all of it taken up by the view of vines turning dormant for the winter. "As soon as you can show me your appetite is back up to what it was before you fell ill."

"But, Mama, I haven't been useful for almost two weeks. I won't have the same appetite I had when I was working dawn to dusk in the vineyard."

"Well then, prove to me you can at least enjoy three meals a day and you'll be free to do what you please."

My spirits lift in hope.

Hope that is quickly dashed by Mama's condition. "Just so you know, I'll be doing the serving. Don't even think of trying to sneak anything by me." She turns to leave. "I'm on to your antics, missy. I know you too well for you to think anything different." Mama's mischievous smile does little to boost my mood, but I grin at her tenaciousness. I inherited the trait from someone in the family, it seems.

Rocking in the porch chair, I tuck the blanket tighter around me and let my mind drift to the activities taking place in the wine cellar. In my mind's eye I imagine the three Russo men, gathered around a table of journals, each of them extolling the virtues of one vintage over another as a course of action to decide upon now.

Nonno appears from the direction of the wine cellar and, for a moment, I think he might be coming to ask my opinion. My input for the wine being plotted in a building I am restricted from accessing until I eat more than my weight in Mama's pasta.

A breath catches in my throat as I watch my grandfather. He hasn't noticed me yet, and I'm thankful for the cloak of invisibility as I sit behind a porch pillar and take in his weary frame. I do the math in my head, eighty-two years old. I've gotten so accustomed to having him here with us, I haven't given his age much thought.

This is my fault. My chin drops to my chest. If only I hadn't worked myself into the ground, so eager to please and accomplish all of it in my first full-hearted attempt, he would look his usual spry self. I mull over how to make this right. How to give Nonno his youthful exuberance back.

I look at the tea in the cup in my hands. It smells like dirt and tastes like grass, but I sip at it anyway, determined to restore myself and help lessen the burden for Nonno. He has been as steady as a rock and my most valiant supporter. I cannot let him down. Not now. Not ever.

When he spots me, he waves a hearty wave, concealing his fatigue from me, even though it is something once seen, I cannot ignore.

"You are looking much better, Sofie." Nonno beams at me and though perhaps an imagined sensation, I can feel the warmth of his love for me radiating through his smile. No wonder the man is such an accomplished winemaker.

"I'm feeling much better," I say, not wanting to give myself, or the knowledge I've recently gained, away. "Mama says I need to eat like three men before I'm allowed back to work. So, tonight I plan to eat from Al's, Papa's, and your plate before finishing my own."

He erupts in a full-on belly laugh that forces him to bend at the waist to catch his breath. A crowbar couldn't pry the grin off my face at the sight of him.

Nonno climbs the steps, once recovered, and kneels beside my chair. "You are more important to me than any wine, Sofie. I want to make sure you understand that."

"I do. Which is why I want to return to the cellar. I want to be useful, not just for me, but for you as well."

"I understand. You are not much different than I was at your age. Eagerness fuels you more than any food will." Nonno winks at me. "But still, you must heed your mama's warning, for I do not wish to be on the receiving end of her wrath should you fall ill again."

"It's funny. You fearing Mama and me fearing Papa." My eyes fall to my tea cup as the words tumble out.

"You have no need to fear your papa. He's a gentle man, misguided at times, yes." Nonno inclines his head, though it looks as if he would rather not say any more on the subject. "But he only wants what is best for you. You must trust me on this, Sofie."

"I'd trust you with anything." I reach a hand out and squeeze his. "I'll trust you with this as well."

Nonno stands, bends at the waist, and places a kiss on top of my forehead. "I am proud of you. I always will be."

He enters the farmhouse with a song on his lips, one that usually invites Mama to dance a few turns around the kitchen before he spins her off to continue on with her chores. I can hear her laughter as Nonno leaves her in a wake of feeling young and jubilant once more, all accomplished in the span of thirty seconds.

Perhaps I was wrong. Nonno isn't showing his age at all. The man will probably live forever.

Thirty-Two

FEBRUARY 1943

NONNO COVERS my eyes with his palms. "Two more steps." He nudges me forward with his words. The crisp winter wind slaps my face with a gust that feels as though it will cut right through my heavy sweater. "Now, step up. That's it." He removes his hands from my eyes. "We are here."

As expected, the inside of the wine cellar comes into view when I open my eyes. "What are we doing here?"

"I have a surprise for you." He moves at a shuffle toward the back of the cellar. "Come, come." He waves me to follow him.

"I'm coming." I laugh and pick up speed. He's faster than he appears. "Why the hurry?"

Oak barrels line the walls and floor, the wine already on its way to becoming Russo Zinfandel. I inhale, the aroma of wine mixed with oak delights my senses.

"I know your disappointment at having missed the harvest and whatnot. So, I told your Papa and Alonso that we would not require their help with the rest."

"The rest?" I run a finger along the smooth edge of a barrel.

"The wine looks perfectly capable of aging in the barrels it's been put into."

"There is much to do before the vintage is ready for bottling. Together, we will tweak and taste and do what is necessary. I will show you why Russo Zinfandel is better than the others." Nonno winks, enjoying the moment as he holds onto his secret a little longer. One I had no idea even existed.

"Are you going to tell me what this secret is, or do I have to guess?"

Nonno laughs, throwing his head back in glee. "These barrels contain grapes from the southern section of the vineyard. You see?" He steps closer to a row of barrels balanced on sturdy beams about a foot above my head. "The label on the wall corresponds to the origin of the grapes."

My head bobs up and down in understanding. "This is about language, then? You are going to teach me what the language of our vineyard is?"

"In a manner of speaking, yes." Nonno's cheeks flush with color. "But there will be some heavy lifting as well."

"Where do we begin?" Not having dressed for work in the cellar today, I remove my sweater and roll up my shirt sleeves.

"First, some preliminary tasting. We will make decisions based on how the wine tastes at this stage and then we will move the wine. Finally, we will add the secret ingredient and let the wine rest until we test it again."

"Wait, did you say we're going to move the wine?" I eye the rows and rows of barrels big enough to fit two of me inside of them and raise my concern. "I have been a vineyard kid all my life, but I can honestly say, I've never seen Papa move the barrels once they're set to age."

"You see, Sofie, there is lots to learn when it comes to being a vintner. This is where the magic happens." Nonno's eyes twinkle with anticipation. "There is a foundation, a school of thought, you might say, that we subscribe to. Russo Zinfandel has always been racked at some point during the aging process, and today, I will teach you how it is done."

Not seeing, or perhaps ignoring, the perplexed expression lining my face, Nonno disappears. He returns moments later with what I assume is the equipment necessary for today's lessons.

We spend the entire day together, moving from section to section, first tasting then making so many decisions my head spins. Among other things, we discuss whether two sections can be combined or if they should remain on their own with additional notes being coaxed out with time and Nonno's experience. I learn that some lots are not to be racked at this time, though understanding the reason behind the decision is not something I've grasped hold of.

I keep two notebooks going. In one, besides the details Nonno added throughout the growing season in terms of terroir, I record the lot and barrel details, today's date, and all decisions made or actions taken. In the second journal, I write copious notes, filling page after page of Nonno's guiding expertise. My hand cramps on more than one occasion as I scribble to keep up with the wisdom he is offering, not wanting to miss a single thing.

After a thorough examination of a section, Nonno teaches me how to rack the wine. First, we remove the wine from its original barrel to a temporary holding barrel. I am tasked with giving the aging barrel a thorough wash to remove all the sediment. Then, we transfer the wine back into its original, now clean, barrel and mark it as complete.

We come up for air when Mama delivers us bowls of stew several hours past the dinner hour. She observes our progress with a warning look. "Neither of you is to work until you drop. Do you hear me?"

"Yes, Mama," I say, poking Nonno in the ribs to bring his attention to Mama and away from the journal he is reading.

"Bed by ten." She scolds us like school children. We both nod in agreement, aware that if we are not in our beds by the ten o'clock hour, there will be a price to pay.

We finish our stew in silence, hunger and dwindling hours motivating us to eat quickly. My eyes scan the cellar, less than half of it visible from my vantage point. Even as a small child playing hide and seek among the barrels, I hadn't perceived the cellar to be as large as it feels today. My enthusiasm deflates when I consider how much more there is to do.

"Why the glum expression?" Nonno puts his empty bowl and spoon on the table beside the coat he shed hours ago.

"I suppose I didn't understand how much work goes into wine at this stage. Papa never let me come around much after the crush. He always said the wine needed time to rest and curious children would not help the situation. All this time, I assumed both the wine and Papa were resting."

I think back to a childhood of harvests. We were kids, and as such, the events took on the feel of a traveling circus. The crush always included Mama putting the half barrel at the edge of the vineyard and Papa filling it with two inches of grapes then allowing Al and I to stomp our feet to our hearts' content. Idyllic, those are the moments I thought I would be recreating as an adult. Not stomping on grapes, per se, but I expected the joy of it all to still be present. All I feel now is in over my head.

"Have you changed your mind about becoming a winemaker?" Nonno's question surprises me.

"Was that your intention? To make me reconsider my path?" My hackles are up in full force.

"Not my intention, no." Nonno tilts his head in thought. "But, perhaps a good question to ask yourself."

"We'd better get back to it if we want to finish another section before ten."

He accepts my words with an acknowledging dip of his chin.

Having found our rhythm, we work in silence, he emptying and filling barrels while I scrub them clean. The thrumming of the brush against the inside of the barrel allows me time to reflect on what I've experienced today.

At twenty-three years old, I hadn't realized my view of vineyard life was a fanciful one. Painted with strokes of rainbow hues, I imagined a make-believe existence that didn't include moving the contents of every single barrel of wine from one to another, not once, but possibly four times over the course of the aging process.

I thought I had known the meaning of hard work. I have prided myself on my willingness to work, having happily toiled in the vineyard for years. My mistake was thinking the farming of the grapes was the most difficult aspect to contend with. How incredibly wrong I was.

Ever since the day Nonno told me that wine, instead of blood, ran through my veins, I assumed the task would come easily to me. I was to be a shining star in the history of the Russo Vineyard. Al must have a less delusional view of the work involved, having seen the goings-on with his own eyes. How could I have been so misinformed?

The sigh slips through my lips, garnering Nonno's attention. I pretend not to notice his concern and keep working. I think back to the years of arguments between Papa and me. Each one of them fueled by the belief that becoming a winemaker is my calling. What would he think if I decided to forgo the family business now? Would he be pleased or disappointed?

The irony isn't lost on me. If Papa had truly wanted to ensure I would lose interest in the vineyard, he should have made me rack wine from an earlier age. One season of wine racking could have been enough to convince me to become a schoolteacher instead of a winemaker.

I pause, brush in hand. Papa never made me rack wine.

Thirty-Three

I CLOSE my eyes and inhale the fruity aroma of the contents of my glass. A light July breeze wafts through the cellar door enhancing the experience of the new vintage before me. A small sip brings to mind blackberry picking with Mama, an end of summer tradition. I let the wine linger, searching for the notes of vanilla and clove, that I insisted we give a try. After deciding racking wine isn't nearly as challenging once you've embraced the process and had the chance to practice it four times in several months, I read everything I could get my hands on about Zinfandel wine.

Despite aging the Zinfandel in the lightly toasted oak barrels, the notes I am seeking remain muddled and barely present. Disappointment over my effort of having spent the better part of four days sorting barrels for the experiment that felt so certain within the confines of my mind, brings a twist to my lips.

Nonno chuckles at my expression. "No good?"

"Unremarkable, but not bad." I offer the concession as a reason not to worry over the potential of lost revenue.

Our second vintage is now complete. Nonno and I agreed to

kccp the first official tasting between ourselves. Preferring to ensure our efforts are worthy of sharing before inviting the rest of the family to sample and comment for themselves, we haven't yet told them the wine is ready.

He raises his glass to his nose and smiles. "Smells like Russo wine, Sofie." I wait for him to taste it, not wanting to get my hopes up.

"*Bene*." His eyes light up. "This is a good effort. Why are you not satisfied?"

Though I suspect he knows the answer, he waits patiently for me to answer.

A huff of defeat precedes the delivery of my words. "The wine is fine. No, it is quite good actually, but..." I pause as I consider my words. "This is not what I set out to achieve."

"Spoken like a true vintner." Nonno chuckles. "Get used to being disappointed, my girl, for it is the life of a winemaker. We are seldom completely satisfied with our own creations."

"Great. A life of constant work with little reward. I look forward to it."

Nonno laughs harder at my barely concealed sarcasm. "You can thank your stubborn streak. It is responsible for getting you into this business."

"Yeah, yeah. Don't I know it?" I take another sip of wine and acknowledge that despite the missing elements I was keen on, the vintage will do nicely. With the rising prices in the grape market, Russo wine will sell well, and for a tidy profit, in 1944.

"What are you two up to?" Al enters the cellar through the open door, a mischievous lilt to his question. "I knew something was up when you snuck out after lunch." He looks over his shoulder. "Papa is heading this way, so you better decide if you're sharing or cowering." Al's gaze lands directly on me.

"I'll head him off so he doesn't get any ideas about not being included from the start. We have no need to ruin a perfectly pleasant day with a misunderstanding." Nonno slips off his stool with a look in my direction. "Sharing?"

"Sharing." The word comes out stronger than I imagine it will. Maybe I am coming into my own with regards to Papa, after all.

"Look at you, all full of confidence." Al bumps my shoulder with his elbow. "I'll go get Mama. She isn't going to want to miss out."

I don't feel confident. In fact, my stomach is informing me that lunch wasn't such a good idea, but I thank my brother anyway as he trots out the door toward the farmhouse.

The four of them arrive together, I'm sure thanks to Nonno's stalling of Papa to lighten the pressure he is more than aware I am feeling in this moment.

"Sofia." Mama is beaming as she walks over and kisses me on both cheeks. "I am so proud of you."

"Mama, you haven't tasted it yet."

"I don't have to. It is wonderful because you made it. I see how hard you work and study. All that effort cannot create an ugly wine. I will make a cake to celebrate." She touches her forehead to mine and I wonder if she is trying to infuse me with as much love as possible in the event my feelings will be hurt once Papa has the chance to taste the vintage.

"You don't have to go to any trouble. Besides, with rations and all, sugar is in short supply. Save it for something truly important."

"Nonsense. I will use applesauce from the pantry to sweeten the cake, and we will celebrate over dinner."

Nonno pours the wine. My heart rate picks up speed, its beat thundering in my ears. Papa takes his time. Smelling, sipping, and yes, is that savoring? I am glued to his every expression, my next breath held hostage within my chest. He tilts the glass, peering at the crimson liquid in quiet contemplation.

"Well, Giovanni." Nonno doesn't mince words. "What do you think?"

"I'm not sure it's the best Zinfandel we have ever made, but it will sell well enough."

Nonno is clearly delighted by Papa's response as he slaps his back and congratulates me for a job well done. He is dancing around the wine cellar, acting like a little boy in an old man's skin.

Feeling myself shrink into my shadow, I do not share Nonno's enthusiasm. I have still not managed to make my father proud.

Mama and Al chime in with their applause and I do what is expected of me. I smile and say thank you, but inside my heart is crumbling into tiny pieces.

One day I won't be able to put the pieces back together again.

After two days of mulling over Papa's reaction to our vintage, I decide brooding will get me no closer to a successful outcome. I spend evenings in my bedroom, poring over my journals, looking for inspiration I can take with me into this year's harvest. I reach for my current journal, its place marked with the heavier cardstock that I picked up but never returned to Nonno's trunk two and half years ago.

I hesitate at first, wondering if it is time to admit to Nonno that I've had his recipe tucked into my journal all this time. Each day, as I record my notes, I have moved the instructions, the ones that continue to tug at the edges of my mind, forward as I write my way through another year of vineyard observations.

I take a sip of our latest Zinfandel, trying to determine how to improve upon it, while scanning his hand printed instructions for the umpteenth time. Each time I see the words *new oak*, my thoughts are baffled by the mere suggestion of it. Nonno has told me countless times that Zinfandel does not need the fuss or the cost of new oak barrels.

Then there is the size of the barrels. Nonno's instructions mention barrels significantly smaller than the ones the Russo wine cellar houses. I suspect it is the recipe's contrary nature to the usual Russo winemaking processes that keeps me returning to it every night.

Nonno has explained to me that reusing our barrels is a benefit in both cost and flavor as traditional Zinfandel does not generally invite toasted oak into the wine. But what if we could change the complexity of the wine by using smaller barrels? It would be a costly experiment, but perhaps there is a way. Tapping my bottom lip with my index finger, I mull the idea over.

I take another sip of wine and I realize that I wasn't likely to fail entirely with our latest vintage by using the lightly toasted oak barrels I spent days sorting and separating. Given their age, finding a sliver of vanilla or clove is an unlikely occurrence. Nonno was teaching me a lesson. I see it now. How foolish of me to not realize sooner. No wonder he was able to have such confidence in my abilities, not to mention a little fun at my expense. *A cleverer man, I don't suspect there was.*

I tuck the information away and consider a question I haven't considered before. If not Zinfandel, then what? I make a mental note to investigate what type of grape would benefit from a smaller barrel. Deciding the time is not ideal to push my luck by suggesting a new varietal be planted in the vineyard, I accept that I'll be making Russo Zinfandel the way Nonno intended for the foreseeable future. Or at least until someone else besides me notices that while grape prices are rising at an alarming rate, Zinfandel hasn't risen as favorably with the wine economy since before Prohibition.

I am intrigued though and with my thoughts focused on the profitability of our vineyard, I grab my pencil and make a list of expenses. Using Nonno's calculations, I compile the numbers I do know, fixed costs being relatively consistent from year to year. In the bottom half of the page, I list a guess of anticipated costs if we were to acquire a fresh planting of vines. With no figures to attach to them, I simply write the type of expense with the goal of finding out the cost of such a venture.

My pencil taps the page. There is little promise of Papa allowing me to spend hard-earned money on something as risky as a new type of wine grape. Even I know, the vineyard has been making do for far too many years to simply hand over the pocket book into my less experienced hands. But what if I could earn the money myself?

My mind begins to hum with an idea. I saw an advert last week when I was in town, researching in the library. The Napa Valley Vintner Society, a recently formed organization focused on the growing and selling of regional wine, is opening a new office. They are looking to fill a part-time position for office work. Surely, I can manage working the vineyard and also in an office a few hours a week. I think of the additional income that could help support my ideas for future plans. An opportunity such as this may be just what we need to ensure the vineyard's success.

Making the decision to inquire at the Napa Valley Vintner Society office tomorrow morning, I go to my narrow clothes closet and rifle through my dresses, searching for something appropriate to wear to a job interview.

Thirty-Four

THURSDAY, MAY 1960

A RUSTLE of the vines catches my attention.

"I have an invitation for you." I turn and see Mr. Parisi waving an arm from the end of the row.

"An invitation?" I look up, gathering my bearings and head in his direction. Having given up on the speech for the time being and seeking a moment of solitude from my over-wrought mind, I ventured into the vineyard. Intent on distracting myself from the acceptance that my future does not include the family vineyard, I set out to walk to the farthest edge of the Parisi estate.

Knowing Mr. Parisi and his ability to put a positive spin on things, he could very well be inviting me to help him with a task he'd like company for. He is crouched low in the row as I approach, examining his vines from the ground up. "What kind of invitation?"

"Don't sound so skeptical. I only mean to invite you to dinner."

"Dinner?" I eye him warily, wondering if he is going to ask me to cook it.

"The Mrs. is away for a few days, visiting her sister. She left more food than I can possibly eat on my own and she's due back tomorrow." Mr. Parisi wiggles his bushy eyebrows. "I wouldn't want Olivia to think I do not appreciate her cooking. What do you say? Help a fellow out and have dinner with me."

Since I haven't even considered what the evening meal might bring for me back at the cottage, I accept his invitation. Eagerly anticipating Mrs. Parisi's lasagna, my steps are swift as we walk up the slope toward the main house.

Seated at the outdoor table with plates of steaming lasagna before us, our conversation flows easily between the weather, the vines, and the wine we are enjoying. The topic shifts to the new Russo tasting room as the sun dips down. Thankful for the cover of a setting sun, I keep my eyes on the horizon in an attempt to hold my emotions in check while the future I always dreamed of becomes the topic of conversation.

When Mr. Parisi places a delicate cannoli, drizzled with chocolate in front of me, I realize I haven't spoken a word in several minutes. "Thank you." I bring my attention back to the table as he lights a candle. Its flickering offers a warm glow of illumination. "This is delicious."

"I've known your Papa since we were boys running around in short pants." He waits for me to meet his eyes in the dim light. "He's my best friend but..." Mr. Parisi pauses a moment in contemplation of what I assume he is trying to say. "I feel I cannot let you remain in the dark any longer."

The hair on my forearms rises in anticipation. I swallow the last bite of cannoli and give him my full attention.

"Your Papa would not agree with me talking out of turn, I can assure you." His hesitant smile morphs into a sad expression. "If Valentino were here though, he'd remind me that you deserve to know. I'm quite sure my son would berate me for not telling you sooner."

A sober smile emerges at the mention of my friend. I lift my glass in toast to the boy we both loved with all our hearts.

"I have stood by and witnessed with my very eyes how your Papa discourages your enthusiasm for the vineyard." Mr. Parisi's head shakes in disagreement.

"I feared from an early age, you took this attitude toward you to somehow be your fault. You must know, I tried to make him see the friction he was creating between the two of you. Many times, we talked about our families. I counseled him to let your natural curiosity flourish and see where it might take you. I was always certain you would make a fine winemaker one day. But I'm afraid when it comes to you, your Papa's pain runs too deep."

I take in a sharp inhale, uncertain of what I'm about to learn. "His pain?" I search the face in front of me, both desiring and fearing the answer to my questions. "What are you not telling me?"

Mr. Parisi's thick fingers turn his wineglass in circles on the table. "Your grandmother passed when we were about seventeen-years-old."

I nod in agreement. The statement confirms what I've known for many years given that Nonno seldom shied away from talking about the love of his life or the importance she played in the success of the vineyard.

"What you may not know is that your Papa blames himself for her death."

The words hang in the air between us like low-lying fog in the vineyard. My thoughts are muddled as the warmth slowly drains from my limbs. "I don't understand. I thought she died of a heart-attack."

"Yes, that's true. It's the reason she was in the vineyard that Giovanni believes is the fault of his actions."

I lean forward, placing my arms on the table to steady myself. "What? How?"

Mr. Parisi tilts his head to examine the darkened sky. I imagine his mind taking him back in time. "Your papa was an adventurous young man. He worked twice as fast as anyone else in the vineyard, always in search of the next idea that would elevate the wine your family made. He was a genius when it came to the innovation of farming practices too. Did you know many of the vineyard's advanced practices that continue to be in use today are due to his creation of them?"

"No wonder he thinks so little of me, given his past accomplishments." It's my lack of ingenuity that has put a wedge between my father and myself.

"You misunderstand me. Your papa does not look down on you, Sofie. He's afraid of burdening you. Afraid you will suffer a similar fate to his own."

I want nothing more than to believe the words, but forty years of experience tells me otherwise.

"Your grandmother was in the vineyard that night because the temperature had dropped rapidly. She was helping your papa by monitoring the smudge pots in an attempt to keep his newest crop of vines safe from the frost. Your grandfather was away overnight, traveling to pick up supplies, so the task was left to your father and grandmother. With a large section of land to cover, they split up and went different directions, lighting the smudge pots as they went. You see, we didn't always have extra help on hand."

Mr. Parisi's head drops to his chin. "Your papa was beside himself. He came racing across the vineyard to our house, wailing and banging on the door for my father to help him. The next morning, his vines were safe, but his mother had perished. The cold was too much for her and when she lied down to rest in the early morning hours, it was her heart that failed."

Tears slide down my face. "I didn't know."

"He has blamed himself ever since. Your grandfather never

did. He resolutely maintained that your grandmother knew what she was doing and even if your father had insisted she return to the house, she wouldn't have listened to him." Mr. Parisi wipes his face with a single swipe of his hand and winks at me. "You can see where you inherit your stubbornness?"

An emotion-filled laugh bursts from my throat. "I imagine it's a family trait."

"Oh, yes. There is no doubt about it. I've known four generations of Russos so far, and I can say with certainty that what began with your grandmother was passed on to your papa, and then to you. If I'm not mistaken, I have noticed the same headstrong nature in Alonso's youngest son. He is sure to make a fine winemaker one day."

Tugging my thoughts back to Papa's resistance to my involvement in the vineyard, I am compelled to ask. "But, how does that explain Papa's insistence that I be excluded from becoming a Russo winemaker?"

"Ah, do you remember your tenth birthday?"

"Of course." I don't elaborate, given the hurt Papa's actions caused me that day.

"He came to me that evening. Told me he saw the fire in your eyes when you sipped your first taste of wine. At ten-years-old you reminded him of himself and that scared him. From that moment on, he was determined that you would not know the same fate as his own. He didn't want your eagerness, your zeal, to put you in the position of choosing the vines over someone you love."

Mr. Parisi is quiet for a few moments, but I know better than to interrupt while emotions are on display. "The first war didn't do him any favors either. His suffering only grew, so he did what he knew to do. He buried it deep within, hiding his pain from the rest of the world. But the day you celebrated your tenth birthday, his pride in you, despite its immense size, couldn't stand up against his fear of you having to live a life with regrets such as the ones he has. The only way he knew to make sure that didn't happen was to ban you from the vineyard. He saw it as the way to protect you from both the desire to achieve and the inevitable pain and disappointment he thought you would experience living the life of a vintner."

I let my head fall into my hands. Papa's words echo in my head, *Sofia, I do not wish for you to bear the weight of the vineyard.* A mixture of relief, worry, hurt, and more swirl around me before my anger asserts itself at the front of the line. "He didn't just ban me from the vineyard. He banned me from his life."

"I'm not sure he realized at the time, the cost to you being shut out. But know this, he did what he thought was right, out of love." Mr. Parisi reaches for my hands, the warmth sending jolts of life up my arms. "Try not to judge him too harshly. You only have one father in this world and despite what it might seem at times, he loves you deeply."

I pull my hands from his as a strangled laugh shoves its way past my throat. "He has an odd way of showing it." My voice rises as resentment rears its head. "I mean, how could he presume to know what is best for my life's path? Don't I get a say?"

Mr. Parisi allows me the space to vent though his downcast eyes tell me of his embarrassment at being the one in the middle of my fractured relationship with my father.

Awareness at the impropriety of my escalating rant nudges me to take a sip of wine and gather myself. "I'm sorry." I tamp down my distraught emotions, heaving the politeness Mama instilled in me to the forefront once more. "Thank you for telling me. I imagine deciding to do so was not easy."

"Your papa came to see me this afternoon too." Mr. Parisi's eyes shift up and scan my reaction. "Your mama insisted he bring your bottle of Pinot Noir to her. Apparently, he hadn't mentioned the times you approached him about a role in the vineyard." Mr. Parisi lets out a low chuckle. "That bit of information did not go over well with your mama. I suspect, after all these years, she assumed you had moved on with your life and all was as it should be."

I incline my head in agreement, realizing my attempt to maintain family harmony by keeping vineyard discussions away from the farmhouse and Mama's listening ears, only worked to my disadvantage.

Mr. Parisi watches me carefully as he continues. "According to your papa, she made him sit at the table until he had given the wine his full attention."

My head lifts a touch higher at the mention of Papa tasting my wine.

Mr. Parisi's expression lifts into a broad, knowing smile. "He admitted that your wine is indeed excellent, which I, of course, already knew."

I beam at the news and the genuine kindness Tino's father has shown me all these years.

"He told me that once your mama was done scolding him for the insensitivity he's shown to you, he was about to be excused, but..."

"But, what?" I lean forward in anticipation.

"Alonso arrived with a slew of his own words to get off his chest."

I cringe inwardly, knowing the heated state my brother was in when he left the cottage. "Oh dear. Papa had a difficult day, it seems."

"He did." Mr. Parisi agrees. "Perhaps it was time, though. We can only stay blind to our mistakes for so long. Eventually, they come back to slap us in the face."

"Yes, I suppose they do." We fall into a comfortable silence, both of us lost in our thoughts.

"Thank you for telling me. I have lots to think through, but I have more context now, and for that I am grateful."

Mr. Parisi shifts in his chair, signaling he is not yet finished. The hair rises on my forearms once more, telling me I have not heard all there is to learn.

"Sofia, there's something else. Your father bought the land your vines are on. Your Pinot Noir is Russo wine."

Thirty-Five

DECEMBER 1944

THE MERRIMENT OF DECEMBER, along with fewer expectations in the vineyard, allows me the occasional lazy afternoon. I have been pressed for hours since beginning work at the Napa Vintner Society last summer, but given the sheer amount of information filtering across my desk every week, I wouldn't dare complain. In taking the job, I've seen both my knowledge of the wine industry and my bank account grow.

Mama and I are decorating for Christmas, the tinsel clinging determinedly to our hands as we attempt to arrange it, strand by strand, onto the tree. Our laughter is interrupted by his cough. A rattling one that sounds as if he has swallowed an old set of keys, yanks me from my holiday cheer.

"Nonno." I knock softly on his back bedroom door. Together, Mama and I peek through the sliver of a crack into the room, darkened by the closed curtains and the low light of winter. "Can I fix you some tea?"

Mama pushes the door open when he doesn't reply. "Salvatore, can you hear me?" She rarely uses his Italian name, preferring instead to call him Nonno as a term of well-earned endearment. "Sofia, get your father. Tell him to ring for the doctor."

"What? No." My protest, fueled by panic rather than disobedience is ignored by Mama.

"Sofia, now," Mama insists, barely glancing in my direction.

I run from the farmhouse, calling to Papa, praying he is nearby.

Hearing the desperation in my voice, Papa comes running from the barn. "Sofia, what is it?" His eyes immediately dart to the farmhouse.

"Nonno. He isn't well. Mama said to call the doctor."

Hours later, we gather together in the living room. Al and Eva, with their tiny one, have joined our despondent little party. Papa sits in his usual chair in the corner, his expression pulled taut with worry. He has barely moved, except to sip from the glass of whisky Al poured him upon arriving.

Mama bounces the baby lightly as she talks and points to the half-decorated tree. Her voice carries a grandmotherly sing song to it, but I can tell her heart is heavy with concern.

Unable to marinate in the gloom any longer, I stand. "I'm going to make Nonno soup. That will make him feel better."

My parents exchange a look of apprehension that I choose to ignore as I make my way to the kitchen. Forming the pasta dough that will provide substance to the soup gives me a sense of purpose and it isn't long before both Mama and Eva join me in the kitchen to relieve their own idle hands.

As the others gather in the kitchen for a bowl of soup and Mama's freshly made bread, I make a tray and deliver it to my grandfather's bedroom.

"Are you awake?" I whisper into the darkness, conflicted as to what I want his answer to be. He needs his sleep, the doctor said as much. But I am desperate to hear his voice and be reassured all is well.

"Sofie, is that you?"

"Yes, Nonno. It's me. I have made your favorite soup." I place the tray on the dresser and turn on the small lamp in the corner of the room. "Do you think you can sit up and have some?"

"You are good to me." His smile falters as a cough takes over. "So good to me."

I help him sit up in bed, offering him one spoonful of soup at a time. He has little appetite and begs off more after only three sips.

"You're going to need to eat to get your strength back." I return the soup bowl to the tray on the dresser. "We'll have you up and about in no time at all."

A slight wave of his hand calls me over to him. "Come, sit."

I sit gently beside him on his bed, placing my hand on his. I notice the softness of his hand's wrinkles as I rub my thumb over the top.

"Sofia, my time is short."

Tears spring to my eyes. "Don't say that. What will I do if you're not here to teach me?"

"You have learned everything you need to know to become a successful winemaker." Nonno's eyes close, fatigue setting in again.

"Please, don't go." My desperation runs like a leaky faucet down my face, dropping with quiet plops onto his favorite quilt. "I can't do it by myself."

I question my ability to carry on as he told me to do while I sit quietly beside him as he falls into slumber. His chest rises and falls in slow methodical movements, giving me hope of his life continuing.

A week later, I am curled up in the chair Papa brought in, reading out loud to Nonno as he rests in bed with his eyes closed. Mama peeks in every few hours to check on both of us, but for the most part, my parents understand my need to be with him every possible moment.

I have ignored all of my obligations, calling the office to let them know I won't be in while asking Al to pick up any slack I may have left in the wake of Nonno's illness. I am closing the novel when he opens his eyes and watches me.

"You must have better things to do than watch an old man sleep."

"I don't, as it happens." I stand and stretch both arms over-head. "How are you feeling?"

His eyes twinkle, lifting my heart with hope. "Right as rain."

"Well, that's good news." I raise a glass of water to his lips. On the heels of my comment, a cough ripples through him, dashing any hopes for a speedy recovery.

"Do you have your journal?" Despite his tiredness, he insists we continue to talk about the vineyard.

"I do." I lift my notebook and pencil from the bedside table.

"Good. Let's talk about what you would like the vineyard to look like in five years."

"Five years?" I mull the timeline over, already knowing what I want but wondering if I am brave enough to ask for it.

Nonno, quick as ever, reads the expression lining my face. "I can tell you have some ideas. Let's get them down. Dreaming is an important part of running a vineyard. You must look into the future, seeking something that doesn't yet exist."

"Well, don't laugh, but..."

"I will never laugh at you for dreaming, Sofie." Nonno settles himself deeper into his pillow.

"I've done research on the use of smaller barrel sizes. I under-stand it isn't conducive for Zinfandel but if I'm to think five years from now, I'd like to see our vineyard boast more than just Zinfandel grapes."

"I see. Tell me your reasons and we can have a proper discussion." A glimmer of excitement flashes in his eyes, and I can see how caring for both his body and his mind is the key to his recovery.

Nonno and I are still talking about grapes when Mama appears an hour later with another tray. Scrambled eggs and a piece of toast. I note the upgrade in the menu as a good sign.

Our conversation shifts, and Nonno tells me about his dreams for the vineyard. "Most of my dreams have come true."

I narrow my eyes on him. "Most of them."

"Yes, all but one, so far. I dreamed of being a vintner from the age of eleven. That dream came true with years of dedication and hard work. Then, we had your Papa, and I dreamed that one day he would take over the family vineyard and he did."

I tilt my head from side to side, deciding whether to mention Papa's abandonment of the vines along the way. I decide better of it and allow him to continue.

"My only remaining dream is for you to continue the tradition of Russo winemaking and it is happening. Every day you spend working toward your goal, you are living the dreams I had for you."

"Your dreams are my dreams, Nonno." I lean forward and kiss his cheek.

"All I ask is that you stay true to what you desire in life. I cannot force my dreams upon you, nor can anyone take your dreams away from you. I do not intend to sound as though it is easy, Sofie. Dreaming is the fun part. There will be challenges and obstacles, and as a vintner, lots of hard work, but if you let your heart guide you, you'll never go wrong."

"There is nothing else in the world I would rather do than become a Russo winemaker." I hear the conviction in my voice and I can't help but believe in Nonno's dream too.

Nonno smiles at me, patting my hand with care. "Now, go on and let an old man sleep."

I squeeze his hand in mine. "I love you."

"My dear, Sofia. I will always love you."

I switch the lamp off on my way out of the room, gathering the remnants of the tray as I go. Looking back over my shoulder, I say a prayer of thanks that Nonno is on his way to better health.

Thirty-Six

FEBRUARY 1945

"ARE you sure you're warm enough?" I tug the blanket wrapped around Nonno's shoulders a little tighter. This afternoon's February chill is doing its best to ruin his requested outing by kicking up a fierce wind that is sure to put both of us to bed with fevers.

The cough, the same one that has kept him bedridden for months, rattles and heaves like a freight train through his body. I place a hand on his back, my meagre attempt to steady him on the cold marble of the vineyard bench.

"Thank you for bringing me here." He looks at me with a dubious expression. "I know your mama didn't agree."

"She didn't." I leave it at that, not wanting to burden him with the terse words Mama and I exchanged yesterday afternoon when I told her of his plans.

"I needed to be here, in the vineyard." His eyes scan the surrounding vines. "One last time. You understand that don't you, Sofie?"

I have no desire to confirm or accept his belief in the end being near, but I appreciate his desire to be in the place he loves most.

"I've never thought the stale smell of sickness trapped in a closed off bedroom does anyone much good."

Nonno chuckles more quietly than usual in what I assume is an attempt to keep his cough at bay. "Did you bring what I asked for?"

I pull the bottle of Russo Zinfandel from the bag before digging to the bottom for two cups. "Are you sure this is a good idea? I had to sneak it out of the house, you know. If Mama finds out, we'll both be in for an earful."

"*Buon vino fa buon sangue.*" He almost sings the words.

"Good wine makes good blood," I repeat in English as I tug the cork free and pour him a small glass. "I'm not sure Mama would agree, given your present state of health."

He takes the glass in his hand, waiting for me to pour my own. "I'm eighty-five-years-old. I have reached the age of not being concerned with what anyone agrees or disagrees with now."

"True enough." I raise my glass to his.

"*Cin cin.*" Nonno's eyes fill with moisture as he clinks his glass to mine. "*Nella botte piccola c'è il vino buono.*"

I've no idea what he has said, but not wishing to interrupt this experience for him, I watch intently as he closes his eyes and sips our wine. He takes his time, letting every note come to life on his palate. His body sways as a soft smile touches his lips.

"This is excellent." Nonno opens his eyes, looking directly at me. "You will find success as a winemaker, Sofia. I am certain of it."

Basking in his praise, I hold his wrinkled hand in mine. Together we sip our wine and let the sounds of the vineyard wash over us. We remain sitting on the marble bench he placed here sixty-one years ago for what seems like hours.

Part of me would love to know what he is thinking as we sit in silence. The other, more apprehensive side of me, would rather believe he has months, if not years to tell me all the stories in his head. I'm certain if we had more time, I could glean more of his knowledge.

It's not just about the wine. Or the vineyard. Or even this year's vintage decisions that have yet to be made, though all of those aspects of my life are what they are because of him. Nonno holds the answers to any question I might have. His is the wisdom I turn to when a new uncertainty appears in my life. Even when I don't ask his opinion, the advice he gives often steers me toward the correct path.

I push aside thoughts of a life without him, determined not to let my fears get the best of me. I search the sky but find little joy in its gray gloom. Nonno shifts beside me and I broach the question, "Should we go in?"

His resigned sigh tells me more than I wish to understand. "If we must."

Sensing this is his final goodbye to the land he worked his life for, I err on the side of compassion. "We can stay a few more minutes." I wrap an arm around his shoulders, using my body as a shield between him and the wind.

Time rushes by too quickly as Nonno and I remain, unmoving, huddled together, both of us holding onto the past and wishing we could start from the beginning all over again.

An hour or more later, Mama's concern has risen to the height of panic as she tromps through the vineyard in search of us. I hear her coming before I see her. Wrapped in Papa's thick woolen coat, her hair escaping from its carefully crafted bun as the wind whips at her back, her relief is evident when both our heads turn in her direction.

"Come, you two." Her words are cut short as Mama moves quickly to help Nonno stand.

Through the lens of a memory, I can hear exactly what she didn't say. I grew up, Nonno and me, being called in from the vineyard as the sun vacated the sky, Mama admonishing us with,

"Come you two. You'll catch your death out here." For once, I fear she may be right.

The walk back to the farmhouse is slow, Nonno pausing every few moments to either cough or look around. I balance Mama's desire to get him safely back home with his own insistence to remain where he stands.

Once settled in bed, Nonno complies with Mama's request to try some soup. I suspect he is doing it to appease her, so I hold my tongue when he winks at me. Nonno is finishing a small bowl of soup when Papa arrives at his bedroom door. Another request made by Mama, I presume.

Al is in the kitchen, scarfing down a bowl of soup by dipping whole slices of bread into the broth. "Hungry?" I tease, as I ladle a small serving for myself.

"How are you holding up?" Al doesn't need to elaborate. The only topic worth discussing is Nonno.

"We are close." The words come out as a squeak while my devastation at losing him bursts forth like an ocean wave. "You'd better say your goodbyes." Moisture gathers in Al's eyes as he reaches for my hand.

As the sky darkens, Mama draws the curtains, the somber mood making each one of us tired. I curl up in the chair beside Nonno's bed, watching like a fly on the wall as each member of my family bids him goodnight. There is a finality in their exchanges and it takes me biting the inside of my cheek to not interrupt their moments with an emotional outburst.

Papa is the last to leave. Looking back one last time with tears streaming down his ruddy, wind-chaffed cheeks. I've never before seen him cry. My heart breaks for him, my mouth tainted with the taste of blood as I bite down in response to his anguish. I see it now. Nonno wasn't mine alone, though he certainly made me feel like that was the case. He is all of ours. He is the one true north in our family and he will desperately be missed by all.

I read from Papa's copy of *A Tale of Two Cities*. My voice is just above a whisper in the low light of the lamp as Nonno drifts off to sleep. My eyes grow heavy, the days and months taking their toll on me. I set the book on his bedside table and tuck the blanket around me as I lean my head against the chair's winged back.

Something in the air shifts, and I wake with a start. The clock on Nonno's bedside table reads ten minutes past three. I sit upright, my eyes adjusting to the darkness. I swear I heard the crack of lightning, but standing to peer beyond the curtain confirms it was my imagination, my dreamlike state, playing tricks on me.

My eyes are drawn to Nonno's bed. His face holds a peaceful expression. Not quite a smile, but an acceptance of sorts. The realization hits me and my eyes dart to his chest where his hands lay folded across his torso. I wait for what feels like an eternity, begging his chest to lift with breath.

I stifle the sob that is desperate to escape and step toward him. Placing a hand over his, the warmth I have often taken comfort in is dwindling. He is gone from our lives, but not from our hearts. I reach for a tissue from the box on Nonno's bedside table and see it there, on top of the book I was reading him. A piece of folded paper that wasn't there when I closed the book. I can't stop my fingers from trembling as I reach for the note. Sliding a finger between the page, I open the note and see Nonno's handwriting. A final letter, just for me.

My dearest, Sofie,

I have said it many times, in wine there is truth. I have known since you were a small child that you will make Russo wine proud. Wine does not tell lies. It is either good or not so good, but it is honest in its telling of itself. This you must embrace. Be honest with yourself, for you will very well face challenges ahead. If you trust in the wine, you will trust in yourself and that will see you through. Follow your heart, Sofie, and you will make excellent wine.

In love and in wine,
Your Nonno
P.S. Nella botte piccola c'è il vino buono

The tears flow so steadily that I don't even bother to wipe them away. I reread Nonno's letter several more times, trying to decipher his Italian message. The phrase is vaguely familiar, not only from his mention of it this afternoon but of something I have heard before. An emotion-filled sigh slips past my lips. I'll never get the chance to ask him its meaning now.

I tuck his letter in between the pages of *A Tale of Two Cities* and gather myself in preparation for waking my parents. I squeeze his hand one final time and silently thank him. I can't even begin to imagine my life without him in it.

Thirty-Seven

APRIL 1945

I FLIP the pages of my journal in a whir of frustration, tearing a page in my haste. I immediately regret my recklessness, pressing a hand to the damage. Since Nonno was laid to rest two months ago, I feel as if I'm a ship lost at sea with nothing and no one to anchor me. I ignore the childish urge to toss the book across the room and force myself to take a steadying breath instead.

I start at the beginning, reading the notes from last spring, trying to recall the details of our plan. The value in Nonno's detailed note-taking has risen dramatically since his absence. I cling to his vineyard journals, imagining him guiding me through each step of the process. But with each passing day, my worry over the decisions I am to make has left me in a state of hesitation.

A light knock at my bedroom door grabs my attention. Al pokes his head in. "What are you up to?"

Seeing my perturbed expression, he steps inside. "Trying to make heads or tails out of spring." My arms flop animatedly against my bed. "I don't understand how I knew exactly what to do. I didn't think twice about it, really, when..."

"When Nonno was here?" He sits on the end of my bed, his head bobbing in understanding.

Sucking in my bottom lip to quell the sadness that is looking for an escape, I nod.

"There is value in someone believing in your abilities that makes things easier. He was that someone for you." Al dips his chin in an attempt to pull my downcast eyes up. "You knew what to do because he believed you did. You were a great team, working together as one. But, all the things he taught you haven't up and disappeared. They're still in there." Al taps a finger to my forehead, forcing a small smile to my lips. "Besides, you don't have to do everything by yourself."

I look at my brother. "Will you help me?"

"Of course, I will. I can hardly believe it took you this long to ask." Al places a playful punch against my arm. "I don't think you'll have to do any of it by yourself, though."

"Why do you say that?" I flip the journal closed, the words written within having lost all semblance of sense.

"Papa asked me to meet him here. He says he has something he wishes to discuss." Al shrugs his shoulders. "I figure it is his plan for how the three of us will work the vineyard side of the land together. He can't expect you to do it by yourself."

"I suppose not." I brighten at the thought of the three of us continuing on with what Nonno and I put into action. "Grape sales are through the roof. There hasn't been a boom like this in decades. This is the perfect time for us to expand the vineyard."

"Alonso." Mama is calling from the kitchen. "Did you want me to make you a sandwich?"

"Yes, Mama. Thank you." Al's eyebrows lift in anticipation. Mama, forever showing her adoration of her son by trying to feed him whenever he is in her presence.

"She does know that Eva cooks for you, right?"

"Shhhh, don't give me away. I am quite capable of inhaling an extra meal if it will make Mama happy."

"Mama or you?" I tease him as we both stand and head toward the kitchen.

"Both of us is an acceptable answer." He fires back over his shoulder.

Mama extends her offer upon seeing both of us in her kitchen. "Sofia, would you like a sandwich?" When it comes to food, Al is forever her first priority, but then again, perhaps she has given up on me and my nibbling ways.

"I'm good, but thanks."

She gives me the *did you eat today* questioning look but says nothing.

The three of us sit at the table, Mama and I sipping tea while Al gobbles his food. "What were you working on?" Mama directs her question to me.

"Just trying to sort out the next step with the vineyard." I wrap both hands around my steaming cup and let its fresh, minty scent waft up to me. "It's a bit overwhelming at times."

Mama pats my hand as the back door opens and closes. "Nonno knew you could handle it. It is up to you now, Sofia."

I appreciate Mama's encouragement and smile into my cup of tea as she rises to make Papa something to eat.

Papa sits down and our conversation shifts from chores to neighbors, to what Mama needs from town tomorrow. I look around the table but the empty chair, Nonno's chair, still sends a dagger through my heart each time I am reminded of his absence. Our family will grow again. With Eva and little Giovanni, Gio for short, and another one on the way. I am confident this kitchen will have many more happy times with lots to celebrate, but for now, I give myself permission to miss him.

This will be a tough year without Nonno, there is no doubt. I take Al's and Mama's words to heart and hold on to them. The vineyard will be just fine if we all work together.

Papa clears his throat as he pushes his empty plate away and rests his hands, folded together in front of him on the table. "I have an announcement to make."

Thirty-Eight

THURSDAY, MAY 1960

MY STEPS ARE SLOW. I can hardly believe it. Mr. Parisi's words spin on repeat through my mind as I walk through the vineyard back to the cottage. Both the pasta and the revelations have left me weary and ready for rest. Papa's exclusion of me when it comes to Russo Wines is not at all what I thought it was.

At the cottage door, I peer over my shoulder, taking in the moonlit vineyard beyond. My Pinot Noir vines stand proud in the distance. Is their strength a result of my work with them or something they've grown into on their own? Maybe Nonno was right. One can only grow into greatness when they've been challenged to rise above the struggle.

I slip through the door, and for the first time in all the years I've lived at the cottage, I wish I had a sofa to collapse onto. I've spent my days and most of my nights, obsessed with wine. The research is never ending. Each new technology requires scrutinizing and every old technique deserves contemplation. The difference between making wise decisions or flying by the seat of one's pants lies in my every spare moment spent hunched over a desk covered in books and papers. Even now, I don't regret a single moment of it.

If pressed, I would answer honestly. The years I've given toward my education, even when faced with a significantly different outcome than I was hoping for, have not been wasted. I am a better person for having intimately known vineyard life. The vines offer many things. Tranquility, inspiration, hope, a work ethic like none other, and the constant reminder of the power of resilience.

The word *resilience* sticks in my craw. I suppose a word can cut two ways. One being positive, the other being, misguided. I think of Nonno and his consistent ability to bounce back. His resilience was a positive force, not only in his life but in the lives of those he loved. Then, on the other hand, Papa's resilience tends to be born out of a desire to ensure the prevention of something he fears. A negative force in more ways than one.

Knowing what I know now, I contemplate the wisdom in looking any further for an answer. Is there even a point? I do not wish to inherit Papa's version of resilience, but perhaps I am stepping a little too close to the edge myself by pushing him with my single-minded view of the situation.

Standing in the threshold between the living room and the rest of the cottage feels akin to my position with Papa. No matter which way I turn, I am unlikely to find the comfort I seek. The clock on the wall reads ten minutes to eleven. My gaze falls to Nonno's trunk. I look away, resisting the urge to dig further and instead pad to the bedroom. Sleep is not likely to find me tonight, but a soft bed to mull over the thoughts running rampant through my mind is much more inviting than the draughty entrance of the cottage door.

Out of habit, I reach for my vineyard journal, sliding Nonno's letter to be a page ahead as I do every night, and record today's findings. I let the methodical nature of a repeated task soften the blow of the words spoken by Mr. Parisi this evening. I felt as if the ground had shifted beneath my feet as he changed my under-standing of everything with six little words. *Your Pinot Noir is Russo wine.*

Several hours after hearing those words, I remain unable to comprehend the statement or its meaning for me and my future. Papa apparently came to his friend, requesting to purchase the small parcel of land where my vines are planted. Al had inadver-tently let my deal with Mr. Parisi slip, telling Papa that I was preparing the land to grow a new varietal. I imagine this striking fear in Papa's heart given the rest of the knowledge I'd gained over tonight's dinner, but Mr. Parisi indicated otherwise.

He reluctantly told Papa of the agreement between us, but Papa persisted, telling him, she is my daughter, I should be respon-sible for her debts. They agreed to keep the purchase of the land a secret from me, Papa insisting my knowing would only serve to sour the grapes. Mr. Parisi kept his side of the bargain, engaging me in Parisi vineyard chores as partial payment for the use of his land.

Thinking back on it now, I realize that Mr. Parisi called me in to help only when absolutely necessary, or when he saw a moment where he could teach me something while he worked the land. Working my debt of borrowed land off has hardly been a burden to me these past few years. I have enjoyed working and learning alongside him. At times, it felt as if Nonno was there and in those moments, all was well with my world.

But Papa owning the land my vines are growing on and now my vintage, is something I'm not sure what to do with. My first thought is that he'll claim the vintage as his own and sell it at the new Russo tasting room. I concede the fact that technically, all of it belongs to him, but it was my hard work and personal paycheck that afforded the new French oak barrels, the vines, and everything in-between. Mr. Parisi allowed me use of much of his equipment and occasionally his crew of laborers helped out but I'm the one who invested in the two things that I am confident make this vintage as good as it is.

My head is swimming with emotions I can't even begin to name. I spent years saving my pennies and making plans. I feel as though I've been tricked under some parental guise of being cared for. My anger toward Papa is at an all-time high.

"How could he?" The question roars out of me before I fall back against the pillow, anguish pouring out of me in shouts and gripes.

Unable to stand it one minute more, I bolt from my bed, bare feet slapping against the wood floor. Brushing my tangled hair from my face, I throw open the front door of the cottage and stride with purpose toward the vines I thought belonged to me.

A shiver runs the length of my spine as a cool evening breeze stirs the canopy of green before me. If I didn't love them so dearly, I'd pull each and every vine out of the ground tonight, just to spite him. All this time, Papa has persisted in keeping me out of his vineyard only to come into mine and kick me out of it.

Thirty-Nine

APRIL 1945

PAPA'S BEAMING expression draws us all in as we wait for his announcement. Mama tilts her head in question while Al leans back in his chair, anticipating what is to come. I find myself holding my breath. I'm hopeful Al is right and Papa wants the three of us to work the vineyard together, but something about his barely concealed excitement makes me wary rather than comforted.

"The time has come to officially begin Alonso's training as a Russo Winemaker." Papa rubs his hands together, eagerness to get started rising within him before he lifts his sandwich to his lips.

"Giovanni." Mama is shaking her head in what I assume is disbelief.

"What?" Papa turns his head in Mama's direction. "I won't be a young man forever. The time has come."

Unaware of the growing tension in the room, Papa stands and places a hand on Al's shoulder. "Together, we will run the vineyard and in time, it will all become yours."

Al can't bring himself to meet Papa's eyes, or mine, for that matter. Instead, he looks down at the kitchen table, not saying a word.

Mama tries again. "But, Sofia. She has kept the vineyard going for so many years now. You can't mean to exclude her."

Papa appears offended at Mama's mention, as if he hasn't already thought of his daughter. "Sofia has better things to do than work in the vineyard. She has a job at the Vintner Society and with the increase in grape prices, it is time for us to expand the vineyard."

"Yes, I understand your desire to settle the future of the vineyard by taking steps now." Mama is treading carefully though I cannot tell if it is out of concern for me, Papa, or herself. "But surely, Sofia will have a role and be welcome to continue her work here?" Mama's words must have hit a nerve as Papa's eyes flash with something unfamiliar but worrying, all the same.

I shrink a little, knowing she is standing up for me. "Giovanni, you must admit that she saw the vineyard through when you weren't willing to. Now that grape prices are increasing, you can't take that away from her."

"Enough." Papa growls out the word. "We agreed many years ago that you would no longer make any decisions regarding the vineyard." Papa's anger is fleeting, a flash in the pan, so to speak. A moment later, his natural, soft-spoken demeanor returns.

"Sofia isn't responsible for making grape prices triple and as I said she has a job. She is not to be burdened with the responsibility of the vineyard." Papa steals a glance in my direction, reminding me of my place in the family. "She also has a roof over her head and plenty of food on the table. Until she decides to marry, she will remain well taken care of by us."

The room falls silent as Papa's final words reverberate around us, none of us able to meet another's eyes. The decision has been made and according to Papa, that is all there is to be said on the topic. Heaven forbid, he should ever think to ask any of us what we want.

I am twenty-five years old and I finally know what I must do. Without a word, I stand from my seat at the table and give Mama's shoulder a light squeeze in appreciation of her support. I do not meet Papa's eyes, I simply turn around and walk out the back door.

* * *

"I cannot stay under his roof any longer."

Mr. Parisi's eyes are filled with sadness as he listens to my request to move into the winemaker's cottage on his vineyard.

He leans against the tractor's wagon, considering my request. "The cottage hasn't been lived in for many years. It will require a lot of attention to be comfortable again. Are you sure you can't make amends with your Papa?"

"I don't have anything to apologize for, otherwise I would." A small sigh escapes my lips. "I realize I'm putting you in a delicate situation, asking this of you, but the cottage was the first place I thought of. Tino always said he was going to move into it one day and that brings me more comfort than you know."

"Oh, Sofia. I'm sorry things have come to this between you and your father. I must be the one to let him know. I suspect he will take the news better coming from me. Perhaps a little separation of space will do you both some good."

I lean toward him and wrap him in an embrace. "Thank you, Mr. Parisi. Thank you. I have money saved, so I won't be a burden on you. I will take care of the cleaning of the cottage. You won't have to do a thing, I promise."

"I'm happy to do whatever you need me to. Please come to me if you need anything at all. I will have the keys ready for you by tomorrow. Once I've spoken with Giovanni, you're free to get started."

Two weeks later, an empty crate lies waiting at the foot of my childhood bed, ready for the final contents of my closet to be tossed into it. The days raced by as I arranged for the departure from my parent's farmhouse. I am happily surprised how easily tasks fell into place once I made the decision to leave.

I asked for and was granted a full-time position at the Vintner's Society, a position that will allow me to be financially independent while maintaining a foothold in the Napa Valley wine industry. Given the necessity to drive into work each day without access to the family pickup truck, I purchased my first automobile, a used 1934 Oldsmobile, for fifty dollars. Al insisted on accompanying me as I made the purchase, wanting to ensure I was buying something suitable, since he would have preferred for me to purchase a newer vehicle for reliability's sake. Given that the war effort has halted the production of cars, that option was not available to me, not that I could afford one, anyway. The only thing that has delayed my move until today, aside from Mama's occasional tearful pleas, is the delivery of my new bed.

As soon as I had the keys to the cottage, I set to work, scrubbing it from top to bottom. I washed every curtain and added a fresh coat of linseed oil to the wood surfaces in the cozy space. Mr. Parisi upgraded the appliances, bringing the kitchen into a new decade, saying it was the least he could do since I insisted on paying my own way, despite my rent being a pittance to what it would cost me in town.

Stretching my arms overhead, my enthusiasm to get going with the day rises within me. Once I've settled into the cottage, I have plans to pour through Tino's notes and use the outbuilding to continue what would have been our experiments with making wine. Mr. Parisi was more than pleased to hear me speak of my plans, even going as far as to offer me grapes from his upcoming harvest to continue my trials.

Sliding my legs from beneath the covers, I tiptoe to my bookshelf, carefully gathering the few books remaining there and place them in the waiting crate. I move toward my bedside table where my eyes are snagged by the copy of *A Tale of Two Cities,* the one I read out loud to Nonno in his final days.

Technically, the book belongs to Papa, but I contemplate taking ownership of it given the memories and Nonno's last letter to me held within its pages. I tell myself I can buy Papa a new copy for Christmas instead as I open the novel and unfold my grandfather's final words.

I draw in a steadying breath, letting my eyes fall to his PostScript. "*Nella botte piccola c'è il vino buono.*" I whisper the phrase, still not recalling what it means. Normally, I'd enlist the help of Mama or Papa for the translation, but I find myself not yet ready to share Nonno's words with anyone else.

A soft knock at the door startles me from my thoughts. Mama pokes her head into the room. "Will you stay for breakfast?" She doesn't wait for me to answer and instead, presses on. "I'm making pancakes."

"I would love to. I'll get these last few crates into the car and then I'll be in to help you." I don't mention the moisture already welling in her eyes or the brave front she is putting on for my benefit. I merely tuck this image of Mama into my heart for safekeeping.

The awareness of the little moments I will miss once I leave my childhood home swirls around me like autumn leaves trapped in a cyclone of air at the back porch door. I decide having Nonno's words close at hand will be important, if not a lifeline, in the coming months.

Lifting my journal from the bedside table, I open it to yesterday's entry. The place is marked by the impromptu bookmark of

Nonno's folded recipe card for wine in smaller barrels. I've been transferring the recipe, a talisman of sorts, with each passing calendar day and journal entry since it caught my attention a few years back.

Deciding Nonno's final words will be far more comforting than instructions for making wine, I tuck his letter into my journal and place the recipe I've yet to make heads or tails out of on top of the pile of books in the crate.

I pull the last few hangers of clothes from my closet and bend at the waist to lay them on top of the books. As the hem of dresses flutter near the crate, Nonno's recipe is bumped to the floor. I move the clothes to the bed and pick up the cardstock instructions.

Not wanting to misplace the instructions that I am certain will one day be important, I grab the copy of *A Tale of Two Cities* and tuck the recipe between the pages and slide the novel further into the crate for safe keeping. I fold the remainder of my clothes on top of the books and make two trips to the car with the final crates.

We are enjoying our pancakes when Al arrives, not hesitating to join us at the table for his second breakfast of the day.

"Have you got everything?" Al asks between mouthfuls.

"I think so." My hand pauses with my fork part way to my mouth. "Well, there is one thing I was wondering about?"

"What's that?" Mama asks, lifting her cup. The aroma of the dark brew wafts into the air. "I told you to take a fry pan and pot."

"It's not that. I was wondering about Nonno's trunk. The one with his journals in it."

Mama's eyes flick up in Papa's direction and I immediately regret speaking out on the topic. I should have known it might be an issue. I admonish myself for creating tension when we were having a perfectly pleasant breakfast together.

Papa gives his permission with a slight nod. "We will put it in the back of the truck." Papa looks to Al as he ropes him into my request. "Alonso will drive it over. He can help you unload it when he arrives."

"Thank you, Papa." I feel the emotions hiding beneath the surface of my skin. Close enough that they tingle, but hidden from sight all the same. "You'll know where it is if you ever need anything from it. Anything at all."

Several minutes later, with breakfast finished and no reason to delay, I look back over my shoulder from my car's door and wave, tucking the smile that is bursting to let loose behind a demure expression. I am not angry. Nor am I upset. I simply understand the only way to make my father proud and prove to him that I'm capable of being the next Russo winemaker is to leave. Time and space are sure to heal wounds while providing me some much needed breathing room to think for myself. The farmhouse grows smaller in my rearview mirror, but the rows of vines are forever imprinted in my memory.

Forty

JANUARY 1954

MY HEAD SNAPS up at the mention of the red *Burgundy* grape. I am putting the finishing touches on my shorthand of this month's meeting when Mr. Zellerbach mentions the French grape known as Pinot Noir in North America. I lean in to listen, having come across the temperamental grape with its thin skin and time-consuming canopy management in my studies. Though the grape has seen small successes in individual wineries since the mid to late eighteen hundreds, its fickle nature has prevented it from gaining a wider breadth of interest in the region.

This could be the one, I think to myself as I linger in the room, delaying my departure in the hopes of learning more. *The one I've been searching for.*

I gather my notebook and pencil and walk back to my desk, thinking back to that day in September when the war with Germany was finally won. Amidst the celebration with Tino's and my family, Mr. Parisi came to me, expectation written on his face. "Now is the time, Sofie. You must do as you promised my son and mark your path to becoming a winemaker."

Goosebumps course through me at the memory of his words

and my subsequent promise to him to resume my wine education. Almost eight years have passed and I have hardly missed a single day of research and study. Two years ago, as Mr. Parisi and I worked side by side during the annual crush of his grapes, I broached the subject of leasing some of the Parisi land for my own plantings. He happily offered me a small plot of land, in exchange for additional help with his vineyard. Help, I am more than happy to offer since being in his company has been one of the greatest benefits of residing at the Parisi winemaker's cottage. Together we work his vineyard, but I alone prepare my borrowed land for vines I do not yet own.

Pinot Noir, I let the name roll off my tongue. Even the sound of it sends a thrill of excitement up my spine. I've considered many grape varietals over the years, but none have elicited quite the response as the thought of Pinot Noir growing in my corner of the Parisi vineyard.

I contemplate the potential issues with Pinot Noir vines. I have never been one to shy away from a challenge, and this particular grape, I have learned, has its fair share of challenges. But I've been paying close attention these years at the Vintner Society and I know a challenge in a vineyard is equal to a well-priced wine on a store shelf. My vintage may be small when compared to others, but it has the potential to be something special in its own right.

Nonno's words of encouragement come back to me, "No vine grows into greatness without first struggling."

Well, since that's the case, Pinot Noir seems like the perfect match for me and my little vineyard.

I briefly wonder what Papa would say before making the conscious decision not to worry myself over such thoughts. I have years to go before we know how my experiment will turn out. In the meantime, he can call me foolish, or even brazen for aiming high with my first solo attempt, but a vintner cannot ignore a great vintage when they see one. Pinot Noir may be my ticket to convincing Papa, once and for all, that I am worthy of becoming the next Russo winemaker and someone he can be proud of.

By the end of the day, I can no longer contain my enthusiasm. I knock on Mr. Hall's office door and make my request. Knowing my ambitions and being delighted by my interest in the grape, my boss makes a phone call and arranges a meeting between Mr. Zellerbach and the two of us.

Three weeks later, we gather in the Vintner Society meeting room to discuss Pinot Noir. Mr. Zellerbach is gracious with his time and knowledge and surprisingly supportive, given the era and the industry, of a woman with an interest in making wine. We bond over techniques and approaches, a friendship forming between us with speed.

By the end of our two hour long meeting, I'm confident knowing Pinot Noir vines are well-suited to my little plot of borrowed land. Mr. Zellerbach has provided his expertise and guidance for me to consider, along with an offer of Pinot Noir cuttings for me to purchase through him. I return to my desk and spend a half hour running the numbers against what I know of the allotment of land I have to work with while the gentlemen continue talking wine and vintages.

With a firm grasp of the expense I'm about to incur, I return to the meeting room ready to seal the deal. A contract is drafted right in front of me with Mr. Hall looking it over to ensure what is agreed upon is included in the paperwork. Mr. Zellerbach signs his name with a flourish before passing the papers to me. I sign my usual, slightly boring, but legible signature and slide the contract to Mr. Hall for him to witness.

As the office closes for the day with many of my coworkers vacating the premises, Mr. Zellerbach reaches into his satchel and pulls out a bottle of his estate's Pinot Noir for us to celebrate with. The three of us, joined together by the mutual appreciation of wine, clink glasses and rejoice in the arrangement we have amicably arrived at. I shake Mr. Zellerbach's hand and thank him for the opportunity.

I am wrapping my coat around me, preparing to leave for the day, when Mr. Zellerbach places the remainder of the bottle of Pinot Noir on my desk. "You take that with you. I'm sure there is someone other than us two old geezers that you'd like to celebrate with."

I laugh in response. "Well, actually, I have another old geezer at home that I'm keen to celebrate with."

The kind man looks at me with sincerity. "I expect great things from you, Sofia Russo. Great things."

"Thank you, sir. I'll do my best." I wave goodbye and thank them again.

Arriving at the Parisi home unannounced is like walking into a party in your honor. Mrs. Parisi plies me with home cooked Italian food while Mr. Parisi asks me question after question about the meeting and the deal. I show him my copy of the contract to purchase the Pinot Noir cuttings, which garners his approval.

We raise a glass of Mr. Zellerbach's Pinot Noir and the three of us drink a toast to those we've loved and lost, and the future that is yet to come. As the deep red wine dances across my tongue, I wonder how this moment would feel if my own family, my own father, were here to celebrate it with me.

Forty-One

FRIDAY, MAY 1960

I PULL the covers up over my head. The early morning light shines like a spotlight on my pillow. Having forgotten to pull the curtains closed last night, my reward is an earlier than intended start to the day. Given last night's news about Papa owning the land my vines are planted on, and the resulting night-long tossing and turning, my reaction to the day's arrival is subdued, at best.

Mr. Parisi's words haunted my dreams all night long, eliciting make-believe images of a distraught Papa as he tried, too late, to save his mother. I saw him racing and frantic through the vineyard. The imagined vision waking me several times as I thrashed within my bed.

Pushing the covers off in a huff, I slide from the bed. I can't imagine how he must have felt. So young and afraid. Nobody should have to live the rest of their life with that kind of experience plaguing them every step of the way. No wonder Nonno allowed him such grace.

My heart softens with the understanding of what his love for the vines has cost him. I wrap myself in my robe and head to the kitchen to make coffee. As the coffee brews, emitting its rich aroma, the pieces in my mind, like a puzzle, begin to fit together.

Coffee in hand, I sit down at my desk. The photograph of Papa and me, tucked into the frame holding the one of Tino and me, tugs my attention. I pluck it from the frame, bringing it closer. We had some good times, clearly, we did. I can hardly refute the photographic evidence of Papa's head thrown back in laughter.

What if Mr. Parisi is right? What if everything changed when Papa recognized our likeness to one another? Maybe my bold, single-minded nature was enough to push him into a protective mode whenever it came to the topic of me and the vineyard. The potential threat he recognized there for both of us might have felt paralyzing.

All this time, I've been fighting against Papa. Which, if I give it a moment's thought means I've been fighting against the ways in which we are similar. I've spent decades trying to convince him to believe in me. But he may have actually believed in me so much that he was scared I'd become just like him.

Maybe that's the solution. If I can find a way to show him that our being alike is a good thing and not a family curse he inadvertently handed down to me, perhaps then we can heal our relationship.

Has fear kept him from allowing the vineyard to really shine? He has been walking a tightrope between success and failure, likely because he believed he didn't deserve success. This realization sheds a light on why a man with an innate talent for vineyard life continued to struggle. I wonder if that is part of the appeal of having Al take over the vineyard. Papa knows my brother's heart isn't in it to the death. Perhaps in some way, that offers him a small sliver of peace.

I think of all the sacrifices he made. How many times did he pick himself up and do what was required while fighting his demons, just so there was food on our table? The challenges he faced were enormous, but in the end it was his own belief that made sure he didn't succeed as he could have.

"Oh, Papa." I feel the shame of not having noticed his suffering. So eager to make my own way in the world, I single-mindedly spent far too much time focusing on how he was impeding my progress. Maybe it is simply the nature of a relationship between a parent and a child. Once the stone is cast, can a daughter ever outgrow her father's expectations of her and become something greater than he anticipated?

As the question simmers within me, I find myself determined to find out. I will do what I must, to demonstrate to Papa that our shared traits are assets instead of the ticking bomb he's assumed them to be. Seeking the reassurance of Nonno's words, I grab my journal from the bedroom and return to my desk, ready to get to work. I slide the letter from within the pages. I take a sip of coffee and brace myself, knowing my grandfather's sentiment has the power to transcend time, space, and even death.

My dearest, Sofie,

I have said it many times, in wine there is truth. I have known since you were a small child that you will make Russo wine proud. Wine does not tell lies. It is either good or not so good, but it is honest in its telling of itself. This you must embrace. Be honest with yourself, for you will very well face challenges ahead. If you trust in the wine, you will trust in yourself and that will see you through. Follow your heart, Sofie, and you will make excellent wine.

In love and in wine,

Your Nonno

P.S. Nella botte piccola c'è il vino buono

My fingers run across his handwriting as I reread it again, his love shines through the years and across the page directly into my heart. Reading the PostScript, I can't help but laugh at myself. After all these years, I still haven't sought out the meaning of his

Italian message. I place the letter open on the desk beside the photo of Papa and me.

Infused with Nonno's words, I turn my attention to the steamer trunk, determined to locate and read through Nonno's earlier journals, the ones that would have been recorded in the aftermath of my grandmother's death. I hope to find the words I need to meet Papa heart to heart and begin our journey back to one another.

Papa's copy of *A Tale of Two Cities* rests on top of Nonno's journals. I must have left it there after I pulled it from my bedroom bookshelf when referencing Nonno's recipe as I prepared the details for an explanation of my Pinot Noir that I never got to deliver to my father.

I lift the novel to place it on my desk, tugging the cardstock with Nonno's written instructions from within its pages. Setting the recipe on the desk beside Nonno's letter, my breath hitches in my chest. A touch of vertigo forces me into the chair with both documents lined up before me.

Like a magnet, I am pulled forward, my eyes moving between Nonno's letter and the recipe. Nonno's instructions, the ones I've used as inspiration for creating my Pinot Noir, all but leap from the cardstock, appearing more weighted when compared to his letter. Without a doubt, the recipe is written in a heavier hand. The last piece of the puzzle clicks into place.

The cottage falls silent around me. I don't utter a sound. The depth of what I've just uncovered is too much for words, but the awareness of the knowledge rumbles through my head like a hurricane. This is Papa's.

Forty-Two

MARCH 1954

DAYLIGHT COULDN'T HAVE COME SOON ENOUGH. The sun is finally peeking above the horizon as I pause for a moment to stretch my back. My calloused hands no longer notice the stiff wooden handle of the shovel they've become one with. I arrived in the vineyard a little after four o'clock. My eagerness to begin the task at hand combined with a restless sleep, drove me to ready myself for the day before a more reasonable hour could appear.

I glance back at the progress I've made in the light of the early morning. The vineyard is outlined by posts marking the beginning and end of each row, running north-south across the land to even out the vine's exposure to the sun. The dim light of a lantern is not an ideal manner in which to dig holes. But, given my time constraint and the Pinot Noir cuttings that have been patiently waiting for me since their arrival at the Parisi vineyard three days ago, I am committed to the back-breaking process that is sure to take up the remainder of my Saturday.

I assess the depth of each hole as I dig. Using the vine spacing decided upon by Mr. Parisi and me, I make my way along the rows, following a string line attached to posts at intervals throughout the row from beginning to end.

Thankful for a week's worth of assistance from Mr. Parisi and his laborers, I can't fathom how long the preparations would have taken on my own. Each morning last week, while I left for the office, they headed onto my borrowed and barren land, prepping the rows by placing the poles and string line to be used as a guide. They'll be back this morning to help dig the remainder of the holes. By this afternoon we should be ready to plant. The mere thought of it sends a jubilant river of excitement through me.

This is the beginning of my life as a full-fledged vintner. From start to finish, it will be my guiding hands, my vision, and likely more than my fair share of worries too, but it will be mine. I've been waiting for this season of my life to begin for what feels like an eternity, and now it is upon me.

If only Nonno could see me now. I'm sure seeing me with my very own vines would make him proud. I may not be able to save Al from a life chained to a legacy he has yet to embrace, but at least I won't have let Nonno down completely. My vines may not grow in the Russo Vineyard, but even Papa can't take away the fact that, due to our shared last name, my vines must also be Russo vines, if only in my own mind.

I fight back against my emotions and return my attention to the row of holes yet to be dug. The steady beat of my shovel hitting dirt lulls me into a reflective mindset. Over the past ten years, I have carefully navigated my way through the minefield that is my relationship with my father and by extension, the Russo Vineyard. For all appearances, everything looks fine from the outside. We are not at all close, having few topics we can discuss without raw emotions getting in our way. But we are polite to one another and given the circumstance that I am excluded from the running of the vineyard, that is all I can hope for.

I offer the assistance of one more body in the vineyard when, and only when, I am asked for help. I keep the conversation of goings-on in my life to the mundane, sharing nothing of my plans on the Parisi estate, except with Al, of course. I never volunteer a suggestion or idea that might prove useful to the family vineyard for fear of stepping on toes. Instead, I filter anything that might be of help through Al, as a method of communication with my father.

Once a month, we gather as a family for Sunday dinner where Mama goes all out, feeding us as though we won't eat again until the next time we meet. I am fortunate to spend time with Al, Eva, and their two boys away from the vineyard at their home in town. Al chooses to drive out to the vineyard each day, a decision I suspect he made as a way of keeping some part of his life separate. I can't say I blame him one bit.

A murmur of voices pulls me from my thoughts. Mr. Parisi and his laborers are music to my ears as their morning banter reaches me in the middle of my digging another hole.

Spotting me, Mr. Parisi waves enthusiastically. "Sofie, what are you doing?" He shakes his head at my early arrival as he comes near. "How long have you been here?"

I walk to the end of the row to meet him. "I couldn't sleep."

He chuckles at my deflection of his question and peers over my shoulder at the extinguished lantern. "I can't imagine it was easy digging in the dark."

I don't say a word, choosing to let him draw his own conclusions.

Mr. Parisi turns to his crew, each of them ready with shovels and wide smiles. I shake hands with the men and thank them for their assistance. With the rows already marked, they know exactly where to start and trek to the farthest section of the vineyard.

A dust cloud rises from the direction of the gravel drive closest to the cottage, a car's movement drawing our attention. I shield my eyes from the sun with one hand and try to make out who could be arriving at this hour.

I know his frame as soon as he steps free from the cloud of dust.

"Al," I whisper, a lump rising in my throat. "He came."

Mr. Parisi pats my shoulder in understanding. "*La famiglia è tutto.*"

"Family is everything," I reply back. "Nonno always said so."

"Your grandfather was one of the wisest men I've ever had the pleasure of knowing. You've done him proud, Sofia. You've done him proud." Mr. Parisi turns to join his crew, already at work at the opposite end of the vineyard.

Al scans the land as he strides up the slight incline toward me. His hands, usually stuffed in his pockets, are full this morning with a thermos in one and a piece of paper in the other. "Good morning."

"Good morning." I tilt my head away from the sun's rays, gaining a better view of his face. "You came."

"You didn't think I would let you make your mark in wine and not be here to witness it, did you?" Al bends at the waist, placing the thermos on the ground.

Appreciation for my brother's understanding of who I am overwhelms me. I drop my shovel and wrap him in an embrace. "Thank you." Joy and relief consume me as years of struggle and heartbreak suddenly feel worth the effort.

"We Russos have to stick together." He whispers in my ear as I pull him close. "Besides, I might learn a thing or two."

We pull apart, both of us with silly grins pasted on our faces. "What's in the flask?" I jut my chin to the thermos on the ground. "Coffee? Please tell me it's coffee?"

Al laughs, his eyebrows lifting in question. "What time did your day start?"

"You don't want to know." I roll my eyes at my own absurdity. "But, seriously, did Eva send you with coffee?"

In true brotherly fashion, Al places a palm on my forehead to keep me arm's length away when I reach for the thermos. "Settle down. This isn't coffee, but I assume you have some? I'll go to the cottage and make a pot." He looks over my shoulder. "How many have we got here?" He counts heads. "I'll be back."

"Wait. If it isn't coffee, what did you bring?"

"This..." Al picks up the flask, not trusting me with its presence, and lifts it to my eye level, "you will have to wait for." He hands me the paper in his other hand. "But you can have this one now."

I take the page and my heart skips a happy beat at the crayon drawing of a person, I presume is me, standing in front of rows of green vines with big purple circles hanging off them. "Aww, this is adorable."

"Gio wanted you to know that this is how he sees his Aunt Sofie, surrounded by vines."

"Please tell him how much I love my drawing." I hand the paper back to Al, not wanting to ruin it with my dirty hands. "Can you put it on the fridge when you go in to make coffee?"

"One track mind, I swear. If it's not wine, it's coffee..." Al's voice trails off as he heads toward the cottage.

I pick up my shovel and head in the direction of Mr. Parisi and the crew working on my behalf. Together, we work our way through the rows, one hole at a time. We break for coffee first, then lunch a few hours later. Mrs. Parisi outdoes herself with platters of sandwiches and jugs of sweet tea, delivered right to the vineyard.

With energies renewed, we pick up our tools and begin again. Al, aside from his trip to the cottage for coffee, hasn't missed a moment of work at my side. For a man who shows little interest in being a winemaker, he certainly has excellent skills for laboring in a vineyard.

By three o'clock, the crew, working with augers at a much faster rate, has completed the majority of the hole digging. Mr. Parisi calls out to me. "Sofie, it is time for the cuttings. We will finish these last rows. You know what to do."

Excitement bubbles up inside me as Al and I head to the storage building where the cuttings have been watered and kept cool while they waited for their new homes to be ready for them. I pull back the tarp and oooh and ahh, like a proud mother goose over her latest hatch.

Al hides a snicker behind a closed fist before grabbing two buckets, one for each of us. We fill our pails with twenty cuttings each before adding some water to prevent them from drying out before their roots find their place in the ground.

"No root stock?" Al asks as we carefully relocate the cuttings.

"We discussed it at length." I roll my eyes. "And, then some. You know how much the threat of Phylloxera instills fear in the hearts of grape growers, but in the end, only a handful of vine-yards in the region are planting with root stock, so we decided to give a full-hearted Pinot Noir try."

Al nods, taking in the information but offering no opinion of his own, something I'm sure he has learned to do around Papa.

When we return to the vineyard, Mr. Parisi is waiting at the spot we chose together. Not too close to the end of the row for the vine's protection, but close enough to spot it from the cottage window. Just as Nonno had done in his vineyard, we left a space around the first vine's location and marked its importance with a pink ribbon.

Misty with emotion and what is likely a goofy grin on my face, I reach into my bucket for what soon will be the first Pinot Noir vine in my little vineyard. "We will do great things together, you and I." I whisper to the vine and place its roots gently into the hole

I dug. I cover the roots with Mr. Parisi's voice guiding me through the hilling of the soil, then I step back.

Two sets of eyes are on me as we gather around the small but hopeful planting. I've been waiting for this day to arrive for what feels like forever. Now that it's here, my excitement mixes with nerves as the responsibility of what I'm embarking on settles over me with a hush of anticipation.

Al opens his thermos and pours three small glasses of red wine, handing one to each of us. "This is the last vintage of Russo Zinfandel that Nonno and you made together. I thought it was only fitting to include him in this milestone."

Fresh tears spring to my eyes and words escape me.

"To you, Sofie." Al raises his glass. "For having the courage to make your dreams a reality."

"To Sofie," Mr. Parisi chimes in, slapping Al on the back with a hearty laugh.

I bring the glass to my nose, inhaling the aroma before taking a sip. My eyes grow wide with delight, as they do each time I taste Nonno's wine.

"I tell you, Alonso, Sofia has wine running through her veins." Mr. Parisi's words strike a chord within me. Nonno used to say the exact same thing.

"What do you think?" Al searches my face.

"I think all this vineyard needs now is a bench."

Forty-Three

FRIDAY, MAY 1960

THE COTTAGE IS quiet around me. Save for the occasional bird chirping beyond the window, the only sound in the room is the thumping of my heart. I can't tear my eyes away from the two pages before me. One in Nonno's hand, the other in Papa's. At first glance, their handwriting is almost identical, but when laid side by side, the subtle differences leap from the page.

All this time I've been using Papa's instructions as inspiration for my Pinot Noir. All this time, it's been Papa's musings I turned to over and over again whenever I needed an infusion of strength to continue. All this time. It's been Papa.

My coffee grows cold beside me, its roast scent dwindling into something stale and burned smelling. I push the mug and its offending odor across the desk. Picking up the photograph of Papa and me, I smile. My affection for my father pushes past any resentment of him. He was with me every step of the way, whether he knew it or not.

He does love the vines, as Nonno said. He loved them so much that it cost him dearly. A daily battle fought between his deepest desire to make exceptional wine and his responsibility to never again cause another harm. Fear has a nasty way of taking over and sucking the joy from one's life.

Forgiveness may take time, but compassion I have at the ready. So ready, in fact, I wonder if I've been holding myself back, waiting for permission to love him again.

Like my father, I've let fear rule my decisions, especially where he is concerned. At the age of ten, I knew I didn't want to feel how I did when his approval was lacking, and so I set forth on a path all my own. A path that took me further away from understanding him. We are more alike than we realize. Mama always used to tell me so. I understand what she means now.

I may have to tame my stubborn side and bite my tongue on occasion, but I find myself coming to terms with doing as Al desperately wants me to and speak with Papa one more time. This time, though, I'll set my pride aside and only bring love into the conversation. We share a love of the vines, Russo wine, and our family. I don't see any reason why we can't share in that together.

I tug my robe free as I race to the bedroom, determination fueling my steps. Today will be a busy day at the tasting room and I have no interest in getting in the way of the preparations. If I can catch him before the others arrive, I can make a start at healing what lies between us.

Running a brush through my hair, I stare at my face in the mirror, weary from a lifetime of resistance and a week's lack of sleep. I shake my head, not believing how long it has taken me to come to terms with what Mama has been telling me all along. *Knowing yourself means being proud of your accomplishments, whether others deem them worthy escapades or not.*

I never needed my father's approval to become a vintner. He may be proud of me or not, I don't know. Either way, his pride in me isn't mine to demand. I understand now, it never was. But it doesn't mean I won't give it one more shot. One more chance to be included in the family vineyard. He doesn't owe it to me and I won't beg for it anymore. I will simply ask. With understanding and compassion, I will ask that he trust me with his dreams and his fears. His heart and his wine.

I swipe a touch of mascara to my eyelashes and grab a sweater from the bedroom closet. Stuffing a piece of toast into my mouth, I chase it with cold coffee to wash it down. In the living room, I spin in a circle, deciding upon what to bring or leave behind. I don't wish to set his teeth on edge by showing up with a truckload of evidence as to why he should choose me. Instead, I settle on a photograph, two pieces of paper and a bottle of Pinot Noir.

Forty-Four

"SOFIA."

Caught by surprise, I snap my head up to see him standing there. On the gravel path that leads to my door, a place I'm certain he has never been before. Papa appears smaller, holding his hat in front of him with both hands.

"Papa, I was—"

"I see you're going out." He apologizes with his eyes. "I can come back later." He hesitates, dropping his gaze to the ground. "If that's convenient for you."

"No." He doesn't let me finish and is bobbing his head in understanding while stepping back toward the driveway with slow steps.

"Wait. I meant, no, you don't have to come back. I was actually on my way to see you." I lift one shoulder in what I hope is an invitation. "Why don't you come in?"

Papa follows me inside.

"Can I get you coffee?" I place the bottle of wine, photograph and pages on the desk before closing the door behind him.

"Coffee would be nice." He looks around the room and I'm

once again reminded of the lack of hospitality in my living room. I hurriedly lug a kitchen chair into the small space before looking up to follow his gaze.

His eyes rest on Nonno's open trunk. Journals, photo albums, and a lifetime of memories stare up at us.

I clear my throat. Having expected to have the short drive to the farmhouse to gather my thoughts, I relish the time it will take to brew the coffee. "I'll be right back then. Make yourself at home." I cringe at the sentiment, knowing there is little in the way of comforts of home in my small living room.

In the kitchen, I rehearse what I hope to say. A few minutes later, as the coffee maker begins to gurgle, I hear the cottage door open then close. The faint sound of footsteps on gravel as he traipses down the path echo through the cottage.

I poke my head into the living room. Empty. He is gone.

I scan the room, wondering what happened to make him up and leave. The photograph of Papa and me on the desk has been moved. My eyes dart to the pages I intended to show him eventually, but with the benefit of conversation to explain myself. He has seen his handwriting with the instructions of his wine-making method. There is no turning back now. I must explain or risk forcing the wedge between us even deeper into the ground.

I am about to chase after him when the sound of footsteps on gravel catches my attention again. This time, they are coming closer. I dash back to the kitchen, catching my breath while letting him settle once more and then bring two cups of coffee into the living room, offering one to him while placing the other on a clutter free corner of the desk.

Together, we sit, he in the kitchen chair and me in the desk chair, spun around to face him. He sips his coffee. "Thank you. This is good."

I laugh nervously. "Well, I don't do much cooking, but coffee I have gotten the hang of. Probably out of necessity." I busy my hands by lifting the coffee cup from the desk.

"It's not the only thing you've gotten the hang of." He lifts the cup to his lips.

I suck in a breath, unable to determine if I'm in for a scolding.

I glance around the room, spotting his copy of *A Tale of Two Cities* sitting on the top of a pile of Nonno's journals. "You saw your recipe?" I sip from my cup, avoiding his eyes.

"I haven't seen that photograph in a very long time. And, my note on a technique I read about. I had to be only sixteen-years-old at the time. I didn't think he kept it." Papa's voice trails off and I imagine him thinking of Nonno and what it must mean to have his father keep something of his like this. "I might have been a little impertinent in my youth." Papa's cheeks flush with color.

"I can't imagine that." I hide a smile with a sip of coffee before returning it to the desk.

"It's true. I had big plans for the vineyard, and your Nonno supported all of them. But..."

Even though I've heard part of the story from Mr. Parisi, I want Papa to tell me. Perhaps, if we have a complete understanding between us, we can heal what has soured our relationship.

"But, what?"

Papa's expression grows somber. "My mother died."

I watch him as he mulls over his thoughts, buying himself time by placing his cup on the floor beside his chair.

"I probably never told you, but she died in the vineyard. She was helping me save my latest idea, a new grape I was eager to test on our land, and the cold was too much for her. She laid down to rest in the early morning hours and she never awoke." A tear slides down his cheek.

I lean forward in my chair, wanting him to hear me. "I am so sorry. I can't imagine how hard that must have been."

Papa's head bobs up and down. "It was my fault. She was in the vineyard because I needed her help. I put the safety of the vineyard above the safety of my own mother."

I give him time to recover himself. A man and his grief are not easily parted. That I am sure of.

"Did you ever ask yourself, if she was in the vineyard out of love instead of obligation? If she was as instrumental to the vineyard as Nonno said she was, then wouldn't she have loved the vines as much as you and Nonno did? Wouldn't she have done whatever it took to ensure their safety?"

Papa looks up, a new understanding occurring to him. "Where did you—"

"Being a Russo woman is something I have experience with. I can honestly say, I would have done just as she did."

His reluctant smile tells me I have struck a chord. "I imagine you would have."

My decision to push forward rises up within me. In order to rebuild a relationship with my father and gain his trust in my abilities as a winemaker, I must put aside my stubborn pride and concede that he was only doing what he thought was best for me. "I was coming to see you this morning."

"Sofia, you..." Papa interrupts but his words falter and he changes tacts. "I tasted your wine. Pinot Noir is a bold choice."

My bottom lip finds its way between my teeth and I instantly feel thirteen-years-old again, waiting for the harsh rebuke that is sure to follow due to an audacious act on my part.

"I know about the deal you made with Mr. Parisi." I blurt the words out immediately regretting the decision to lead with this particular announcement. "You own the land my vines are growing on." I etch the injury out of my voice. "I think I understand the reason, but I'd like to talk with you about it."

"I did not come to argue with you." Papa's face is lined with what I read as regret.

"What I meant to say is, I'm sorry we have fallen out, Papa. I'm sorry if the things I said hurt your feelings. I never intended to hurt you."

"Sofia, please. I only want to tell you that you've done well."

His gaze falls to the floor. Like a parched vineyard in need of rain, my heart hungrily soaks up his words. When he lifts his head to speak again, I raise a palm to halt him. "I need to say this. Please let me."

Papa agrees with a dip of his chin.

"You are more important to me than the vineyard." A sob lodges in my throat at my admission. "I love the vines, Papa. You know how much I love them. But, even so, I love you more. Just as I imagine your mother did."

Moisture gathers in Papa's eyes, making it even more challenging for me to continue.

"I can do great things with wine, and I will attempt to do so, even if it means I do it alone." I let out a long, slow breath, allowing my words to settle. "I won't argue against your decision to pass the vineyard down to Al. That's your right to do so, and it wasn't mine to demand. I understand that now. But I would like you to consider something. Maybe there is a way for all three of us to work together. When I was a little girl, all I wanted was to spend time with you."

Papa's tears are flowing freely now, matching mine drop for drop.

"You spent most of your time in the vineyard, so that, too, is where I wanted to be. I looked up to you. You were my hero—" I take in a sharp breath, an attempt to cut off the emotion in my words before continuing. "And then one day, you weren't."

A shadow falls across his face.

"Heaven knows, I tested you. Pushed you to the limits with my stubbornness. All I ever wanted was a relationship with you, through the vines. That was all I ever wanted. All I want, still."

"Sofia, I came here to apologize to you." Papa washes a hand over his tear-stained face. "I let you down in uncountable ways through the years. Yet, you have turned into a strong, independent woman, and a fine vintner as well. All of it despite my lack of encouragement or support. I was wrong to try to squash your determination. It is a wonderful and necessary characteristic to have as a winemaker."

"You think I'm a fine vintner?" My voice is barely a whisper.

Papa reaches behind his chair and pulls out a bottle. "I know you are." He hands me the bottle, the Russo Vineyard label looking familiar but different.

Pulling it closer, I recognize Al's newest logo design, the one where he drew roots and wings as a nod to the two of us. I'm running a finger across the drawing, admiring its detail when I see it. *Pinot Noir* in a bold swirling script. Then just below it in small straight script, Vintner: Sofia Russo. A hand flies to my open mouth in surprise. "But, how?"

"You are a Russo winemaker. This is your wine. This is where your name should go."

I spring up from my chair, unable to contain myself. Papa rises to meet me. Stepping forward, my first bottle of labeled Russo wine clutched tight in one hand, I wrap him in a hug so fierce I feel as though we've melded into one. "Thank you, Papa." I whisper into his shoulder. "Thank you."

He pulls back to meet my eyes. "No, Sofia, it is I who owe you the thanks." Papa squeezes my hand in his. "I'm proud of you. I have never been prouder of you than I am today. Not..." he shakes his head lightly, "because of the wine, though that is a huge accomplishment in itself. I'm proud of you for having the strength to stay true to yourself, to your dreams, even if your Papa didn't do much to help you along the way."

"If we join forces." I squeeze his hand with certainty. "Together, we can make Russo wine, Papa. Together."

Forty-Five

AN HOUR LATER, I am settling myself on Nonno's marble bench, unable to take my eyes off my name on the bottle of Russo wine. Several men are helping Papa as they move the patio tables and chairs into position on the new stone laid for outdoor wine tastings. Nonno's bench has been relocated to the front entrance of the tasting room. A nod, I presume, to the man who started it all.

We finished our coffee, dried our faces, and then I returned to the vineyard with Papa, his list of tasks not made easier by the emotional, but long overdue, conversation between us. I find myself in a mild state of shock, unsure of how exactly I became the next Russo winemaker.

"He finally listened." Al startles me from behind.

I jump up and wrap my arms around his tall frame. "How did you do it? I can barely believe it. I—I don't know what to say."

Al takes the bottle from my hand and examines the label. "I think, in the end, it was a combination of pressures. Apparently, unbeknownst to me, Mama had a few words for him before I arrived. We weren't the only ones thinking something needed to change." He shrugs his shoulders sheepishly. "I suspect if I had known, I wouldn't have pushed him so hard. Maybe it's better I didn't know." He hands the bottle back to me. "It all worked out in the end."

A slight breeze has me folding my arms around myself. "But, how did you label a bottle of my wine? Wait." The pieces click into place. "You didn't want the second bottle for yourself? You wanted it to do this?"

Al's grin is as mischievous as a four-year-old with a slingshot. "I knew you were going to let things lie. The fight had gone out of you and I don't blame you one bit for saying enough is enough. But, I couldn't. Not when the vineyard's success depends on you. If I'm being honest, I was afraid to be the one to run the family's legacy into the ground. I know you wouldn't let that happen, and then there is, of course, your actual talent and instinct for making wine."

Tilting my head to the side, I invite him to continue.

"I went home and finished the design, with Eva's help. Then I went to a friend of mine and had him make it into a label. With the labeled bottle in hand, I came to the house and asked Papa to consider the options. By that point, he had already tasted your Pinot Noir. Seeing it with a label, maybe that was all the push he needed to see you as the vintner you are."

"Thank you, Al." I step forward and embrace him again, giving him an extra squeeze of my appreciation. "What does this mean for you?"

His laugh is boisterous and lighthearted. "I'm not out of a job, if that's what you're asking. We still have to sort some things out, but it's not like the vineyard can't use all of our help. None of us has to do it alone anymore." Al's expression turns serious. "Eva is convinced I can make a business out of designing wine labels. I think it's something I can work at on the side."

"Little squares of paper." The words whisper past my lips as I see how our paths led us to where we are. "You've been creating wine labels your whole life. It's about time you were recognized for your talent."

Papa joins us, wrapping an arm around each of our shoulders.

"That reminds me. I've been meaning to ask if you know what this means?" I tug Nonno's letter from my back pocket and point to the PostScript. "Any idea? I swear I've heard it before. Do you remember Nonno using this phrase?"

Papa reads the letter silently. "He left this for you?"

I nod, emotions rising to the surface again. "It was the last thing he ever told me."

Papa's Italian is laced with affection. "*Nella botte piccola c'è il vino buono.* In small barrels, there's good wine." Papa's head shakes slowly from side to side. "He was quite a man."

"What does it mean?" Al and I exchange a look, neither of us recognizing Nonno's words.

Papa's smile grows wide. "Your Nonno wasn't one to sit idly by when he saw what needed doing. He was giving you a nudge, Sofia, to continue with your efforts. It is an Italian proverb similar to the sentiment, good things come in small packages."

I glance at Al, trying to figure out what I'm missing. "I still don't understand."

Papa points to Nonno's letter. "My mother said the same thing to him when she arrived from Italy. She had brought with her—"

I interrupt my father as I remember Nonno's story. "The vines. She brought the vines that started the Russo Vineyard."

"That's right." The strain that has lined Papa's face for the past several years seems to fade into a more relaxed version of the man before me. "She was telling Nonno that starting small was not to be dismissed. Starting with a few vines, with a small vintage, would lead to great things. Nonno was telling you the same thing, Sofia. He was telling you to take a chance."

My head snaps up at the revelation. "Papa, your recipe said the exact same thing. It is what has intrigued me all these years. Small new French Oak barrels."

Papa's laughter makes my heart fill with joy. "So it does." Papa repeats the phrase, his voice soft with contemplation. "In small barrels, there is good wine."

"Did someone say wine?" Mama is heading toward us with a tray of meats, cheeses, olives, and bread.

The four of us move to the new patio, Papa doing the honors of opening and pouring the wine while Mama dishes out the picnic lunch, the aroma of the fresh focaccia adding to the sensation of feeling at home once again.

I pause, waiting for someone to give the toast. I catch Papa's eye and he inclines his head slightly, both of us thinking the same thing.

"*In vino veritas.*" I raise my glass to the middle of the table.

Without missing the cue, Al continues Nonno's family tradition. "In wine there is truth."

We clink glasses as my anticipation of what comes next swirls within my mind.

Forty-Six

AUGUST 1960

I CATCH the first glimpse of sun as it rises between the canopy of vines. Early morning in the vineyard continues to be my favorite daily ritual. The scent of the earth mixed with the sweet Napa air is the perfume that lures me from my slumber in the early morning hours. Having resigned my job at the Napa Valley Vintner Society, I am free to dedicate my days and my nights to Russo wine.

Nonno's habits have rubbed off on me. Having been back at the family vineyard every day for the past few months, I have caught myself, on more than one occasion, talking to the vines as I stroll the rows. I haven't decided if my chatting up the vines offers a benefit to grape production yet, but I'm comforted by my grandfather's presence during the quiet of the early day, either way.

Coffee cup in hand, I've made a routine out of visiting every corner of every section on a rotating schedule. Just like when I was a small child, I have made it my goal to explore the entirety of our family's land. Reacquainting myself with the land has already proved itself a worthy investment of time.

Last week, I visited the section of land where Papa planted his plum trees long ago. Though the trees still produce fruit, their dwindling numbers and aging trunks gave me reason to pause. My first thought was Cabernet Sauvignon. The wine, its attributes that lean toward flavors of plums, along with the increasing interest in the grape in the Napa Valley, all have me considering a new varietal in Russo wine.

I return to the tasting room, kicking my boots off at the back door before sliding into my new office in stocking feet. Tucked in the back of the building, I have a view of the vineyard and a bookshelf lined with resources. I pull the biggest book from the shelf and set it on my desk with a light thud. Today's mission is to assess the land I've earmarked against the growing needs for the new grape.

There isn't an aspect of vineyard life that I don't relish, but discovering something new is one of the best feelings of all. A new wine means new experiments, new journals, more challenges, and a new story for Russo wine. There is nothing more exciting than that.

I tuck one leg underneath me as I lean my elbows on the desk and open the book, eager to begin the research. My eye catches the framed speech that sits on the corner of my desk. Its job is to act as a reminder of what is most important to me.

My Nonno was a wise man, famous for quoting Italian proverbs, insistent that a reference to wine and bread was sure to resonate with our daily life. He told me once, that a vine must struggle in order for it to thrive. There is no success without struggle, he insisted. He also said, people were a lot like vines.

Until recently, I assumed he was referring to our big successes in life. You know, the ones where you hit that home run or your achievements are recognized by a group of your peers. All nice things, of course. But it wasn't until I sat down to write these words that I real-

ized growing into greatness is less about our accomplishments and more about our willingness to bend and shift and mold our lives in the ways that show care and attention to who and what we love.

A vine is never judged by one vintage alone. Nor should a person be judged by one action. Just like our wine, we are a combination of hard work, sacrifice, determination, and love. My father is a great example of having lived a life full of integrity. He is not a boastful man, nor is he a simple one. But, his passion for wine thrums through him and if there is one thing I do know, it is the life of a grape farmer is a calling. Those who answer the call do so with the understanding that success is not a guarantee.

I let the words settle over me, remembering my commitment to my family, the vineyard, and the wine. There is always something that needs doing in a vineyard, and each of us has our roles.

For all his talk of handing over the family legacy, Papa continues to be involved in the day-to-day operations of the vineyard and business. I am thankful to have him near and can't help but smile with him following along behind me. Working side by side, he has surprised me with his open-minded approach and I know there is still much I have to learn from him.

Al pokes his head into the room. "Hey, Sis, did you see that sketch I left on your desk?"

I pick up the paper. "This is great."

Al embraced the role of marketing director the moment Papa offered it to him. In addition to heading up the tasting room and helping in the vineyard whenever all hands are needed, he has managed to elevate the Russo brand in a matter of a few months with his designs, labels, and advertising efforts.

"If I've got your approval, I'll drop it at the printers today."

"You don't need my approval, Al." I lower my eyes in mock admonishment.

"You're the head winemaker, so yeah, I kind of do." He

doesn't give me the opportunity to refute him as he ducks back out of my office to carry on with his day.

Eagerness to get started on a new project sends a shiver of delight through me. I tug the reference book toward me and begin to read about Cabernet Sauvignon.

Forty-Seven

SEPTEMBER 1963

"I'M IN HERE."

A light autumn breeze lifts the papers on my desk in a flutter as Papa appears in the doorway of my office.

"Alonso said you wanted to see me." His eyes land on the bottle waiting on top of my desk.

"I do. We have some tastings to do and I could use your help." I gesture for him to sit in the chair behind my desk as I stand to take the smaller chair across from him.

"I should have brought your mama. You know how much she enjoys seeing what you've made."

I laugh at his words. The same ones that used to make me feel like a kindergartener bringing home a finger painting, now bring me only joy. Looking back, his comment was only ever intended as a compliment.

"She can taste the next round. This one is for us." I open the unlabeled bottle with a pop and pour a sample into both of our glasses.

I raise the glass in my right hand, giving it a swirl. I notice how it clings to the sides a moment longer than I anticipate before cascading like a waterfall toward the base of the glass.

My glass catches the light coming in from beyond the window, drawing me into the magic that happens when light meets the crimson liquid. I swirl my glass again, watching it dance and delighting in its deep, rich color with a subtle hint of purple at its edges.

We both record our impressions of the look and behavior of the wine on the sheets in front of us.

With a nod from Papa, I lift the glass to my nose and inhale its fragrance. Black cherry and a hint of spice. Once again, we note our findings. I sniff again and add a touch of smoke to my list.

Together, we take a sip. My eyes grow wide with delight. The full body nature of the wine offers a layer of indiscernible flavors at first as it rolls across my tongue. I raise my glass to take another look at the color, then sip again. First it is blackberry and then... There it is, the slight essence of plum I was looking for. The longer the wine rests on my palate the deeper the flavors present themselves and I find myself in awe of such an experience. Right down to the oakiness and slight tang of the wine, I have an awareness of the decisions we made along the way as they seep into each sip.

I am contemplating how I can possibly describe the new Russo varietal as I know I must, but words escape me. I look at Papa in hopes of finding an answer there.

"What do you think?"

"The Cabernet Sauvignon is a complicated wine." Papa smiles at me with a twinkle in his eye. "Just like its creator."

I can't help but laugh. Reaching across the desk, I clink my glass with his in celebration of another Russo success. "Like father, like daughter."

Papa's smile is warm and approving. "Like father. Like daughter. Like wine."

Author Notes

Researching and writing this novel was an incredible four-year exploration through wine and history. Though I had an appreciation for it, I was a novice when it came to wine, drinking only a few varieties of white wine for most of my adult life. When I was welcomed into the homes, offices, vineyards, and tasting rooms of several Napa Valley wineries where I asked a plethora of questions, I was introduced to more than the history of the region. I fell in love with the people, the land, the lifestyle, the wine, and the process of winemaking. From the terroir to the bottling to the tasting, I found myself eager to learn more. I am pleased to report I am now a red wine enthusiast, who is expanding her wine tasting repertoire on a regular basis.

It is important to note that the commercial industry of Napa Valley winemaking as we know it today, though long lived, is actually more recent in terms of true commercialization. The Napa Valley began to see growth through the 1960s but it was the Paris Tasting* of 1976 that put the Napa Valley on the worldwide stage. *For a glimpse into how the Paris Tasting came to be, look for the 2008 movie *Bottle Shock*.

When the story came to me, I knew immediately the Russo family would be Italian. Thankfully, history backed up my imagination and research confirmed that many European grape farmers descended on the Napa Valley with the intent to make wine comparable to those of their homelands. I'd say they definitely succeeded.

Sofia Russo also arrived in my mind's eye fully formed and ready to tackle the world of wine. She was tenacious right from the start and I suspect it was her enthusiasm for wine that drew me to her. Women have been involved in wine throughout Napa's history but much like most male dominated industries, they were few and far between. Mrs. Josephine Tychson was the first woman in California to own and with the assistance of a foreman, grow and operate an estate vineyard after her husband's death. Sadly, in the end she was forced to sell her vineyard due to the phylloxera outbreak of 1893. Tychson Cellars has evolved through the years and has its own unique history existing now as Freemark Abbey in St. Helena.

While visiting the region, I was intrigued by the wineries that remained open during Prohibition. I interviewed three different wineries, all of whom remained operational during the thirteen years the Volstead Act was in place. I was delighted to learn of three different approaches to how families and vineyards stayed afloat during those trying years. I have done my best to include a nugget of each vineyard's story within the pages of the novel. For more details on my research into Prohibition and wine, subscribe to my newsletter to receive an eBook copy of *At the Corner of Fiction and History, facts and follies that inspire the stories.*

A few things became the norm as the reality of Prohibition settled in. Winery owners closed, some walking away from their land and homes completely. A few remained in operation with sacramental wine licenses. Several continued to operate "illegally" or on the cusp of legality. Some planted table grapes or heartier varieties that were suitable for long distance travel back east. Others plowed under their vines entirely and planted other crops including plum trees and walnuts. Despite the term "prune trees", still being common among old timers in the Napa Valley today and also throughout much of my research, I refer to these trees as "plum" so as not to confuse readers. A prune simply being a dehydrated plum.

The Napa Valley Vintner Society does exist and was a helpful and accommodating resource as I dug into the details. If you would like to know more about current and historic events in the region, be sure to check out their website at napavintners.com. Their newsletter is also an enjoyable resource for quick escapes, virtually speaking, to the beautiful Napa Valley.

When it comes to wine math, I have to say that I felt a little like I imagined Alonso might have in the story. Though I do not live with dyslexia, numbers are far less favorable to me than words are. A few YouTube videos on wine math acted as a very good reminder that running a vineyard is not for the faint of heart and requires more skills than I ever realized. The term, dyslexia has been in use since 1877 where the term meant "difficulty with words" or "word blindness".

I invoked artistic licence when it came to the use of smudge pots in 1900. The early morning scene when Nonna (Sofia and Alonso's grandmother) passes away in the vineyard after spending the night keeping the smudge pots burning in order to save the vines would not have occurred in 1900. Smudge pots weren't in use until 1907 and only became common in fields and vineyards after a disastrous freeze in 1913 wiped out entire crops in Southern California.

Pinot Noir, the same vines Sofia planted on her borrowed piece of land, was first planted in California in 1953 by the very real Mr. James Zellerbach of Hanzell Vineyards located in Sonoma Valley. Though their encounter is fictional, I wanted to give a nod of thanks to the man who introduced the grape and many other vineyard advancements to the region as I do enjoy a glass of Pinot Noir. During my research, I was delighted to discover Pinot Noir is the healthiest red wine due to its high concentration of resveratrol, which is an antioxidant that lowers bad cholesterol and high blood pressure.

Though grafting of vines to phylloxera-resistant rootstock was an option in 1954, I chose to have Sofie plant the vine as is to take out a lengthy explanation of the process. I should note that by the 1950's, less than 30% of California grapevines were grafted onto phylloxera-resistant rootstocks. Overtime, the California grapevine industry has transitioned primarily to grafted vines.

My reference of *A Tale of Two Cities* is twofold. The memorable first line of the story, "It was the best of times, it was the worst of times..." was what ran through my head as I considered poor Papa as he welcomed twins into his family at the very same time his livelihood was stolen out from under him with Prohibition. Then again, the Dickens' novel became poignant when I was reminded that one of the morals of the story is *things are not always as they seem*. I thought it fitting that Papa's favorite novel mirrored Sofia's knowledge of her father.

Speaking of Papa, if you are a native Italian speaker, you will notice that I have used the American spelling of Papa and Mama throughout the story instead of the accented Italian spelling. The reason for this is Sofia and Alonso are second generation Italian Americans and thus they would have referred to their parents with the sentiment of the era in the United States. They refer to Nonno in Italian because that was his preference, being a first generation Italian American.

I mention Sofia and Al receiving lollypops after their yearly doctor appointment. The modern version of the hard candy on a stick has existed since 1908 but was not actually trademarked as such until 1931.

Nonno quotes "good wine makes good blood". This is one of the most used among the Italian proverbs about wine. I read that almost every "nonno" in Italy will swear that a good glass of wine is the way to remain healthy. I'll raise a glass to that!

Sofia talks about hanging vines on the farm gate. The idea for this part of the story came from the Italian proverb, *il buon vino non ha bisogno di frasca* which translates to *good wine needs no leafy branch* and corresponds with the proverb, *actions speak louder than words*. This lesser-known Italian proverb is tied to the old tradition of disposing of a surplus of the previous year's wine in order to make room for the current year's harvest. Italian winemakers would request permission to sell their overstock wine directly to consumers at reduced prices and once approved by authorities to do so, would hang a leafy bundle of branches at the farm gate to let passersby know that they had wine for sale. Hence, a good wine would not need a leafy branch as it presumably would be revered and likely sold out prior to the current year's harvest.

Acknowledgments

I owe a debt of gratitude to the many vineyard workers and winemakers of the Napa Valley. They are humble enough to call themselves grape farmers but what they create are moments that enrich the lives of many. Each time we raise a glass in celebration, we will think of you.

Thank you to the Bartolucci family of Madonna Estate who welcomed us in while sharing their stories, vineyard history, and exceptional wine over the course of an enjoyable afternoon. Our visit was like settling into a conversation with old friends. Thank you, Buck, Susan, and Brette, for your hospitality and your willingness to answer my many questions. I am now a red wine enthusiast because of Madonna Estate Pinot Noir.

Thank you to Beaulieu Vineyard and Nicolas Roux for our behind-the-scenes tour and exceptional BV winetasting. We thoroughly enjoyed learning about Georges de Latour, the historic winery, and sacramental wine during Prohibition. In addition to learning of where to go to experience the "old" Napa vines, seeing actual bottles of BV sacramental wine was the cherry on top of a wonderful day.

Thank you to the Nichelini Family Winery and Diane Patterson for inviting us into the historic Nichelini family home where, like a true historian, she detailed the family's journey and the evolution of the vineyard. Sharing personal photographs and touching memories, I was inspired to include a mention of the wall that had been notched out to make room for the invention of the telephone. That shared moment will remain with me. Thank you, Diane.

There is something magical when two history enthusiasts connect. I am thankful for the detailed assistance from Kelly O'Connor, research librarian at the Napa County Historical Society who not only answered all of my questions as they came up but also set aside a research table for me and then proceeded to cover it with research material in anticipation of my arrival in Napa. To say I was in research heaven is an understatement. Thank you, Kelly!

Several of the above-mentioned individuals also steered me toward the St. Helena Public Library where my husband asked about an online resource. I have spent hours scouring Napa Valley Daily Register newspapers from the 1920s to 1960 and am eternally grateful for the online resource the library provides. Thank you to the librarians for creating such a database.

Special thanks to Aram Chakerian and Jesse Ramer of the Napa Vintners for their guidance in kick starting my research and putting me in touch with some of the above mentioned individuals.

Thank you to Copperfield's Books in downtown Napa for making it tremendously difficult to walk away from the excellent selection of books on Napa history. Several of them now line my bookshelves.

This story would not have made it into readers hands if it was not for my three wonderful editors. Robinette Waterson, Lucy Cooke, and Jamie Mc Gillen. Thank you for backing this story with your time and attention to detail.

Thank you to my cover designer, Ana Grigoriu-Voicu for another cover that speaks to the heart of the story.

To my advanced readers, you are the glue that holds me together as release day nears. Your insightful comments, typo spotting genius, and enthusiasm for the stories I write makes my heart swell. Thank you for all that you do!

To public librarians everywhere, thank you for loving books, supporting authors, and embracing the hunt for random historical queries.

When it comes to writer friends, I am truly blessed. Each one of you is instrumental in bringing joy and inspiration into my writing. Thank you for joining me in stories and in life. Carla Young, Kelsey Gietl, Diana Lesire Brandmeyer, Kate Thompson, Michelle Cox, Gloria Mattioni, Sayword Eller, Kerry Chaput, Jen Craven, Maggie Giles, Jenn Bouchard, Colleen Temple, Caitlin Moss, Sharon Peterson, and my HNS afterparty friends. Together, we learn, laugh, and support one another in all the best ways.

On a personal note, thank you to my family and friends who understand my headspace when a deadline is looming and who celebrate each milestone reached. I look forward to raising a glass with each one of you.

Special thanks to Justin for reading random chapters at a moment's notice. Huge thanks to Dave, for keeping M & M's on hand for those long writing days and for the daily walks that clear my head and hopefully help counteract all those M & M's.

And to you, thank you for taking time out of your day to read *Growing into Greatness*. I hope the story made you laugh, cry, and explore your own thoughts on family, challenging times, and the human desire to grow into something great.

About the Author

A writer from a young age, Tanya E Williams loves to help a reader get lost in another time, another place through the magic of books. History continues to inspire her stories and her insightful view into the human condition deepens her character's experiences and propels them on their journey. Ms. Williams' favorite tales, speak to the reader's heart, making them smile, laugh, cry, and think.

Also by Tanya E Williams

Becoming Mrs. Smith

Stealing Mr. Smith

A Man Called Smith

All That Was

Welcome to the Hamilton

Meet Me at the Clock

Milton Keynes UK
Ingram Content Group UK Ltd.
UKHW011918120724
445613UK00002B/29